DEATH OF A BLUE MOVIE STAR

Death of a Blue Movie Star

Jeffery Deaver

CORONET BOOKS
Hodder & Stoughton

Copyright © 1990 by Jeffery Wilds Deaver

This right of Jeffery Wilds Deaver to be identified as the Author
of the Work has been asserted by him in accordance with the
Copyright, Designs and Patents Act 1988.

First published in Great Britain in 2001 by Hodder and Stoughton
First published in paperback in 2001 by Hodder and Stoughton
A division of Hodder Headline

A Coronet Paperback

10 9 8 7 6 5 4

A CIP catalogue record for this title
is available from the British Library.

ISBN 0 340 79312 0

Printed and bound in Great Britain by
Clays Ltd, St Ives plc

Hodder and Stoughton
A division of Hodder Headline
338 Euston Road
London NW1 3BH

For Wiz, Chris,
Charlotte and Isabel

I call for a theater in which the actors are like victims burning at the stake, a signaling through the flames.

—ANTONIN ARTAUD

CHAPTER ONE

Rune had walked past the movie theater and was three blocks away when the bomb went off.

No way was it construction-site dynamite—she knew *that* from living for several years in urban-renewing Manhattan. The noise was way loud—a huge, painful bang like a falling boiler. The turbulent black smoke and distant screams left no doubt.

Then sirens, shouts, running crowds. She looked but couldn't see much from where she stood.

Rune started toward it but then stopped, glanced at a watch—of the three on her wrist, it was the only one that worked. She was already late getting back to the studio—was due a half hour ago. Thinking: Hell, if I'm going to get yelled at anyway why not come back with a good story to take the sting out of it.

Yes, no?

Go for it. She walked south to see the carnage.

The blast itself wasn't all that big. It didn't crater the

floor and the only windows it took out were the theater's
and the plate glass in the bar one address up. No, it was
the *fire* was the nasty part. Wads of flaming upholstery
had apparently arced like those tracer bullets in war movies and had ignited wallpaper and carpeting and patrons'
hair and all the recesses of the theater the owner'd probably been meaning to get up to code for ten years but just
hadn't. By the time Rune got there the flames had done
their job and the Velvet Venus Theater (*XXX Only, The
Best Projection In Town*) was no more.

Eighth Avenue was in chaos, closed off completely between Forty-second and Forty-sixth Streets. Diminutive
Rune, thin and just over five feet, easily worked her way
to the front of the spectators. The homeless people and
hookers and three-card monte players and kids were having a great time watching the slick choreography of the
men and women from the dozen or so fire trucks on the
scene. When the roof of the theater went and sparks cascaded over the street the crowd exhaled approval as if
they were watching the Macy's fireworks over the East
River.

The NYFD crews were good and after twenty minutes
the fires were "knocked down," as she heard one fireman
say, and the dramatic stuff was over. The theater, a bar, a
deli and peep show had been destroyed.

Then the crowd's murmuring disappeared and everyone watched in solemn quiet when the medics brought
out the bodies. Or what was left of them.

Rune felt her heart slamming as the thick green bags
were wheeled or carried past. Even the Emergency
Medical Service guys, who she guessed were pretty used
to this sort of thing, looked edgy and green at the gills.
Their lips were squeezed tight and their eyes were fixed
ahead of them.

She eased closer to where one of the medics was talking to a fireman. And though the young man tried to

sound cool, slinging out the words with a grin, his voice was shaky. "Four dead, but two are mystery stiffs—not even enough left for a dental."

She swallowed; nausea and an urge to cry were balanced within her for a moment.

The queasiness returned when she realized something else: Three or four tons of smoldering concrete and plaster now rested on the same sidewalk squares where she'd been strolling just minutes before. Walking and skipping like a schoolgirl, careful to miss the cracks to save her mother's back, glancing at the movie poster and admiring the long blonde hair of the star of *Lusty Cousins*.

The very spot! A few minutes earlier and . . .

"What happened?" Rune asked a pock-faced young woman in a tight red T-shirt. Her voice cracked and she had to repeat the question.

"A bomb, a gas line." The woman shrugged. "Maybe propane. I don't know."

Rune nodded slowly.

The cops were hostile and bored. Authoritative voices droned, "Move along, come on, everybody. Move along."

Rune stayed put.

"Excuse me, miss." A man's polite voice was speaking to her. Rune turned and saw a cowboy. "Can I get by?" He'd walked out of the burnt-out theater and was heading for a cluster of officers in the middle of the street.

He was about six two. Wearing blue jeans, a work shirt and a soldier's vest stiff with plates of armor. Boots. He had thinning hair, swept back, and a mustache. His face was reserved and somber. He wore battered canvas gloves. Rune glanced at his badge, pinned to his thick, stained belt, and stepped aside.

He ducked under the yellow police tape and walked into the street. She edged after him. He stopped at a blue-and-white station wagon stenciled with BOMB SQUAD and leaned on the hood. Rune, slipping into eavesdropping range, heard:

"What've we got?" a fat man in a brown suit asked Cowboy.

"Plastic, looks like. A half ki." He looked up from under salt-and-pepper brows. "I can't figure it. No I.R.A. targets here. The bar was Greek." He nodded. "And the Syndicate only blows things up after hours. Anyway, *their* M.O. is, if you want to scare folks, they miss protection payments, you use Tovex from a construction site or maybe a concussion grenade. Something that makes a big noise. But military plastic? Sitting right next to the gas line? I don't get it."

"We got something here." A patrolman came up and handed Cowboy a plastic envelope. Inside was a scorched piece of paper. "We're going fishing for latents so if you could be careful, sir."

Cowboy nodded and read.

Rune tried to get a glimpse of it. Saw careful handwriting. And dark stains. She wondered if they were blood.

Cowboy glanced up. "Are you someone?"

"My mother thinks so." She tried a fast smile. He didn't respond, studied her critically. Maybe trying to decide if she was a witness. Or the bomber. She decided not to be cute. "I just wondered what it said."

"You're not supposed to be here."

"I'm a reporter. I'm just curious what happened."

Brown Suit offered, "Why don't you be curious someplace else."

Which ticked her off and she was about to tell him that as a taxpayer—which she wasn't—she paid his salary but just then Brown Suit finished reading the note and tapped Cowboy's arm. "What's this Sword?"

Forgetting about Rune, Cowboy said, "Never heard of them but they want credit, they can have it till somebody better shows up." Then he noticed something, stepped forward, away from the station wagon. Brown Suit was looking elsewhere and Rune glanced at the message on the burned paper.

The first angel blew his trumpet, and there followed hail and fire, mixed with blood, which fell on the earth; and a third of the earth was burnt up. . . .
                              —A Warning from the Sword of Jesus

Cowboy returned a moment later. A young priest was behind him.

"Here it is, Father." Cowboy handed him the plastic envelope. The man touched his ear above his Roman collar as he read, nodding, his thin lips pressed together. Solemn, as if he were at a funeral. Which, Rune figured, he just about was.

The priest said, "It's from the *'Revelation to John.'* Chapter eight, verse . . . seven, or six maybe. I'm not—"

Cowboy asked, "What's that about, 'Revelation'? Like getting inspiration?"

The priest gave a polite, noncommittal laugh before he realized the cop wasn't joking. "What it's about is the end of the world. The Apocalypse."

Which is when Brown Suit noticed Rune, looking through the crook of Cowboy's arm. "Hey, you, move along."

Cowboy turned, but didn't say anything.

"I've got a right to know what's going on. I walked by there just a minute ago. I could've been killed."

"Yeah," said Brown Suit. "But you weren't. So count your blessings. Look, I'm getting tired of telling you to get out of here."

"Good. 'Cause I'm getting tired of hearing it." Rune grinned.

Cowboy reined in a smile.

"Now." Brown Suit stepped forward.

"Okay, okay." Rune walked away.

But slowly—just to show they weren't going to bully her *too* much. Her leisurely departure let her overhear something the young priest was saying to Cowboy and Brown Suit.

"I hate to tell you this but if that note has to do with the bombing it's not such good news."

"Why not?" Cowboy asked.

"That verse? It's about the *first* angel. In the whole passage there are seven angels all together."

"So?" asked Brown Suit.

"I guess that means you've got six more to go until God wipes the slate clean."

In the office of L&R Productions, on Twenty-first Street, Rune took a beer from the fridge. It was an old Kenmore and one of her all-time favorite objects. On the door was a raised pattern like the grille of a 1950 Studebaker and it had a big silver handle that looked like it belonged on a submarine hatch.

Looking at her reflection in a scabby mirror above the receptionist's desk, she saw her muted black-and-green portrait, lit by the fluorescence of the office: a girl in a red miniskirt, printed with silhouettes of dinosaurs, and two sleeveless T-shirts, one white, one navy. Her auburn hair was pulled back in a ponytail, which made her round face somewhat less round. In addition to the watches, Rune wore three pieces of jewelry—a double-terminated crystal on a chain, a single fake-gold earring in the shape of the Eiffel Tower and a silver bracelet in the shape of two hands clasped together, which had been broken and soldered together. The little makeup she had put on that morning had vanished in the sweat of the August afternoon and the spewing water from an open hydrant on Thirty-first Street she couldn't resist dunking her head under. Rune wasn't much for makeup anyway. She did best, she felt, with the least attention. When she got elaborate with her looks, she turned sophisticated into clowny, svelte into whorish.

Her theory of fashion: You're short and occasionally you're pretty. Stick to the basics. T-shirts, boots and dinosaurs. Use hair spray only to kill flies and to paste things into scrapbooks.

She rubbed the cold beer bottle against her cheek and sat down at the desk.

The L&R office was a good reflection of the cash flow of the company. Gray steel furniture, circa 1967. Peeling linoleum. Stacks of yellowing invoices, storyboards, art directors' annuals and papers that had grown the dense fur of city grit.

Larry and Bob, her bosses, were Australians, documentary film makers, and—Rune's opinion on most days—maniacs. As producers of commercials for Melbourne and New York ad agencies they had developed something more than their massive artistic egos; they were, in their own words, *accurate* words, "bloody fucking good." They ate like farm animals, belched, lusted over blondes with big boobs and indulged in gloomy moodiness. In between doing TV commercials they now produced and shot some of the best documentaries that ever ran on PBS or England's Channel 4 or at the Film Forum.

Rune had wheedled a job here, hoping some of their magic would rub off.

It was now a year later and not much had.

Larry, the partner with the longer beard, walked into the office. His uniform of the day: boots, black leather pants and a black, blousy Parachute shirt, every button of which his gut tested.

"About bleedin' time. Where've you been?"

She held up the Schneider lens she'd picked up at Optirental in Midtown. He reached for it but she held it from his grasp. "They said you're behind on your account—"

"Me account?" Larry was deeply stung.

"—and they wanted a bigger deposit. I had to give them a check. A personal check."

"Right, I'll add it to your envelope."

"You'll add it to my *pocket*."

"Look, you can't keep being late like this, luv. What if we'd been shooting?" He took the lens. "Time is money, right?"

"No, money is money," Rune countered. "I'm out some and I want you to pay me back. Come on, Larry. I need it."

"Get it out of petty cash."

"There's never been more than six dollars in petty cash since I've been working here. And you know it."

"Right." He examined the lens, a beautiful piece of German optics and machinery.

Rune didn't move. Kept staring at him.

He looked up. Sighed. "How fucking much was it?"

"Forty dollars."

"Jesus." He dug into his pocket and gave her two twenties.

She smiled curtly. "Thank you, boss."

"Listen, luv, I've got a big pitch meeting going on—"

"Not another commercial, Larry. Come on. Don't sell out."

"They pay the rent. And your salary. So . . . I need four coffees. One light, one regular, two sweet. And two teas." He looked at her with a gaze of refined kindness, forgiving her the sin of asking for reimbursement. "Another thing—I wouldn't ask if I didn't need it, but me sports coat . . . you know, the black one? It's at the cleaners and I've to go—"

"No laundry. I'm a production assistant."

"Rune."

"Write it down and read it. Assisting with production. Does not mean assisting with dry cleaning."

"Please?"

"Produce and laundry. Very different. Night and day."

He said, "Let you use the Arriflex next time out."

"No laundry."

"Jesus."

She finished the beer. "Larry, I want to ask you about something."

"I just gave you a raise."

"There was this bombing? In Midtown. A porn theater got blown up."

"Not a place you frequent, I 'ope."

"I walked by just before it happened. It looks like this religious group did it. Some right-wing fanatics or something. And what it is, I want to do a film about it."

"You?"

"A documentary."

When she was in her characteristic slouch Rune came to Larry's second button down. Now she stood up and rose almost to his collar. "I came here to learn how to make films. It's been eleven months and all I do is get coffee and pick up equipment and coil cables on the set and drop off film and walk Bob's mangy dog."

"I thought you liked him."

"He's a wonderful dog. That's not the point."

He looked at his Rolex. "They're waiting for me."

"Let me do it, Larry. I'll give you a producing credit."

"Bloody generous of you. And what do you know about documentaries?"

She forced her small mouth into a smile that impersonated admiration. "I've been watching you for almost a year."

"Balls. All you got is balls. You got no film technique."

"Two outa three," Rune said.

"Look, luv, not to make myself into a flamin' genius

but I got fifty, sixty resumes sitting in me desk right now. And most of them're dying for the privilege of getting me fuckin' laundry."

"I'll pay for the film myself."

"All right. Forget the laundry. I got a roomful of people need caffeine." He put a crumpled five in her hand. "*Please* get some coffee."

"Can I use a camera after work?"

Another glance at the watch. "Fuck. All right. But no camera. The Betacam."

"Aw, Larry, *video*?"

"Video's the wave of the future, luv. You buy your own friggin' tape. And I'm checking the Arris and the Bolexes every night. If one's missing, even for a half hour, you're fired. And you do the work on your own time. That's the best you're getting."

She smiled sweetly. "Would you like some biscuits with your tea, mate?"

As she turned to leave Larry called, "Hey, luv, one thing . . . This bombing, whatever 'appened, the news'll do the story up right."

Rune nodded, seeing that intensity she recognized in his eyes when he was on a set shooting or kicking around ideas with Bob or the cinematographer. She paid attention. He continued. "Use the bombing like a 'ook."

"A hook?"

"You want to make a good documentary, do a film that's about the bombing but not about the bombing."

"It sounds like Zen."

"Fucking Zen, right." He twisted his mouth. "And three sugars for me tea. Last time you bleedin' forgot."

Rune was paying for the tea and coffee when she remembered Stu. She was surprised she hadn't thought about him before this. And so she paid the deli guy two bucks of her own money, which is the way she looked at Larry's change, to have somebody deliver the cartons to L&R.

Then she stepped outside and trudged toward the subway.

A low-rider, a fifteen-year-old beige sedan, churned past her. The horn sang and from the shadows of the front seat came a cryptic solicitation, lost in the ship's diesel bubbling of the engine. The car accelerated away.

God, it was hot. Halfway to the subway stop, she bought a paper cone of shaved ice from a Latino street vendor. Rune shook her head when he pointed to the squirt bottles of syrup, smiled at his perplexed expression, and rubbed the ice over her forehead, then dropped a handful down the front of her T-shirts. He got a kick out of it and she left him with a thoughtful look on his face, maybe considering a new market for his goods.

Painful hot.

Mean hot.

The ice melted before she got to the subway stop and the moisture had evaporated before the train arrived.

The A train swept along under the streets back up to Midtown. Somewhere above her was the smoking ruin of the Velvet Venus Theater. Rune stared out the window intently. Did anyone live down here in the subway system? She wondered. Maybe there were whole tribes of homeless people, families, who'd made a home in the abandoned tunnels. They'd be a great subject for a documentary too. *Life Below the Streets.*

This started her thinking about the hook for her film. *About the bombing but not about the bombing.*

And then it occurred to her. The film should be about a single person. Someone the bombing had affected. She thought about movies she liked—they were never about issues or about ideas in the abstract. They were about people. What happened to them. But who should she pick? A patron in the theater who'd been injured? No, no

one would volunteer to help her out. Who'd want to admit he'd been hurt in a porn theater. How 'bout the owner
or the producer of porn films. *Sleazy* came to mind. One
thing Rune knew was that the audience has to care about
your main character. And some scumbag in the Mafia or
whoever made those movies wasn't going to get much
sympathy from the audience.

About the bombing but not . . .

As the subway sped underground the more she
thought about doing the document the more excited she
became. Oh, a film like this wouldn't catapult her to fame
but it would—what was the word?—*validate* her. The list
of her abortive careers was long: clerking, waitressing,
selling, cleaning, window dressing. . . . Business was
not her strength. The one time Rune had come into some
money, Richard, her ex-boyfriend, had thought up dozens
of safe investment ideas. Businesses to start, stocks to buy.
She'd accidentally left his portfolio files on the merry-go-
round in Central Park. Not that it mattered anyway because she spent most of the money on a new place to live.

I'm not good with the practical stuff, she'd told him.

What she was good with was what she'd *always* been
good with: stories—like fairy tales and movies. And despite her mother's repeated warning when she was
younger ("No girl can make a living at movies except you-
know-what-kind-of-girl"), the odds of making a career in
film seemed a lot better than in fairy tales.

She was, she'd decided, born to make films and this
one—a real, grown-up film (a *documentary:* the ground-
zero of serious films)—had in the last hour or two became
vitally important to her, as encompassing as the air pressure that hit her when the subway pounded into the tunnel. One way or another, this documentary was going to
get made.

She looked out the window. Whatever subterranean

colonies lived in the subways, they'd have to wait a few more years for their story to be told.

The train crashed past them or past rats and trash or past nothing at all while Rune thought about nothing but her film.

. . . *but not about the bombing.*

████

In the offices of Belvedere Post-Production the air-conditioning was off.

"Give me a break," she muttered.

Stu, not looking up from *Gourmet,* waved.

"I do not believe this place," Rune said. "Aren't you dying?"

She walked to the window and tried to open the greasy, chicken-wire-impregnated glass. It was frozen with age and paint and wormy strips of insulating putty. She focused on the green slate of the Hudson River as she struggled. Her muscles quivered. She groaned loudly. Stu sensed his cue and examined the window from his chair, then pushed himself into a standing slump. He was young and big but had developed muscles mostly from kneading bread and whisking egg whites in copper bowls. After three minutes he breathlessly conceded defeat.

"Hot air outside's all we'd get anyway." He sat down again. He jotted notes for a recipe, then frowned. "Are you here for a pickup? I don't think we're doing anything for L&R."

"Naw, I wanted to ask you something. It's personal."

"Like?"

"Like who are your clients?"

"That's *personal*? Well, mostly ad agencies and independent film makers. Networks and big studios occasionally but—"

"Who are the independents?"

"You know, small companies doing documentaries or

low-budget features. Like L&R . . . You're grinning and you're coy and there's an old expression about butter melting in the mouth that I could never figure out but I think fits here. What's up?"

"You ever do adult films?"

He shrugged. "Oh, porn? Sure. We do a lot of it. I thought you were asking me something inscrutable."

"Can you give me the name of somebody at one of the companies?"

"I don't know. Isn't this some kind of business-ethics question, client confidentiality—"

"Stu, we're talking about a company making films that're probably illegal in most of the world and you're worried about business ethics?"

Stu shrugged. "If you don't tell them I sent you, you might try Lame Duck Productions. They're a big one. And just a couple blocks from you guys."

"From L&R?"

"Yeah. On Nineteenth near Fifth."

The man's huge Rolodex spun and gave off an afternoon library smell. He wrote down the address.

"Do they have an actress who's famous in the business?"

"What business?"

"Adult films."

"You're asking me? I have no idea."

"When you super the credits in the postproduction work, don't you see the names? Whose name do you see the most?"

He thought for a minute. "Well, I don't know whether she's famous but there's one actress for Lame Duck that I see all the time. Her name's Shelly Lowe."

There was a familiarity about the name.

"Does she have a narrow face, blonde?"

"Yeah, I guess. I didn't look at her face very much."

Rune frowned. "You're a dirty old man."

"You know her?" he asked.

"There was a bombing in Times Square, this porn the-ater. . . . Did you hear about it?"

"No."

"Just today, a couple hours ago. I think she was in one of the movies that was playing there when it happened."

Perfect.

Rune put the address in her plastic leopard-skin shoul-der bag.

Stu rocked back in his chair.

"Well?" Rune asked.

"Well what?"

"Aren't you curious why I asked?"

Stu held up a hand. "That's okay. Some things are best kept secret." He opened his magazine and said, "You ever made a *tarte aux marrons*?"

CHAPTER TWO

■■■ *Contrasts.*

Rune sat in the huge loft that was the lobby of Lame
Duck Productions and watched the two young women
stroll to a desk across the room. Overhead, fans rotated
slowly and forced air-conditioned breezes throughout the
place.

The woman in the lead walked as if she had a degree in
it. Her feet were pointed forward, her back straight, hips
not swaying. She had honey-blonde hair tied back with a
braided rope of rainbow-colored strings. She wore a white
jumpsuit but saved it from tackiness by wearing sandals,
not boots, and a thin, brown leather belt.

Rune examined her closely but wasn't sure if this was
the same woman she'd seen in the poster. In that photo,
the one on the front of the porno theater, her makeup had
been good; today, this woman had a dull complexion. She
seemed very tired.

The other woman was younger. She was short, face

glossy, a figure bursting out of the seams of her outfit. She had a huge, jutting—and undoubtedly fake—bust and broad shoulders. The black tank top showed a concise waist; the miniskirt crowned thin legs. There was no saving this cookie from tack; she had spiky high heels, feathery and teased hair sprayed with glitter and purple-brown makeup, which did a fair job minimizing the effect of a wide, Slavic nose.

Wouldn't be a bad-looking woman, Rune thought, if her mother dressed her right.

They stopped in front of her. The shorter one smiled. The tall blonde said, "So you're the reporter from, what was it, *Erotic Film Monthly*?" She shook her head. "I thought I knew everybody from the industry mags. Are you new with them?"

Rune started to continue the lie. But impulsively she said, "What I am is dishonest."

Which got a faint smile. "Oh?"

"I lied to the receptionist. To get in the front door. Are you Shelly Lowe?"

A momentary frown. Then she gave a curious smile and said, "Yes. But that's not my real name."

The handshake was strong, a man's grip, confident.

Her friend said, "I'm Nicole. That *is* my real name. But my last name isn't. D'Orleans." She gave it a Gallic pronunciation. "But it's spelled like the city."

Rune took her hand carefully; Nicole had inch-long purple fingernails.

"I'm Rune."

"Interesting," Shelly said. "Is it real?"

Rune shrugged. "As real as yours."

"Lot of stage names in our business," Shelly said. "I lose track sometimes. Now tell me why you're a liar."

"I thought they'd kick me out if I was honest."

"Why would they do that? You a right-wing crazy? You don't look like one."

Rune said, "I want to make a movie about you."

"Do you now?"

"You know about the bombing?"

"Oh, that was terrible," Nicole said, actually shivering in an exaggerated way.

"We all know about it," Shelly said.

"I want to use it as sort of a jumping-off point for my film."

"And I'm the one you want to jump to?" Shelly asked.

Rune thought about those words, thought about disagreeing with her but said, "That's about it."

"Why me?"

"Just a coincidence really. One of your pictures was playing when the bomb went off."

Shelly nodded slowly, and Rune found herself staring at her. Nicole was scrunching her broad, shiny face at the mention of the explosion and the deaths in the theater, closing her eyes, practically crossing herself, while Shelly was simply listening, leaning against a column, her arms crossed.

Rune's thoughts were muddled. Under Shelly's gaze she felt young and silly, a child being indulged.

Nicole took a package of sugar-free gum from her pocket, unwrapped a stick and began to chew. Rune said, "Anyway, that's what I want to do."

Shelly said, "You know anything about the adult-film business?"

"I used to work for a video store. My boss said the adult films gave us the best margin."

She was proud of herself for that, saying something about *business*. Margin. A mature way to talk about fuck films.

"There's money to be made," Shelly said. Hers were eyes that sent out a direct light. Pale blue laser beam. They were intense at the moment but Rune sensed they were switchable—that Shelly could choose in an instant to be probing or angry or vindictive by a slight touch to the nerves. Rune assessed too that her eyes wouldn't dance with humor and there was a lot they chose not to say. She wanted to start her documentary with the camera on Shelly's eyes.

The actress said nothing, glanced at Nicole, who chewed her gum enthusiastically.

"Do you two, like, perform together?" Rune blushed fiery red.

The actresses shared a glance, then laughed.

"I mean . . . ," Rune began.

"Do we work together?" Nicole filled in.

"Sometimes," Shelly said.

"We're roommates too," Nicole said.

Rune glanced at the iron pillars and tin ceiling. "This is an interesting place. This studio."

"It used to be a shirtwaist factory."

"Yeah? What's that?" Nicole asked.

"A woman's blouse," Shelly said, not looking down from the ceiling.

Shelly is tall and she isn't a stunning beauty. Her presence comes from her figure (and eyes!). Her cheekbones are low. She has skin the consistency and the pale shade of a summer overcast. "How did I get into the business? I was raped when I was twelve. My uncle molested me. I'm a heroin addict—don't I cover it up well? I was kidnaped by migrant workers in Michigan. . . ."

Nicole lit a cigarette. She kept working on the gum too.

Shelly looked down from the tin panels at Rune. "So this would be a documentary?"

Rune said, "Like on PBS."

Nicole said, "Somebody wanted me to do one once, this guy. A documentary. But you know what he really wanted."

Shelly asked, "Still hot out?"

"Boiling."

Nicole gave a faint laugh, though Rune had no idea what she was thinking of.

Shelly walked to a spot where cold air cascaded on the floor. She turned and examined Rune. "You seem enthusiastic. More enthusiastic than talented. Excuse me. That's just my opinion. Well, about your film—I want to think about it. Let me know where I can get in touch with you."

"See, it'll be great. I can—"

"Let me think about it," Shelly said calmly.

Rune hesitated, looked at the woman's aloof face for a long moment. Then dug into her leopard-skin bag, but before she found her Road Runner pen Shelly produced a heavy, lacquered Mont Blanc. She took it; felt the warmth of the barrel. She wrote slowly but Shelly's gaze made her uneasy and the lines were lumpy and uneven. She gave Shelly the paper and said, "That's where I live. Christopher Street. All the way to the end. At the river. You'll see me." She paused. "Will I see you?"

"Maybe," Shelly said.

■■■■■

"Yo, film me, momma, come on, film me."

"Hey, you wanna shoot my dick? You got yourself a wide-angle lens, you can shoot my dick."

"Shit, be a microscope what she need for that."

"Yo, fuck you, man."

Walking out of the Times Square subway, Rune ignored her admirers, hefted the camera to her shoulder and walked along the platform. She passed a half-dozen beggars, shaking her head at their pleas for coins, but she dropped a couple of quarters into a box in front of a young South American couple giving a tango demonstration to the rattling music of a boom box.

It was eight p.m., a week after she'd first met with Shelly and Nicole. Rune had called Shelly twice. At first the actress had been pretty evasive about doing the film but the second time she'd called, Shelly had said, "If I *were* to do it would you give me a chance to review the final cut?"

From her work at L&R, and her love of movies in general, Rune knew that the final cut—the last version of the film, what was shown in the theaters—was the Holy Grail of the film business. Only producers and a few elite directors controlled the final cut. No actor in the history of Hollywood ever had final cut approval.

But she now said, "Yes."

Instinctively feeling that it was the only way she could get Shelly Lowe to do the film.

"I'll let you know in a day or two for sure."

Rune was now out looking for atmosphere footage and for establishing shots—the long-angle scenes in films that orient the audience and tell them what city or neighborhood they're in.

And there was plenty of atmosphere here. Life in the Tenderloin, Times Square. The heart of the porno district in New York. She was excited at the thought of actually shooting footage for her first film but remembered the words of Larry, her mentor, as she was heading out of L&R studios that night. "Don't overdo it, Rune. Any friggin' idiot can put together ninety minutes of great atmosphere. The *story's* the important thing. Don't ever bleedin' forget that. The story."

She eased into the swirl and noise and madness of Times Square, the intersection of Seventh Avenue, Broadway and Forty-second. She waited at the curb for the light, looking down at the accidental montage embedded in the asphalt at her feet: a Stroh's bottle cap, a piece of green glass, a brass key, two pennies. She squinted; in the arrangement, she saw a devil's face.

Ahead of her was a white high-rise on the island of concrete surrounded by the wide streets; fifty feet up, the day's news was displayed along a thick collar of moving lights. ". . . *SOVIETS EXPRESS HOPE FOR . . .*"

The light changed and she never saw the end of the message. Rune crossed the street and passed a handsome black woman in a belted, yellow cotton dress, who was shouting into a microphone. "There's something even better in heaven. Amen! Give up your ways of the flesh. Amen! You can win the lottery, you can become a multi-millionaire, billionaire, get everything you ever wanted. But all that gain cannot compare with what you'll find in heaven. Amen! Give up your sinful ways, your lusts. . . . If I die in my little room tonight, why, I'd praise the good Lord because I know what that means. That means, I'm going to be in heaven tomorrow. Amen!"

A few people chorused with *amens*. Most walked on.

Farther north in the Square, things were ritzier, around the TKTS discount ticket booth, where one could see the huge billboards that any out-of-towner who watched television would recognize. Here was Lindy's restaurant, with its famous and overpriced cheesecake. Here was the Brill Building—Tin Pan Alley. Several glossy, new office buildings, a new first-run movie theater.

But Rune avoided that area. She was interested in the southern part of Times Square.

Where it was a DMZ.

She passed a number of signs in stores and arcades and theaters: STOP THE TIMES SQUARE REDEVELOPMENT PROJECT. This was the big plan to wipe the place clean and bring in offices and expensive restaurants and theaters. Purify the neighborhood. No one seemed to want it but there didn't seem to be organized resistance to the project. That was the contradiction of Times Square; it was a place that was energetically apathetic. Busyness and hustle abounded but you still sensed the area was on its way out. Many of the stores were going out of business. Nedick's—the hot dog station from the forties—was closing, to be replaced by slick, mirrored Mike's Hot Dogs and Pizza. Only a few of the classic Forty-second Street movie theaters—many of them had been grand old burlesque houses—were still open. And all they showed was porn or kung fu or slasher flicks.

Rune glanced across the street at the huge old art-deco Amsterdam Theater, which was all boarded up, its curvaceous clock stopped at five minutes to three. Of which day of which month of which year? she wondered. Her eye strayed to an alleyway and she caught a flash of motion. Someone seemed to be watching her, someone in a red jacket. Wearing a hat, she believed. Then the stranger vanished.

Paranoid. Well, this was the place for it.

Then she walked past dozens of small stores, selling fake-gold jewelry, electronics, pimp suits, cheap running shoes, ID photos, souvenirs, bootleg perfumes and phony designer watches. Hawkers were everywhere, directing bewildered tourists into their stores.

"Check it out, check it. . . . We got what you need, and you gonna like what we got. Check it out. . . ."

One store, the windows painted black, named Art's Novelties, had a single sign in the window. LEISURE PRODUCTS. YOU MUST BE TWENTY-ONE TO ENTER.

Rune tried to peek inside. What the hell was a leisure product?

She kept walking, listing against the weight of the camera, sweat running down her face and neck and sides.

The smells were of garlic and oil and urine and rotting food and car exhaust. And, brother, the crowds . . . Where did all these people come from? Thousands of them. Where was home? The city? The burbs? Why were they here?

Rune dodged out of the way of two teenage boys in T-shirts and Guess? jeans, walking fast, in an arm-swinging, loping roll, their voices harsh. "Man, mothafuckah be mah boss but he don' own me, man. You hear what I'm sayin', man?"

"Fuck no, he don' own neither of us."

"He try that again, man, an' I'll deck him. I mothahfuckin' deck him, man. . . ."

They passed her by, Rune and her camera, as she taped a visual history of Times Square.

A place like no other in New York.

Times Square . . .

But every Magic Kingdom needs its Mordor or Hades and tonight as Rune walked through the place she didn't feel too uneasy. She was on her quest, making her movie. *About the bombing but not about the bombing.* She didn't have to justify the creepy place to anyone or worry about anybody's shoes but her own and she was careful where she put her feet.

Behind her, a huge snort.

Fantastic! Knights!

Rune turned the camera on two mounted policemen, who sat rod-straight in their saddles, their horses lolling their heads and stomping solid hooves into the piles of granular manure under them.

"Hey, Sir Gawain!" Rune called. They glanced at her, then decided she wasn't worth flirting with and continued to scan the street with stony gazes that streamed from under the visors of their robin's-egg-blue helmets.

It was when she looked down from the tall, chestnut horse that she saw the red jacket again. It vanished even more quickly than earlier.

A chill ran through her, despite the heat.

Who was it? she wondered.

No one. Just one of the ten million people in the Magic Kingdom. And she forgot about it as she turned the corner and walked up Eighth Avenue toward the site of the former Velvet Venus Theater.

Along this stretch she counted six porn theaters and

adult bookstores. Some had live dancers, some had peep shows where for a quarter or a token you could watch films in little booths. She stuck the camera through the door and shot a sign (ONLY ONE PERSON PER BOOTH. IT'S THE LAW AND OUR POLICY. HAVE A NICE DAY) until a big guy selling tokens shooed her away.

She got some good footage of commuters on their way to the Port Authority and their homes in suburban Jersey. Some glanced in the windows; most wore glazed faces. A few businessmen turned quickly into the theaters, not pausing at all, as though a gust of wind had blown them through the door.

It was then that a humid wind carried a sour stink of burn to her. From the theater, she knew. Rune shut off the camera and strolled up the street.

Still spooked. The paranoia again. But she still could hear, in her memory, the terrible bang of the explosion. The ground moving under her. Recalling the bodies, the *parts* of bodies. The terrible aftermath of the bomb and the fire. She glanced back, saw no one watching her.

She continued along the street, thinking: The press coverage of the event had been good. *News at Eleven* had devoted ten minutes to the incident and the story had been a hook for a *Time* magazine article on the trends in adult films ("Hard Times for Hard-Core?") and one in the *Village Voice* on the conflict the bombing presented to the First Amendment ("Disrespecting Religion and Abridging the Press"). But, as Larry had predicted, those were all spot news stories, hard news. Nobody was doing a human-interest piece on the bombing.

Come on, Shelly, she thought. You're the key. I need you. . . .

As she approached the ruins of the theater Rune paused, resting her hand on the yellow police tape. The odor was stronger than the day of the bombing. She al-most gagged on the air, thick with the smell of wet, scorched upholstery. And something else—a sickening cardboardy scent. It would have to be the scorched bodies, Rune figured, and tried to force the image out of her thoughts.

Across the street was another theater. The neon said: THE FINEST IN ADULT ENTERTAINMENT. COOL, COMFORTABLE AND SAFE. Rune assumed that patrons were not much soothed by the illuminated reassurance and that business was slow.

She turned back to the destroyed theater and was startled by motion. Her first thought: Shit, he's back. Whoever was following her through Times Square.

A man's face . . .

Panic took her. Just as she was about to turn and run she squinted into the shadows and got a better look at her pursuer. He wore jeans and a navy-blue windbreaker that said NYPD in white letters on the chest. It was Cowboy. The guy from the Bomb Squad.

She closed her eyes and exhaled slowly. Tried to steady her shaking hands. He sitting on a folding chair, looking at a white sheet of paper, which he folded and put into his pocket. She saw a thin brown holster on his right hip. Rune lifted the camera and shot a minute or so of tape, opening the aperture wide to get some definition in the gloom.

He looked at the camera. She expected the man to tell her to get lost. But he merely stood and began walking through the ruined theater, kicking at debris, bending down occasionally to examine something, training his long black flashlight on the walls and floor.

The image in the viewfinder of the heavy camera faded. Dusk had come quickly—or perhaps she just hadn't noticed it. She opened the lens wide but it was still very dim and she didn't have any lights with her. She knew the exposure was too dark. She shut the camera off, lowered it from her shoulder.

When she looked again into the building Cowboy was gone.

Where had he disappeared to?

She heard a scuttling of noise near her.

Something heavy fell.

"Hello?"

Nothing.

"Hey?" Rune called again.

There was no answer. She shouted into the ruins of the theater, "Were you following me? Hey, Officer? Somebody was following me. Was it you?"

Another sound, like boots on concrete. Nearby. But she didn't know where exactly.

Then a car engine started. She spun around. Looking for the blue-and-white station wagon, emblazoned with BOMB SQUAD. But she didn't see it.

A dark car pulled out of an alley and vanished up Eighth Avenue.

Uneasy once more. No, damn scared, for some reason. But as she looked over the people on Eighth Avenue she saw only harmless passersby. People on their way to the theaters. Everybody lost in their own worlds. Nobody in the coffee shops and bars paid her any mind. A horde of tourists walked past, obviously wondering why the hell their tour guide was leading them through *this* neighborhood. Another teen, a mean-looking Latino, propositioned her harmlessly and walked on when she ignored him, telling her to have a nice night. Across the street a man in a wide-brimmed hat carrying a Lord & Taylor shopping bag was gazing into the window of an adult bookstore.

Nobody in a red jacket, nobody spying on her.

Paranoia, she decided. Just paranoia.

Still, she shut down the camera, put the cassette into her leopard-skin bag and headed for the subway. Deciding that she'd had enough atmosphere for one night.

In the alley across the street from what was left of the Velvet Venus a bum sat beside a Dumpster, drinking from a bottle of Thunderbird. He squinted as a man stepped into the alley.

Hell, he's gonna pee here, the bum thought. They *always* do that. Have beers with their buddies and can't make it to Penn Station in time so they come into my alley and pee. He wondered how the guy'd feel if the bum walked into *his* living room to take a leak.

But the man didn't unzip. He paused at the mouth of the alley and peered out over Eighth Avenue, looking for something, frowning.

Wondering what the man was doing here, why he was wearing that wide-brimmed, old-fashioned hat, the bum took another sip of liquor and set the bottle down. It made a clink.

The man whirled around quickly.

"Got a quarter?" the bum asked.

"You scared me. I didn't know anybody was there."

"Got a quarter?"

The man fished in his pocket. "Sure. Are you going to spend it on booze?"

"Probably," the bum said. Sometimes he'd hustle the crowds at the commuter stations by saying, "Help the blind, help the blind. . . . I want to get blind drunk." And people gave him more money because he'd made them laugh.

"Well, I appreciate honesty. Here you go." The man reached down with a coin.

As the bum began to take it he felt his wrist gripped hard by the man's left hand.

"Wait!"

But the man didn't wait. Then there was a slight stinging feeling on the bum's neck. Then another, on the other side. The man let go of his wrists and the bum touched his throat, feeling two flaps of skin dangling loose. Then saw the razor knife in the man's hand, the bloody blade retracting.

The bum tried to shout for help. But the blood was gushing fast from the two wounds and his vision was going black. He tried to stand but fell hard to the cobblestones. The last thing he saw was the man reaching into his Lord & Taylor shopping bag, pulling out a red windbreaker and pulling it on. Then stepping out of the alley quickly as if he were, in fact, late for his commuter train home.

CHAPTER THREE

The next morning Rune was lying in bed—well, a bunk—listening to the sounds of the river. There was a knock on her front door.

She pulled on her jeans and a red silk kimono, then walked to the front of the boat. She opened the door and found she was looking at Shelly Lowe's back. The actress was examining the water lapping under her feet as she stood on a small gangway painted egg-yolk yellow. She turned and shook her head. Rune nodded at the familiar reaction.

"It's a houseboat. You live on a houseboat."

Rune said, "I used to make wisecracks about having water in the basement. But the material's limited. There aren't a lot of houseboat jokes."

"You don't get seasick?"

"The Hudson River isn't exactly Cape Horn." Rune stepped back to let Shelly into the narrow entryway. In the distance, along the roof of the pier to the north, a flash

of color. Red. It reminded her of something disturbing.
She couldn't remember what.

She followed Shelly into the boat.

"Give me a tour."

The style: nautical suburban ranch, mid-fifties. Downstairs were the living room, kitchen and bath. Up a narrow staircase were two small rooms: the pilot house and
bedroom. Outside, a railing and deck circled the living
quarters.

The smell was of motor oil and rose potpourri.

Inside, Rune showed her a recent acquisition: a half-
dozen Lucite paperweights with flecks of colored plastic
chips in them. "I'm very into antiques. These are guaranteed 1955. That was a great year, my mother tells me."

Shelly nodded with detached politeness and looked
around the rest of the room. There was a lot to put politeness to the test: turquoise walls, a painted vase (the scene:
a woman in pedal pushers walking a poodle), Lava lamps,
kidney-shaped plastic tables, a lampshade made out of
Bon Ami and Ajax cleanser cartons, wrought-iron and
black-canvas chairs you sank down into like hammocks,
an old Motorola console TV.

Also: an assortment of fairy-tale dolls, stuffed animals
and shelves filled with old books.

Shelly pulled a scaly, battered Brothers Grimm off the
shelf, flipped through and replaced it.

Rune squinted at Shelly, studying her. A thought occurred to her. She laughed. "Know what's weird? I've got
a picture of you."

"Me?"

"Well, sort of. Here, look."

She took a dusty book from the shelf and opened it up.
Metamorphoses.

"Some old Roman dude wrote these stories."

"Roman?" Shelly asked. "As in Julius Caesar?"

"Yeah. Here, look at this picture."

Shelly glanced at the color plate of a beautiful woman being led out of a dark cave by a man playing a lyre. The caption read: *Orpheus and Eurydice*.

"See, you're her. Eurydice. You look just like her."

Shelly shook her head, then squinted. She laughed. "I do, you know. That's funny." She looked at the spine of the book. "This is Roman mythology?"

Rune nodded. "It was a sad story. Eurydice died and went down to Hades. Then Orpheus—he was her husband, this musician guy—went to rescue her. Isn't that romantic?"

"Wait. I've heard that story. It was an opera. Didn't something go wrong?"

"Yeah, those Roman gods had weird rules. The thing is he could take her out of the Underworld as long as he didn't look back at her. That makes a lot of sense, right? Anyway, he did and that blew the whole thing. Back she went. People think myths and fairy tales have happy endings. But they don't all."

Shelly gazed at the picture for a moment. "I collect old books too."

"What kind?" Rune assumed erotica.

But Shelly said, "Plays mostly. In high school I was president of the drama club. A thespian." She laughed. "Whenever I tell somebody in the Industry—I mean, the porn business—tell them that, they say something like, 'What's that, a dyke with a speech problem?' " She shook her head. "My profession's got a pretty low common denominator."

Rune clicked on an ultraviolet light. A black-light poster of a ship sailing around the moon popped out into three dimensions. It was next to purple-and-orange tie-dye hangings. "I mix my eras. But you don't want to get too locked in, do you now? Never be too literal. That's my motto."

"Avoid it at all costs." Shelly had climbed up to the

pilot house and was pulling the whistle cord. There was no noise. "Can you take this thing out for rides?"

"Naw, it doesn't drive," Rune said. "Oh, no wait, I'm supposed to say *she*. She doesn't drive."

"Drive?"

"Well, sail or whatever. There's a motor, but it doesn't work. My old boyfriend and I were driving up along the Hudson and we found it—I mean, *her*—moored near Bear Mountain. She was for sale. I asked the owner to take me out for a spin and he said the motor didn't work so we went out for a tow. We did a lot of haggling and when he agreed to throw in the Formica dining room set I had to get it."

"You pay to dock it here?"

"Yep. You pay the Port Authority. They still run the docks even though they don't have much ship traffic anymore. It's pretty expensive. I don't think I can stay here forever. But it'll do for now."

"Is it safe?"

Rune pointed out one of the picture windows. "That's still a working pier so this whole area's chained off. The security guards and I are friends. They keep an eye out. I give them good Christmas presents. It's really neat, owning a house. And there's no grass to mow."

Shelly gave her another wan smile. "You're so . . . enthusiastic. And you actually live on a houseboat in Manhattan. Amazing."

Rune's eyes sparkled. "Come here. I'll show you what's amazing." She walked out onto the small gray-painted deck. She clung to a railing and dipped her foot into the opaque oily water.

"You going swimming?" Shelly asked uncertainly.

Rune closed her eyes. "You know that I'm touching the exact same water that's lapping up on the Galápagos Islands, and in Venice, and in Tokyo and Hawaii and Egypt? It's so neat. And—I haven't figured this out yet—it may very well be the same water that splashed against the *Nina, Pinta* and *Santa Maria* and against Napoléon's ships. The same water they used to wash away the blood after Marie Antoinette got the axe. . . . I'm guessing that it might be. . . . That's the part I'm not too clear on. Does water, like, die? I remember something from science class. I think it just keeps recirculating."

Shelly said, "You have quite an imagination."

"I've been told that before." Rune jumped back on deck. "Coffee? Something to eat?"

"Just coffee."

They sat in the pilot house. Rune was putting peanut butter on her toast while Shelly sipped black coffee. The woman may have been a celebrity in the flesh trade but today she looked just like a Connecticut housewife. Jeans, boots, white blouse and a thin, light blue sweater, the arms tied around her neck.

"Find the place okay?" Rune asked.

"Wasn't hard. I would've called first but you didn't give me a number."

"I don't have a phone. When I tried to get one the New York Bell guys drove up, laughed and left."

A moment passed and Shelly said, "I've been thinking about the film. Even after you agreed to the final cut approval I didn't want to do it. But something happened that changed my mind."

"The bombing?"

"No," Shelly said. "What happened was I had a bad fight with one of the guys I work for. I don't want to go into the details but it brought a lot of things into focus. I realized how sick I was of the business. I've been in it too long. It's time to leave. If I can get some legitimate public-ity, if people can see that I'm not a bimbo, maybe it'll help me get legitimate jobs."

"I'll do a good job. I really will."

"I had a feeling about you." The pale blue laser beams

of her eyes fired out. "I think you're just the person who could tell my story. When can we start?"

Rune said, "How's now? I've got the day off."

She shook her head. "I've got some things to do now but why don't you meet me this afternoon, around, let's say, five? We can do a couple hours of work. Then tonight there's a party this publisher's giving. Most of the companies publishing skin magazines are also into adult films and video. There'll be a lot of people from the business there. Maybe you could talk to them."

"Excellent! Where do you want to do the filming?"

She looked around the room. "How's here? I feel very comfortable here."

"It's going to be a great interview."

Shelly smiled. "I may even be honest."

After Shelly'd left, Rune was at the window. She caught another glint of red from the roof of the pier across the spit of slick water.

And she remembered the color.

The same as the jacket or windbreaker of the person she'd seen—or thought she'd seen—in Times Square, following her.

She went into her bedroom and dressed.

Five minutes later the red was still there. And five minutes after that she was on her way toward the pier, running low, crouched like a soldier. Around her neck was a big chrome whistle, the kind football referees use. She figured she could get 120 decibels easy and scare the hell out of anybody looking to give her trouble.

Which was fine for skittish attackers. For the others Rune had something else. A small, round canister. It contained 113 grams of CS-38 military tear gas. She felt its comfortable weight against her leg.

She hurried along the highway. The river water gave

off its rotten-ripe smell, riding on the humidity that the clouds—now covering the sky—had brought. The day became still. Several church bells chimed. It was exactly noon.

Rune twisted through the gap in the chain link and walked slowly up to the pier. It rose three stories above her and the facade was weathered down to the bare wood in many places. She could make out part of the name of the shipping line across the top, in a dark blue paint that she associated with old-fashioned trains. *America* was one word. And she saw, or thought she did, a faint blue star.

The twelve-foot wooden doors looked imposing but were off their track and Rune easily slipped through a seam into the darkness.

It was ratty and spooky inside. At one time these piers had been the places from which the great liners had sailed to Europe. Then they'd been used for cargo ships until Brooklyn and New Jersey docks took over most of that business. Now, they were mostly just relics. A barge half the size of a football field had appeared one day, moored next to Rune's houseboat, while she'd been at the studio. But that was the only commercial shipping traffic in the neighborhood.

Rune had been to this particular pier a couple of times since she'd docked the boat along this stretch of river. She'd stroll around, imagining what the luxurious liners of the nineteenth century must've been like. She also wondered if some of the ships had dropped off contraband (gold bullion was a front-runner) that had never been found. Pirates, she knew, had sailed the Hudson River, not far from here. She wasn't surprised that she found no chests of gold. The only salvage was empty cardboard boxes, lumber and big pieces of rusty machinery.

After she'd decided there was no plunder Rune would come occasionally to picnic with friends on the roof and watch the giants in the clouds play above the city until they disappeared over Brooklyn and Queens. Sometimes she'd come just to be by herself and feed the gulls.

In the portion of the pier farthest into the water there were warrens of rooms. These had been offices and the off-loading docks and were boarded up now. Whatever light snuck in did so through the grace of the carpenters' sloppy nailing. This portion of the pier contained the rickety staircase that led up to the roof.

And this portion of the pier was what she now slipped into. Rune eased through the back of the pier and started toward the stairs slowly. At the foot of the stairwell the floor of the pier had given way; a ragged hole three feet across led down into darkness. Water lapped. The smell was sharp and foul. Rune stared through the gloom at the hole and edged slowly past it.

She listened carefully on her way up but there was no sound other than distant traffic and the water on the pilings and the wind that meant the storm would hit pretty soon. Rune paused at the top landing. She pulled the white tear gas canister from her pocket and pushed the door open.

The roof was empty.

She stepped outside, then walked carefully along the rotting tar paper and gravel, testing each square in front of her. At the edge, she walked back toward the front of the building to the spot where she thought she'd seen the guy.

Rune stopped and looked down at her feet.

Okay, so it's *not* my imagination. She was looking at footprints in the tar. They were large—a man's shoe size. And were smooth, like conservative business shoes, not sneakers or running shoes. But aside from that, nothing. No cigarette ash, no discarded bottles. No cryptic messages.

As she stood there a sprinkling of rain began and she

hurried back to the stairs. She started down slowly, reaching out with her foot to find the flooring in the dimness.

A noise.

She paused on the second-floor landing. Stepped through an open doorway into the dark, abandoned office. Her hand gripped the tear gas canister firmly. Her pupils, contracted from the brightness, couldn't take in enough light to see anything.

But she could hear. Rune froze.

He's here!

Someone was in the room.

Nothing specific told her—no popping boards, no whispers, no shuffles of feet. The message was transmitted maybe by a smell or maybe by some sixth-sense radar.

The wave came back with a message: Whoa, honey, he's big and he's pretty damn close.

Rune didn't move. The other figure didn't either though twice she heard the air of his breath across his teeth. Her eyes became accustomed to the dark and she looked for a target and slowly lifted the tear gas.

Her hands began to quiver.

No, not one but two of them.

And they were ghosts.

Two pale forms. Humanlike, vague, undefined. They both stared at her. One held a thick, white billy club.

She aimed the canister at them. "I've got a gun."

"Shit," a man's voice said.

The other voice, also male, said, "Take the wallet. Take *both* wallets."

Her vision was improving. The apparitions turned into two naked, crew-cut men in their mid-thirties. She began to laugh when she saw what the club was; it was now considerably smaller.

"Sorry," she said.

"This isn't a mugging?"

"Sorry."

Heavy-duty indignation. "Well, I just want you to know you scared the living hell out of us. For your information, this room happens to be reserved."

Rune asked, "How long have you been here?"

"Too long, apparently."

"For the last hour or so?"

The anger became giddy relief. One of the men nodded toward his friend and said, "He's good but he's not *that* good."

The other, more sober: "Forty-five minutes?"

"Closer."

Rune asked, "Did you hear anybody come down from the roof?"

"Yeah, I did. Fifteen minutes ago. Then you go up, then you come down. Grand Central Station today."

"Did you see him?"

"We *were* a little busy. . . ."

Rune said, "Please? It's important."

"We thought he was cruising but we weren't sure. You have to be kind of careful."

Sure. No telling what kind of degenerate you'll meet while having sex in deserted piers.

"So we kept mum."

"What did he look like?"

"Medium build. But otherwise I have no idea." Turning to his companion: "Do you? . . . No, we don't have any idea."

Rune said, "Did you see what he was wearing? A jacket?"

"A red windbreaker. Hat, an old-fashioned one. Dark slacks, I think," one voice said.

"Tight." From the other.

"You *would* notice that."

Rune said, "Well, thanks."

As she left she heard them whispering. Something

about not exactly being in the mood anymore. "Well, you can *try*."

She started the descent to the first floor.

Feeling her thudding heartbeats slow.

Rune laughed. *This room is reserved.* Why didn't they pick a more romantic—

He got her from behind.

At the foot of the stairs, as she was stepping carefully around the hole, the hand grabbed her ponytail and jerked her backward. She saw a gloved hand, holding a razor box cutter, start for her neck. She grabbed his wrist and dug in hard with her short nails. It deflected the knife and for a moment they grappled for it. She knew if she let go of the banister she'd fall but there was no other way to get the tear gas with her other hand; it was deep in her pocket.

Rune released her grip and as she tumbled into her attacker she grabbed the canister and, without aiming, pushed the button. A cloud sprayed out between them, blinding them both. She cried out in pain as the attacker spun away, hands over his face.

But he didn't let go and Rune felt herself being pulled backward. Eyes shut, she reached out but grabbed only air and fell in panic and confusion. Her breath exploded from her lungs as she hit the floor hard on her back. She twisted onto her stomach, then was up on one knee, scrabbling away from him. The man bent down quickly and gripped her around the neck. He wasn't strong. But he had surprise on his side—and desperation. He kicked her in the chest, again knocking her windless. She curled into a ball, gasping. Vaguely she saw his blurry form groping for the razor knife. She smelled old wood and salt water and motor oil and rot, and she tasted salt—maybe her tears, maybe blood.

Christ, her eyes stung. Like alcohol.

She too began looking for her weapon, slapping her hand on the floor, trying to find the canister of tear gas.

He gave up on the knife and looked at the floor near them. Then he grabbed her by the collar and dragged her toward the jagged black opening that led down to the Hudson. A roar was in her ears. He pushed her head, then her shoulders into the hole. He gripped her belt and she started to go in.

CHAPTER FOUR

▮▮▮▮▮ Rune lashed out with her boot and came close to catching his groin but her aim was bad. She hurt him only slightly and he just grunted angrily and drove a fist into her back.

She gave a faint scream. Tears ran. The rotten, fishy scent of the water rose from the water and choked her.

He kicked boards into the hole to widen it; they fell into darkness. He pushed her farther and farther in.

It was so dark beneath her!

She got a hand on the banister and held tight. But this was just a minor inconvenience; he kicked her hand and easily broke her grip.

I'll swim . . . But can I see the light of the surface? What if there's no way to swim out from underneath, what if there's just a pipe that goes a hundred feet down?

He dropped to his knees and took her by the hair with one hand, then reached out with the other toward the edge of the hole to get a good grip and fling her into it.

"Hell-o? Ohmygod!"

A man's voice.

The attacker froze.

"Jesus, what's going on?" the other man, from upstairs, asked. They'd either given up on their tryst or finished it and had come to investigate the noise.

The man let go of Rune and glanced up the stairs. She twisted away from him, as he leapt back, panicking. She rolled away from the foot of the stairs. When the attacker turned back toward her, reaching forward, what he was looking at wasn't Rune but a tiny hissing nozzle.

The stream of tear gas caught him in the nose.

Breathe it, sucker, breathe!

The man gasped, covered his eyes and took a wild swipe at her. Rune fired again. He stumbled past her, shoved her hard into the hole that led to the river and then ran into the warehouse.

His pounding footsteps faded, then vanished.

Rune pulled herself from the hole and collapsed onto the floor, frozen. She pressed her eyes shut against the terrible pain. Her nose and throat burned violently. She rested her face against the wooden floor as her breathing calmed and she smelled grease, felt the coolness of fresh air returning.

"Oh, my God," one of the men said. They were dressed now. "Are you all right? Who *was* he?"

They helped her to her feet.

"Did you get a look at him?" she asked.

"No, just saw that jacket."

"It was red," his friend answered. "Like I said. Oh, and the hat."

"You have to call the police. . . . What's that smell? It's terrible."

"Tear gas."

A pause. "Just who *are* you?"

Rune rose to her feet slowly, thanked them. Then stumbled through the warehouse out into the daylight.

When she got to a pay phone she called the police. They showed up pretty quickly. But, as she'd expected, there wasn't much they could do. She didn't have a detailed description of the attacker. Probably white male, medium build. No hair color, no eye color, no facial characteristic. A red windbreaker, like in *Don't Look Now*— that scary movie based on the Daphne du Maurier story. Which Rune deduced neither of the responding cops had seen or read, judging by the blank look on their faces.

They said they'd check into it, though they weren't happy that she'd had a canister of CS-38, which was illegal in the city.

"You have any idea why he'd want to do it?"

She supposed it might have something to do with her movie and the porn theater and the Sword of Jesus. She told them this and the look on their faces told her that, as far as they were concerned, the case was already a dead end. They flipped their notebooks closed and said they'd have a patrol car cruise past occasionally.

She asked them again how many men they were going to put on the case but they just looked at her blankly and told her they were sorry for her troubles.

And then they confiscated the tear gas.

━━━━━━

After cleaning up, putting hydrogen peroxide on the scrapes and digging a new tear gas canister out from under the sink, Rune went to L&R Productions.

" 'ey, what've we got 'ere?" Bob asked, examining her face.

She wasn't about to tell him that the injuries might have to do with her movie—since it was L&R's Betacam that would be at risk if she got machine-gunned down on the street.

"Guy hassled me. I beat the crap out of him."

"Uh-huh," Bob said skeptically.

"Listen, after work, I need to borrow the camera again. And some lights."

Bob, in a lecturing mood, said to her, "You know what this is, Rune?" Rubbing the large video camera as if it were a blonde's rump.

"Larry said it was okay. I've used it before."

"Humor an old man, luv. Tell me. What is it?"

"It's a Betacam video camera, Bob. It's made by Sony. It has an Ampex deck. I've used one about fifty times."

"Do you know how much they cost?"

"More than you'll ever pay me in my lifetime, I'll bet."

"Ha. It's worth forty-seven thousand dollars." He paused for dramatic effect.

"Larry told me that the first time he loaned it to me. I didn't think it'd gone down in value."

"You lose it, you break it, you burn out the tube, you pay for it."

"I'll be careful, Bob."

"Do you know what forty-seven thousand dollars will buy?" he asked philosophically. "A man could take forty-seven thousand dollars, move to Guatemala and live like a king for the rest of his life."

"I'll be careful." Rune began numbering storyboards for a TV commercial estimate that Larry and Bob were bidding on next week.

"Like a king for the rest of his days," Bob called out, retreating into the studio.

■

Rune set the Sony up on the deck of her houseboat, next to a single 400-watt Redhead lamp. She tore bits of silver gaffer tape from a large roll and with them mounted a pink gel on the black metal barn doors of the lamp. It put a soft glow on Shelly's face.

To master cinematography, luv, you master light, Larry had told her.

She added a small fill lamp behind Shelly.

Rune also found she was picking up the lights of the city over the actress's head, without any flare or after-image.

Looking through the eyepiece, she thought, Totally excellent.

Thinking too: It also looks like I know what I'm doing. She was very eager to impress her subject.

As she'd been stuffing the storyboards into an envelope Rune had been thinking up questions for Shelly. Jotting them on a yellow pad. But now, as she turned the light on and started the tape rolling, she hesitated. The questions reminded her of her journalism course in high school.

Uhm, when did you get started in the business?

Uhm, what're your favorite movies, other than adult movies?

Did you go to college and what did you major in?

Shelly, though, didn't need any questions. Rune got the opening shot she'd been planning all along—an ECU, extreme close-up, of those reactor-blue eyes—then pulled back. Shelly smiled and began to talk. She had a low, pleasing voice and seemed wholly in control, confident, like those feisty women senators and stockbrokers you see on PBS talk shows.

The first hour or so Shelly discussed the pornography industry in a matter-of-fact, businesslike way. Adult films were experiencing a reluctant death. They were no longer chic and trendy, as some had proclaimed them to be in the seventies. The excitement of illicit thrills was gone. The religious right and conservatives were more active. But, Shelly explained, there were other factors that helped the business. Certainly AIDS was a consideration. "Watching sex is the safest sex." Also,

people tended to be more faithful now; with fewer affairs, couples experimented more at home. You didn't
have to go to some stinky theater in a tawdry part of
town. You and your partner could watch sexual acrobatics in your own bedroom.

The mechanics for viewing porn had changed too.
"VCRs're the biggest contributor to the new popularity,"
she explained. Porn, Shelly felt, was meant for the video
medium. "Fifteen years ago, the heyday of big-production
porn, the budgets for a film sometimes hit a million dollars." There were elaborate special effects and constructed
sets and costumes and ninety-page screenplays that the
actors memorized. They were shot on 35mm film in Tech-
nicolor. The producers of the classic *Behind the Green Door*
actually campaigned for an Oscar.

Now, porn was virtually homemade, with dozens of
small companies in the business. They shot on tape, never
on film. A producer was somebody with five thousand
bucks, a good source of coke and six willing friends. There
were few superstars like John Holmes or Annette Haven or
Seka or Georgina Spelvin. Shelly Lowe was as famous as
anyone. (With a tough glance at the camera: "Hell, I've got
five hundred films under my belt. So to speak.") But stars'
fame was limited to New York and California mostly. In
Middle America Shelly Lowe was just another face on the
boxes of tapes offered for rental in curtained-off corners of
family video stores. If she'd been in the business in the
mid-seventies she would have done live appearances at
theater openings across the country. Now, that didn't happen.

Making a film was easy: A three-person crew rented a
loft or took over somebody's apartment for two days, set
up the camcorders and lights and sound, shot six to ten
fuck scenes and twenty minutes of transitions. The script
was a ten-page story idea. Dialogue was improvised. In
the postproduction house two versions were edited. Hard-

core for sale to the adult theaters, mail order, peep shows and video stores; soft for sale to the cable stations and in-room hotel movie services. Movie theaters weren't the biggest outlet for adult films anymore; they went out of business or put in video projection units, then went out of business anyway. But people rented porn tapes and took them home and watched them. Four thousand X-rated videos were made every year. They had become a commodity.

"Mass production. It's the era of pornography as Volkswagen."

"What about you? Like personally?" Rune asked. "You get forced into the business? Were you like kidnaped? Molested when you were ten?"

Shelly laughed. "Not hardly. I wanted to do it. Or maybe I should say that the pressures were subtle. I wanted desperately to act but I couldn't get any legit jobs. Nothing that paid the rent. Porn was the only job I could get. Then I found that not only was I acting but I was making great money. I had control. Not only creative control but sexual control too. It can be a real high."

"Weren't you exploited?"

Shelly laughed once more, shook her head. Looked straight into the camera. "That's the myth of pornography. No, we're not poor farm girls who get enslaved. Men have the power in legitimate films but in porn it's the other way around. Just like with sex in real life: It's the *women* who're in control. We have what men want and they're willing to pay for it. We make more money than men do, we dictate what we do and what we don't do. We're on top. Forgive the joke."

Surprise in Rune's voice: "So you like the business?"

A pause and the sincere eyes glazed back easily into the Betacam's expensive, glossy lens. "Not exactly. There's one problem. There's no sense of . . . beauty. They call them erotic films but there's nothing erotic about them.

Erotic connotes emotional stimulation as well as physical. Close-ups of people humping isn't erotic. I think I said this to you before: The business has a real low common denominator."

"So why have you stayed with it?" Rune asked.

"I do some legitimate theater now. Not much but every once in a while. And most I've ever made has been four thousand dollars a year. Making porn, I made a hundred twelve last year. Life's expensive. I took the path of least resistance."

Shelley slumped an inch and Rune noticed something. The tough, flirty woman who'd begun talking, the Shelly with the facts and figures, the Shelly with the newscaster's grit in her voice, wasn't the same person who was talking now. This was someone different: softer, sensitive, thoughtful.

Shelly sat up, crossed her legs. She looked at her watch. "Hey, I'm beat. Let's call it a wrap for tonight."

"Sure."

The hot lights went dark and made tapping noises as they cooled. Immediately Rune felt the chill of the evening envelop them.

"How did it go, you think?" Rune asked. "I thought it was super.

Shelly said, "You're a very easy person to talk to."

"I'm not even using any of my questions." Rune sat in the lotus position and flapped her knees up and down like butterfly wings. "There's so much material . . . and we've hardly started talking about you yet. You're so good."

"You're still interested, we can go to that party."

"You bet."

Shelly asked, "Use your phone?"

"Sorry, remember? I'm Miss Incommunicado."

"A ship-to-shore radio. That's what you need. Then let's stop by the studio for a minute? I've got to see if

there's a shoot scheduled for tomorrow." She noticed
Rune's small JVC camcorder. "Why don't you bring that.
You can do some taping at the party."

"Great." Rune packed the small camera. "You think
they'll mind?"

Shelly smiled in a way that was also a shake of her
head. "You'll be with the star, remember?"

———

Lame Duck Productions' soundstage was only three
blocks from Rune's company.

Both were located in Chelsea, a neighborhood that
changed block by block—while L&R's building sat next
to an overpriced, gentrified restaurant, Lame Duck's
squatted in a gray and greasy stretch of Korean importers
and warehouses and coffee shops. Rune smelled garlic
and rancid oil as they walked along the street. Cobblestones shone through the asphalt. Battered cars and delivery vans waited for another day of abuse on the streets of
New York City.

They walked into the lobby of the building, stained
with the residue of a thousand halfhearted moppings.
Shelly said, "I'll be right down. I just have to check the
scheduling board. Is it too dark to shoot some exteriors?"
She nodded toward the video camera.

Rune said she would.

The security guard said, "Oh, Miss Lowe, phone message for you. It says urgent."

Shelly took the pink message slip, read it. She said to
Rune. "Be right down."

Rune wandered along the sidewalk outside. She held
the camera to her eye but the low-light warning flashed
through the eyepiece. She put it back into her bag. The
garlic was making her hungry and she wondered what
there was to eat at pornographic film parties.

Food, like everybody else, girl. What do you think? Shelly's just like anybody else. She—

"Hey, Rune!" Shelly's voice filled the street.

Rune looked up but in the gloom couldn't see which window she was calling from. Then she saw the actress outlined in a third-floor window. She called back, "What?"

"I'm shooting at eleven tomorrow. You want to watch?"

"I guess," she said quickly and then just as quickly realized that she did not in fact want to see the shoot. "You think it's okay?"

"I'll make it okay. Let me make this call. I'll be right down." She vanished inside.

This could be totally weird. What was the set like? Would the crew seem bored? Did the sets turn into one big orgy? Maybe some of the actors would proposition her—though if all the actresses were tall and blonde and beautiful like Shelly *that* probably wouldn't be a problem. Did men and women just walk around naked on the—

The ball of flame was like a ragged sun, so bright that Rune instinctively threw her arms up over her eyes, just saving her face from the bits of concrete and glass and wood that hurtled into the street, on the heels of a roar so loud that the slap of the concussion landed like knuckles all over her body.

Rune screamed—in terror at the thundering volume and in pain as she slammed into a battered Chevy van parked on the curb.

Smoke rising, flames . . .

For some time Rune lay in the gutter, her head wedged against the concrete curb, her face resting in a patch of oily water. The ringing in her ears so loud she thought a steam pipe had ruptured.

God, what happened? A plane crash?

Rune sat up slowly. She brushed at her ears. They felt cottony, stuffed with ash. She snapped her fingers near them; she couldn't hear a sound. Not her fingers, not even the huge Seagrave fire truck as it braked to a halt ten feet from her, whose siren was probably screaming loudly.

She stood, supporting herself on the van. She was dizzy. She waited for the sensation to pass but it didn't and she wondered if maybe she had a concussion.

Rune wondered too if there was something wrong with her vision—because she found she was focusing perfectly on two things at the same time: one near, the other far away.

The close object was a feather of thin paper, gilt-edged and printed with fine lettering. It sailed decorously down past her cheek and slipped away in the uneasy current of air.

The other thing Rune could see all too clearly, even through the column of black smoke, was the hole in the third floor of the building in front of her—the cavern that had been the office where Shelly Lowe had been standing to shout to Rune what would be, apparently, the last words she'd ever say.

CHAPTER FIVE

Their faces were stone.

Rune sat in the back of an NYPD patrol car, the door open, her feet on the ground outside, and wiped at her tears. She was aware of the two men who stood five feet away, watching her, but she didn't return their gaze.

The fire was out. A foul, chemical reek filled the air and a film of smoke hung over the street like an oily fog.

Rune's face and elbows had been cleaned and bandaged by the EMS attendants. They used Band-Aids. She thought they would've used something more elaborate but they just scrubbed the skin, slapped on flesh-colored strips and went upstairs. They walked slowly. No one up there needed their talents.

She pressed the shredded wad of Kleenex into her eyes one final time and looked up at the men, who were dressed in dark suits. "She's dead, isn't she?"

"You're shouting," one of the detectives said.

She couldn't hear her own voice—her ears were still

numb. She repeated the question, trying to talk more softly.

The question surprised them. One had an expression that could have been a faint smile. He said something she couldn't hear. Rune asked him to repeat it. He said, "She's extremely dead."

It was confusing, talking to them. She caught fragments of phrases, missed others. She had to look at their eyes to make sense of what they were asking.

"What happened?" she asked.

Neither of them responded. One asked gruffly, "What's your name, miss?"

She told them.

She heard: "Not your stage name, honey, not the one you use when you're up on the silver screen, your real name." He gazed at her coldly.

"Rune is my real name. Wait. . . . You think I worked with Shelly?"

"Work? You call it *work*? What does your mother say about your career?"

Anger burst in her face. "I'm not a porn actress."

The other smiled. "Well, I guess that's not too hard to figure out." His eyes scanned her body. "So whatta you do for the company? Get coffee? Do makeup? Give the actors head to get 'em up before the shoot?"

She started up. "Listen—"

"Sit down." He waved her back into the car. "I've got a lot better things to do with my time than talk to one of you people." His partner didn't seem as angry but he wasn't stopping the man's tirade. "You want to do this kind of bullshit with your life, encouraging people to get diseases and things, fine. It's a free country. Just don't expect me to like you and tell you how sorry I am your friend got blown the fuck up. Now, I wanna ask my questions and get the hell outa here. So tell me what you saw." A notebook appeared.

She was crying again, messy, sniffling tears, as she told them what happened, about the party they were going to, about Shelly getting a phone message, Rune waiting for her downstairs.

Rune said, "I saw her in the window, then the room exploded." She closed her eyes. The blast replayed in slow motion; she opened her eyes again. The scene continued, vivid, in her mind. "It was . . . it was so *loud*."

The one who was taking notes, the mean one, nodded and slipped his pad into his coat pocket. "You didn't see anybody else?"

"No."

He turned to the other with a feigned frown of thought. "Maybe we should take her up to see the body. She could ID it."

"Yeah, with that blast, the ME's office'll have a bitch of a time. You can be a big help. Come on, Miss Porn, you've got a strong stomach, don't you?" He took her by the arm, pulled her from the car.

The other was grinning. "Half her skin's blown off and the rest is pretty burnt." He pushed her toward the doorway.

A voice behind them: "Howdy, gentlemen. What's up?"

Cowboy stood on the sidewalk, moving his knuckles slowly along the rim of his baseball cap. He glanced at Rune, then back to the cops.

A detective nodded toward her. "Eyewitness. We were just—"

Rune pulled away, stepped toward Cowboy. "They were going to make me go upstairs and look at Shelly's body."

Cowboy's brow creased. "Were they?"

One of the cops shrugged, a grin on his face.

Cowboy said, "They took it out ten minutes ago, sent it to the ME's office. You guys saw it go."

The detectives grinned. "Having a little fun is all, Sam."

He was nodding, not pissed, but not smiling back either. "You finished with her?"

"Guess."

"Mind if I talk to her for a bit?"

"She's all yours." The detective turned to her. "We'll want you to sign a statement. Where can we get in touch with you?"

Rune gave them the phone number of L&R Productions.

Climbing into their unmarked car, one detective said, "I hope you consider this a lesson, young lady. Get your life together."

"I wasn't—," Rune began. But they slammed the doors and sped off.

Cowboy was studying her face. "Not too bad."

"What do you mean by that?"

"The cuts, I mean. You were lucky. It'd been on ground level, you might not have made it."

Rune was staring at the smoldering hole, where firemen had set up portable lights in metal cages hanging from scorched wires and conduit.

"What was her name?" he asked.

"Shelly Lowe. That was her stage name. She was an adult-film star."

"That was a studio?"

"Lame Duck Productions."

He nodded, looking up at the hole in the side of the building. "Another porn bombing."

"They"—she nodded at the detectives who'd just left—"thought I worked for them."

"They were giving you the shock treatment. They do the same thing with kids they find with drugs, and hookers and drunk drivers. You humiliate them, they're supposed to change their wayward lifestyle and go back to school or go on the wagon and join the church. I did it myself when I was a portable."

"A what?"

"A beat cop."

She walked a foot or two toward the building, staring at the opening. "I didn't work with her. I'm doing a documentary about her. I don't do those kind of films."

"I've seen you before."

"I was at the other bombing, the theater, and I saw you. Then again last night."

"I saw somebody with a camera. I didn't recognize you."

"I asked you something and you didn't answer me."

"I didn't hear," he answered. He touched his ear. "Hearing's not so great. Been doing bomb work for a few years now."

"I'm Rune." She stuck out her hand.

His fingers were narrow, but thick with calluses. "Sam Healy."

Healy motioned for her to step back as several blue-and-white police cars pulled away. Rune noticed that most of the police were gone. Just a half-dozen fire trucks were left. And the blue-and-white Bomb Squad station wagon.

He stood with his hands on his hips, looking at the shattered wall. He paced up and down.

"Why is everyone gone?"

Healy stared at the bricks. He asked, "Did you see a flash?"

"A flash? Yeah."

"What color was it?"

"I don't remember. Red or orange, I guess."

He said, "Did you feel a chemical irritation, like tear gas or anything?"

"It smelled pretty bad but I don't think so."

"No one threw anything through the window?"

"Like a hand grenade?"

"Like anything," he said.

"No. Shelly called out the window, asked me a question. Then she went to make a phone call. It blew up a minute later. Less, maybe."

"Phone call?"

"She got a message that she was supposed to call someone. The guard might know who. But I'm sure the detectives talked to him."

Healy was frowning. He said in a soft voice, "They sent the guard home. He didn't know anything and didn't say anything about a message. Or the detectives *said* he didn't. Hey, wait here a minute, okay?"

He was walking back to the station wagon on his long legs. He spoke on the radio for a few minutes. She saw him put the receiver back on the dash. A young officer came up to him and handed him a plastic bag.

When he returned to Rune she said, "Second angel?"

He gave a surprised laugh.

"I was looking over your shoulder last week."

He nodded. Then debated and showed her the plastic sleeve.

The second angel blew his trumpet, and a great mountain, burning with fire, was thrown into the sea, and a third of the sea became blood. . . .

This too was from the Sword of Jesus. He slipped it into his attaché case.

Rune said, "What I was asking a minute ago—where is everybody? You're almost the only cop left."

"Ah, the word has come down." Healy looked at the crater again.

"Word?"

He nodded toward the smoking building. "If, say, a cop'd been killed in there. Or a kid or a nun or pregnant lady, well, there'd be a hundred cops and FBI here right now." He looked at her, the kind of glance parents give their kids during birds-and-bees lectures to see if the message is getting across.

It didn't seem to be and Healy said, "The word is we're not supposed to waste too much time on people like this. In the porn industry. Understand?"

"That's ridiculous." Rune's eyes flashed. "What about those people in the theater? Don't you care about them?"

"We care. We just don't care too much. And you want to know the truth about the patrons at the Velvet Venus? A couple of them were innocent bystanders, sure. But two were wanted on drug charges, one was a convicted felon who jumped parole, one was carrying a ten-inch butcher knife."

"And if a nun'd been walking by outside when it went off, or on that sidewalk there, she'd be just as dead as Shelly Lowe."

"True. Which's why I'm saying the we're not going to *stop* investigating. We're just not going to waste resources."

Rune was spinning the silver bracelet on her wrist. "You talk like Shelly wasn't a real person. She was, and somebody killed her."

"I'm not saying I feel that way."

"Would it give you any more incentive if you knew she was trying to get out of the business?"

"Rune—"

"Somebody kills you and it's a crime. Somebody kills Shelly Lowe and it's urban renewal. That sucks."

A Fire Department inspector walked up to them, larger than life in his black-and-yellow gear. "We're going to have to put supports in before anybody can go up, Sam."

"I've got to do the postblast."

"Have to wait till tomorrow."

"I wanted to finish up tonight."

Rune walked away. "Sure, he wants to take five minutes or so and look for clues."

"Rune."

". . . then get back to protecting nuns."

Healy called after her. "Wait." The voice was commanding.

She kept going.

"Please."

She slowed.

"I want to ask you some questions."

She stopped and turned to him and she knew that he could see her thick tears in the swinging glare of the firetruck lights. She held up a hand. Angrily she said, "Okay, but not tonight. Not now. There's something I've got to do and if I don't go now I won't ever. The detectives have my number."

She thought maybe Healy called something to her. She wasn't sure; her hearing was, at the moment, a lot worse than his. But mostly she was concentrating on where she was going and had absolutely no idea how she was going to handle what she now had to do.

■

Nicole D'Orleans, however, had already heard the news.

Rune stood in the doorway of the apartment in a high-rise in the Fifties, watching the woman lean against the doorjamb, exhausted by the weight of sorrow. Her face was puffy. Along with the tears, she'd scrubbed away some of the makeup, but not all. It made her face lopsided.

Nicole straightened up and said, "Like, sorry. Come on in."

The rooms were cool and dark. Rune smelled leather and perfume and the faint fumes of the vodka that Nicole had been drinking. She glanced at the blotches of modern paintings on the wall, the theatrical posters. She noticed some framed signatures. One looked like it said George Bernard Shaw. Most she didn't recognize.

They walked into a large room. A lot of black leather, though not kinky the way you'd think a porn star's apartment would be. More like some millionaire plastic surgeon would have. There was a huge glass coffee table that looked like it was three inches thick. The carpet was white and curled around the toes of Rune's boots. She saw packed bookshelves and remembered the way she and Shelly had looked through some of Rune's books just that morning and she wanted to cry. But forced herself not to because Nicole seemed to be pulling up just shy of hysterical.

The woman had her mourning station assembled. A box of Kleenex, a bottle of Stoly, a glass. A vial of coke. She sat down in the nest of the couch.

"I've forgotten your name. Ruby?"

"Rune."

"I just can't believe it. Those bastards. They're supposed to be religious but that's not the way good Christians ought to be. Fuck 'em."

"Who told you?" Rune asked.

"The police called one of the producers. He called everyone in the company . . . Oh, God."

Nicole blew her broad nose demurely and said, "You want a drink? Anything?"

Rune said, "No. I just came by to tell you. I was going to call. But that didn't seem right—you two seemed close."

Nicole's tears were streaming again but they were the sort that don't grab your breath and her voice remained steady. "You were with her when it happened?" She hadn't heard Rune's refusing a drink, or had decided to ignore it, and was pouring Stoly over small, half-melted ice cubes.

"I was in the street, waiting for her. We were going to a party."

"The AAAF party, sure."

The memory of which set off another jag of tears.

Nicole handed Rune the drink. She wanted to leave but the actress looked at her with such wet, imploring eyes that she eased into the hissing leather cushions and took the offered glass.

"Oh, Rune . . . She was one of my best friends. I can't believe it. She was here this morning. We were joking, talking about the party—neither of us really wanted to go to it. And she made breakfast."

What should I say? Rune thought. That it'll be all right? Of course it won't be all right. That time heals all wounds? Forget about it. No way. Some wounds stay open forever. She thought of her father, lying in a Shaker Heights funeral home years ago. Death changes the whole landscape of your life, forever.

Rune sipped the clear, bitter drink.

"You know what's unfair?" Nicole said after a moment. "Shelly wasn't like me. Okay, I do a pretty good job. I've got big boobs so men like watching me and I think I know how to make love pretty good. And I like what I do. I make good money. I've even got fans send me letters. Hundreds of 'em. But Shelly, she didn't like the business. It was always like she was carrying around a, you know, burden of some kind. She would've done something else if she had a chance. Those religious nuts . . . It's not fair they picked her."

Nicole stared at the bookcases for a moment. "You know, one time we went to this movie about this hooker who was also a blues singer. She had a terrible life, she was so sad. . . . Shelly said that was her, that's how her life was. Blue. We saw it twice, and, boy, did we cry."

Which is what she did now.

Rune set the vodka down and put her arm around Nicole's shoulders. What a pair *we* are, she thought. But there was nothing like tragedy to bring out sisterliness.

They talked for another hour until Rune's head began to ache and the cuts on her face began to throb. She said she had to leave. Nicole was sentimental drunk and still segued into tears every few minutes but she also would be asleep in a few minutes. She hugged Rune hard and took her number at L&R.

Rune waited for the elevator to take her down to the shiny marble lobby of the building.

Thinking how it was really sad that now with Shelly gone, Rune wouldn't be able to make the movie that would tell everyone about her—about how she was really a serious person, despite what she did for a living, how she wanted to rise above it.

But then she thought: Why not?

Why *couldn't* she make the film?

Sure she could.

And remembering something that Nicole had said, about the blues, suddenly the title for her film came to mind. She thought about it for a minute and decided that, yes, that was it. *Epitaph for a Blue Movie Star.*

The elevator arrived. Rune stepped in, rested her face against the cool brass plate holding the buttons and sent the car on its journey to the first floor.

CHAPTER SIX

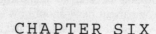 Just look like you know what you're doing and he won't stop you; he'll let you right in.

Life is all a question of attitude, Rune knew.

She was wearing a blue windbreaker. On the back, in white, were the letters NY. She'd stenciled them on that morning with acrylic poster paint. She kept the Sony Betacam on her shoulder as she walked past the uniformed policeman standing in the lobby of Lame Duck Productions. She nodded in a distracted way, cool, a civil servant nod, confident he'd let her pass by.

He stopped her.

"Who're you?" he asked, a guy who looked like—what was his name?—Eddie Haskell on *Leave It to Beaver.*

"Film unit."

He looked at her black stretch pants and high-top Keds.

"Never heard of it. What precinct you out of?"

"*State* police," she said. "Now, you don't mind, I got five other CSs to do today."

"What's a CS?" Eddie didn't move.

"Crime scene."

"CS." He was nodding. "Shield?" he asked.

Rune reached into her purse and flipped open an ID wallet. On one side was a bright gold badge and on the other was an ID card with a sullen photo of her. It gave her name as Sargant Randolf. (The man who sold her the ID an hour before, in an arcade in Times Square, had said, "Your name's Sargant? My generation, they named kids weird things too. Like Sunshine and Moonbeam.")

Eddie glanced at it, shrugged. "You gotta use the stairs. Elevator's broke."

Rune climbed to the third floor. The scorched smell assaulted her again and turned her stomach. She stepped through the door into what had been an office. She lifted the heavy camera and started shooting. The scene wasn't what she expected, wasn't like in the movies where you see a little smoke damage, chairs knocked over, broken glass.

This was pure destruction.

Whatever furniture was in the room had been blown to shreds of wood and metal and plastic. Nothing was recognizable except a blistered file cabinet that looked as if a huge fist had slammed into it. The acoustical tile on the ceiling was gone, wires hung down and the floor was a frozen black sea of paper, trash and chunks of debris. The walls were crisp bubbles of blackened paint. Heat still rose from piles of damp black cloth and papers.

She panned slowly.

This is where Shelly Lowe's life ended. This is how it ended. In flames, and—

A voice behind her asked, "What do you think?"

The camera drooped and she shut it off.

She turned and saw Sam Healy, standing in another

doorway, sipping coffee from a blue deli cup. She liked that. Asking what he'd asked, rather than "What the hell're you doing here?" Which is probably what he should've been asking.

Rune said, "I think it looks like Hades, you know, the Underworld."

"Hell."

"Yeah."

Healy nodded toward the hallway. "Why'd he let you up here?"

"I reasoned with him."

Healy walked up to Rune and spun her around slowly, looking at the letters on her back. "Cute. What're you, impersonating a bus driver?"

"Just shooting some tape."

"Ah. Your documentary."

She looked at a small suitcase on the floor next to him. "What're you doing here? I thought the word was, keep your distance. Remember the *word*?"

"I'm just a grunt. I collect the evidence. What the D.A. does with it is his business."

She looked at a number of plastic bags sitting next to his attaché case. "What kind of evidence've you—"

Another voice cut through the room. "That's her."

Eddie the cop.

It was that kind of emphasis on *her* that Rune had heard before. It usually came from teachers, her parents and bosses.

Rune and Healy looked up. Eddie was with another man, heavyset. He looked familiar. Yeah, that was it—at the first bombing, the theater: Brown Suit.

"Sam." He nodded at Healy, then said to Rune, "I'm Detective Begley. I understand you're with the New York State Police. Could we see your ID again, please?"

Rune frowned. "I never said that. I said I wanted to do some tapes *of* the state police. For the news."

Eddie shook his head. "She showed me a shield."

"Miss, you know it's a crime to have a badge?"

"It's a crime for *some* people to have a badge."

Healy said, "Artie, she's with me. It's okay."

"Sam, she can't go flipping shields around." Begley turned to her. "Either open your bag or we'll have to take you to the precinct."

"The thing is . . ."

Eddie took the leopard-skin bag and handed it to Begley. He rummaged through the dull-clinking carnival of junk. He searched for a minute or two, then grimaced and dumped the contents out on the floor. There was no badge.

Rune pulled out all her pockets. Empty.

Begley looked at Eddie, who said, "I saw it. I know I did."

Healy said, "I'll keep an eye on her, Artie."

Begley grunted, handed her bag to Eddie and ordered him to fill it back up.

"She had a shield," he protested.

Begley said to Healy, "Got a positive ID on the body from dentals. It's that Lowe woman all right. Nobody else hurt. And you were asking last night about her phone call?"

Healy nodded.

"The security guard doesn't remember who the message was from. And the phone company's still running pen registers, trying to find out who called who. As soon as we know anything else we'll let you know."

"Thanks."

Begley left. Eddie finished refilling Rune's bag. With a cold glance at Rune he too left.

Rune turned and saw Healy reading her ID.

"You spelled Sergeant wrong."

She reached for it and he lifted it above her reach.

"Begley's right. You get caught with this, it's a misde-meanor. And wising off to a cop'll get you the maximum sentence."

"You picked my purse."

He slipped the fake-leather wallet into his pocket. "Bomb Squad's got steady hands." He finished his coffee.

Rune nodded after Begley. "You were asking them to check out phone calls and things? Sounds to me like you're more than just a grunt."

A nonchalant shrug. "You leave the camera off and I'll show you what I got."

"Okay."

They walked to a crater in the concrete floor. Rune slowed as she got close. Streaks of white and gray led outward from it. Above them was a black mess of a dome where the explosion had destroyed the acoustic-tiled ceil-ing. In front of Rune was the gaping hole where the outer wall had been.

Healy pointed to the crater. "I measured it. We can tell from the size how much explosive there was." He held up a small glass vial with cotton in it. "This has absorbed the chemical residue in the air around the site. I'll send it over to the police lab in the Academy near Second Avenue. They'll tell me exactly what kind of explosive it was."

Rune's hands were sweating and her stomach was knotted. This is where Shelly had been standing when she'd turned to make her call. This is where she'd been standing when she died. Maybe in this very spot. Her legs went weak. She backed away slowly.

Healy continued, "But I'm sure it was composition four. C-4 it's usually called."

"You hear about it in Beirut."

"The number one choice among terrorists. It's military. You can't buy it from commercial demolition suppliers. It looks like dirty white putty, kind of oily. You can mold it real easily."

"Was it like hooked to a clock or something?"

Healy walked to his attaché case and picked up one of the plastic bags. It contained bits of burnt metal and wires.

"Junk," Rune said.

"But *important* junk. It tells me exactly how the bomb worked, how she was killed. It was in the phone she called from. Which was on a wooden desk right about there." He pointed to a space on the floor near the crater. "The phone was a new-model Taiwanese import. That's significant because in the old Western Electric phones most of the space was take up by the workings. There's a lot of empty space in new phones. That let the killer use about a half pound of C-4."

"That's not so much."

Healy smiled grimly. "Oh, yes it is—C-4's about ninety-one percent RDX, which is probably the most powerful nonnuclear explosive around. It's a trinitramine."

Rune nodded, though she had no idea what that was.

"They mix that with a sevacate and an isobutylene, oh, and a little motor oil—those are for stability, so it doesn't go off when you sneeze. You don't need very much at all for a very, very big bang. Detonation rate of about twenty-seven thousand feet per second. Dynamite is only about four thousand."

"If you haven't sent it to the lab how do you know it's C-4?"

"I pretty much knew when I walked in. I could smell it. It was either that or Semtex, a Czech explosive. I also found a bit of plastic wrapper—with a U.S. Army code on it. So it'd have to be C-4, and old C-4 because it didn't completely detonate."

"What set it off?"

He was absently examining burnt pieces of metal and plastic in the bag, squeezing them, sliding them around.

"The C-4 was molded around an electric detonating cap attached to a little box that contained a battery and a radio receiver. The wiring was also connected to the switch that closes the circuit on the phone—so the device wasn't armed until someone picked up the receiver. That's the problem with radio detonation. You always run the risk that somebody, police or fire or a CB operator, will hit your frequency by mistake and set the charge off while you're planting it. Or when there's somebody in the room you don't want to kill."

Rune said, "So Shelly picked up the phone, called the number, and whoever was on the other end—what?— used a walkie-talkie to set it off."

"Something like that." Healy was staring out the window.

"And that's the phone number your friend's trying to find out."

"Only he's not as enthusiastic as he ought to be."

"Yeah, I kind of saw that. Hey, there're phone booths on the corner," Rune said. Nodding out the window. "Would he've been nearby? So he could see Shelly go inside."

Healy said, "You're a born cop."

"I want to be a born film maker."

"So I already called somebody at your unit this morning."

"My unit?"

He glanced at her jacket. "CS. Crime scene. It's on their list to dust all the phones that have a clear visual path to the building here."

Definitely not a grunt. Or a techie. He sounded like a real detective.

Rune said, "So somebody followed us here. . . . You know, there was someone spying on Shelly and me, near where I live. I went to see and he beat me up."

Healy frowned, turned toward her. "You report it?"

"Yeah, I did. But I didn't get a good look at him."

"What *did* you see?"

"Broad-brimmed hat—kind of tan color. He was me-dium build. Wore a red jacket. I thought I saw him earlier too. Around the theater that night I saw you. A week after the first bomb."

"Young, old?"

"Don't know."

"Red jacket . . ." Healy wrote some lines in a note-book.

Rune poked at the metal bits through the plastic bag. "You know what's kind of funny?"

Healy turned to her. "That this is the kind of setup you use when you want to kill someone specific? Is that what you're thinking?"

"Well, yeah. That's exactly what I was thinking."

Healy nodded. "This is what the Mossad and PLO and professional hit men use. You just going to make a state-ment, like the FALN or the Sword of Jesus, you leave a timed device in front of the office. Or in a movie theater."

"This bomb, was it different from the one in the the-ater?"

"A bit. This was remote-detonated, that one was timed. And the charge was different too. This was C-4. That was C-3, which is about as powerful but leaves dangerous fumes and is messier to work with."

"Isn't that suspicious? Two different explosives?"

"Not necessarily. In the U.S., good explosives are hard to find. Dynamite's easy—hell, southern states, you can buy it in hardware stores—but, like I told you, C-3 and C-4 are strictly military. Illegal for civilians to buy. You can only get them on the black market. So bombers have to take what they can get. A lot of serial bombers use different materials. The common elements are the target and mes-sage. I'll know more when I talk to the witness—"

"What witness?"

"A guy who was hurt in the first bombing. He was in the theater watching the movie."

Rune said, "And what was his name again?"

"No *again* about it. I don't give out the names of witnesses. I shouldn't even be talking to you."

"Then why are you?"

Healy looked out the gap. Traffic moved slowly by on the street. Horns screamed and drivers hooted and gestured, everyone in a hurry. A half-dozen people stood outside, gawking up at the hole. He looked at her for a moment, in a probing way that made her uncomfortable. "What they did here"—Healy nodded at the cratered floor—"that was real slick. Real professional. I were you, I'd think about a new subject for your film. At least until we find this Sword of Jesus."

Rune was looking down, playing with the plastic controls on her Sony. "I have to make my film."

"I've been in ordnance disposal for fifteen years. The thing about explosives is that they're not like guns. You don't have to look the person in the eyes when you kill them. You don't have to be anywhere near. You don't worry about hurting innocent people. Hurting innocent people is *part* of the message."

"I told Shelly I was going to make this film. And I am. Nothing's going to stop me."

Healy shrugged. "I'm just telling you what I'd want you to do, you were my girlfriend. Or something."

Rune said, "Can I have my wallet back?"

"No. Let *me* destroy the evidence."

"It cost me fifty bucks."

"Fifty? For a phony shield?" Healy laughed. "You're not only breaking the law, you're getting ripped off in the process. Now get out of here. And think about what I said."

"About the Mossad and bombs and C-4?"

"About making a different kind of movie."

Son of a bitch.

That night, home from work, Rune stood in the doorway of her houseboat and looked at the damage. Every drawer was open. The thief hadn't been very careful—just dumping clothes helter-skelter, opening notebooks and dressers and galley drawers and looking under futons. Clothes, papers, books, tapes, food, utensils, stuffed animals . . . everything everywhere.

Son of a bitch.

Rune pulled a new tear gas canister out of a closet near the door and walked through the boat.

The burglar had left.

She stepped into the middle of the mess, picked up a few things—a couple of socks, the book of Grimms' fairy stories. Her shoulders slumped and she set the objects on the floor again. There was too much to do, and none of it was going to get done tonight.

"Damn."

Rune turned a chair right side up and sat on it. She felt queasy. Somebody had touched that sock, touched the book, touched her underwear and maybe her toothpaste. . . . Throw them out, she thought. She shuddered from the sense of violation.

Why?

She had valuables, fifty-eight Indian head nickels, which she thought were the neatest coins ever made and would have to be worth something. About three hundred dollars in cash, wadded up and stuffed in an old box of cornflakes. Some of the old books would be worth something. The VCR.

Then she thought: Shit, the Sony.

L&R's camera!

Hell's bells it cost forty-seven thousand dollars shit Larry's gonna sue me double shit.

Enough for a man to live in Guatemala for the rest of his life.

Shit.

But the battered Betacam was just where she'd left it.

She sat for ten minutes, calming down, then started to clean. An hour later a good percentage of order had been restored. The burglar hadn't been particularly subtle. To unlock the door, he'd pitched a rock through one of the small windows looking out on the Jersey side. She swept the glass up and nailed a piece of plywood over the opening.

She'd thought about calling the cops again, but what would they do?

Why bother? They'd be too busy protecting nuns and the mayor's brother and celebrities.

She was just finishing cleaning when she glanced at the Betacam once more.

The door on the video camera's recording deck was open and the cassette of Shelly was gone.

The man in the red jacket had robbed her.

A moment of panic . . . until she ran to her bedroom and found the dupe tape she'd made. She cued it up to make sure. Saw a bit of Shelly's face and ejected the cassette. She put it in a Baggie and slipped it into the cornflakes box with her money.

Rune locked the doors and windows, turned out the outside lights. Then she made herself a bowl of Grape-Nuts and sat down on her bed, slipped the tear gas canister under a pillow, and lay back against the pile of pillows. She stared at the ceiling as she ate.

Out the window, a tug honked its deep vibrating horn. She turned to look and caught a glimpse of the pier. She remembered the attack, the man in the red windbreaker.

She remembered the terrible burst of explosion, the pressure wave curling around her face.

She remembered Shelly's blonde head turning into the room to die.

Rune lost her appetite and put aside the bowl. She climbed out of bed and walked to the kitchen. She opened the phone book and found the section on colleges and universities. She began to read.

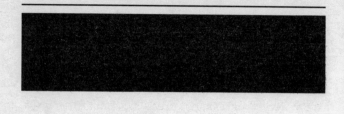

CHAPTER SEVEN

The problem was that his voice kept trailing into silence as he answered her questions.

As if everything he said brought to mind something else he had to consider.

"Professor?" Rune prompted.

"Right, sure." And he'd continue on for a few minutes. Then the words would meander once again.

His office was filled with what must have been two thousand books. The window overlooked a patch of quadrangle grass and the low sprawl of Harlem beyond that. Students strolled by slowly. They all seemed dreamy-eyed and intense. Professor V.C.V. Miller sat back in his creaky wooden chair.

The camera didn't bother him in the least. "I've been on TV before," he told her when she'd called. "I was inter-viewed for *Sixty Minutes* once." His subject was compara-tive religion and he'd written a treatise on the subject of

cults. When Rune had told him she was doing a documentary on the recent bombings he'd said, "I'd be happy
to talk to you. I've been told my work is definitive." Making it sound like *she* should be happy to speak to *him*.

Miller was in his sixties, hair white and wispy, and he
always kept his body three-quarters to the camera, though
his eyes locked right onto the lens and wouldn't let go—
until his voice grew softer and softer and he looked out
the window to contemplate some elusive thought. He
wore an ancient brown suit flecked with the dandruff of
cigarette ash. His teeth were as yellow as little ivory Buddhas and so were his index finger and thumb, where he
held his cigarette, even though he didn't inhale it while
the camera was running.

Rune found the monologue had wandered into Haiti
and she was learning a number of things about voodoo
and West African Dahomean religion.

"Do you know about zombies?"

"Sure, I've seen the movies," Rune said. "Somebody
goes to an island in the Caribbean and gets bit by this
walking-dead gross thing, yuck, with worms crawling
around, then he comes back and bites all his friends
and—"

"I'm talking about real zombies."

"Real zombies." Her finger released the trigger of the
camera.

"There is a such a thing, you know. In Haitian culture,
the walking dead are more than just a myth. It's been
found that *houngans* or *mambos*—the priests and priest-
esses—would appear to induce death by administering
cardiopulmonary depressants. The victims seemed to die.
In fact, they were in suspended animation."

("Rune," Larry'd told her, "the interviewer is always in
control. Remember that.") She said, "Let's get back to the
Sword of Jesus."

"Sure, sure, sure. The people that're responsible for these pornography bombings."

Rune said, "What do you know about them?"

"Nary a thing, miss."

"You don't?" Her eyes strayed to the bookshelves. What was this "definitive" stuff.

"No. Never heard of them."

"But you said you knew most of the cults."

"And I do. But that doesn't necessarily mean they don't exist. There are thousands of cult religions in this country. The Sword of Jesus could be one that has a hundred members who read from the Bible and talk fire and brimstone—of course, all the while writing off their tithes on their income taxes."

He got an ash into the round ceramic ashtray on his desk before it fell to the floor.

"Say they did exist. You have any thoughts on them?"

"Well, I guess . . ." The volume went way down. Eyes out the window again.

"Professor?"

"Sorry. It's surprising."

"What is?"

"The killings. The violence."

"Why's that?"

"You see, in America, we can't escape the heritage of religious tolerance. We're so damn proud of it. Oh, we'll lynch a man because he's black, persecute him because he's a Communist, despise him because he's poor or because he's Irish or Italian. But his religion? No. That is not a prejudice that flies in America, the way it would in Europe. And you know why? Nobody really cares about religions here."

"But what about Jim Jones? He was American."

"People may kill to *protect* their religion. And these Sword of Jesus people, if there is such a thing, unquestionably come from conservative, military backgrounds

and a love of firearms and hunting. They'd kill abortion-
ists. But, see, that's to save lives. Killing purely to further a
system of morality . . . Well, I could see some Islamic
sects, some primitive religions doing that. But not in
America, not a Christian group. Remember, Christians
were the folks that brought you the Crusades, and the
reviews were not good at all. We've learned our lesson."

"Would you have any idea where I could find out if
they're real?"

"You're talking to the best source, young lady, and I'm
afraid I can't help very much. Is this going to be network?"

She said, "Maybe even in the movie theaters."

A caterpillar of ash fell onto his shiny pants and he
brushed it away to join the other fractured, gray bodies at
his feet. "I have tenure, you know, but still, every bit
helps. Now, if you still have some tape left would you like
to hear about the Sioux Sun Dance ceremony?"

■

In his most cheerful Down Under lilt, Larry was saying,
"What it is, what it is, we're gonna give you a raise."

Rune was unplugging the tungsten lights. They'd just
finished interviewing people for a documentary on day-
care centers. Rune was exhausted. She'd been up until
three that morning poring over books about cults—and
finding nothing about the Sword of Jesus—and rewatch-
ing Professor Miller's less-than-helpful tape. Now she
paused and stifled a yawn. Looked at her boss.

This *was* Larry, wasn't it?

Occasionally, when she had a hangover or was tired or
it was early in the morning, she had trouble telling them
apart. Bob, she had to remember, was a little smaller, with
a trimmer beard and a tendency toward beiges and
browns, while Larry wouldn't be found south of Dutchess
County in anything but black.

"A raise?"

He said, "We figure it's time you took on a few more things."

Her stomach gave an excited lurch. "A promotion? I get to be a cameraman?"

"Something like that."

"How *much* 'like that'?"

"We were thinking: an administrator."

Rune began coiling the electric wires into loops. After a moment she said, "I worked for an administrator once. She wore her hair in a little bun and had glasses on a metal chain and her blouses had little embroidered dogs on them. I got fired after about three hours. Is that the sort of administrator you have in mind?"

"Serious work is what I'm saying, luv."

"You're firing Cathy and you want me to be a secretary. Oh, this is, like, too gross for words, Larry."

"Rune . . ."

"Forget it."

His face was a massive grin and he would have been blushing if he knew how. "Cathy's leaving, right. That part is true."

"Larry, I want to make films. I can't type, I can't file. I don't *want* to be an administrator."

"Thirty bucks more a week."

"How much are you saving by firing Cathy?"

"I didn't bleedin' fire her. She's going on to a better opportunity."

"Unemployment?"

"Ha. Tell you what, we'll give you forty more a week and all you 'ave to do is 'elp out a little in the office. When you feel like it. Let the files stack up, you want."

"Larry . . ."

"Look, we just won the bid for this big advertising job. That company we were going after. House O' Leather. You 'ave to 'elp us out. You'll be first production assistant. We'll let you shoot some footage."

"Advertising? You shouldn't do that crap, Larry. What about your documentaries? They're honest."

"Honesty 'as its place, luv, but what it is, this agency's paying us a two 'undred thousand fee plus fifteen percent markup on production. Please . . . Just 'elp us out for a bit."

She waited a moment while she muscled up some coyness. "Larry," she said. "You know I'm working on this documentary. About the bombing—but not about the bombing."

"Yeah, right." His mouth curled a portion of a millimeter.

"Maybe, when it's finished, you could talk to some of the programming people you know. Put in a good word for me."

"Rune, you think you're gonna send a tape to PBS and they're gonna bleedin' show it? Just like that?"

"Pretty much."

"Lemme see it first. Maybe, you got some good footage, we could go in and work with it."

"Not it, *me*. Work with *me*."

"Sure, *you*'s what I meant to say."

"You can introduce me to some distributors?"

"Yeah. Might 'appen."

"All right, fair enough. You want an administrator, I'll do it."

Larry hugged her. " 'ey, way to go, luv."

Rune finished coiling the wires. She made sure the coils were even but not too tight. That was one thing they'd taught her at L&R, and she appreciated it—how to take care of your equipment.

Larry asked, " 'ey, what kinda hook d'you come up with for that film on the bombing? A bio of that girl got killed?"

"That's what it *was* going to be about, but not any-more."

"What's it's about now?"

"It's going to be about finding a murderer."

━━━━━

Rune sat on Nicole D'Orleans's couch, sinking so far into the luxurious leather that her feet were off the ground.

"This is very embryonic, you know. They oughta sell these to therapists. Get right back, you know, to the womb, sitting here."

Nicole wore a purple minidress with a scooped neck showing six inches of taut cleavage, purple glittery stockings, white high-heel shoes. When she walked she loped forward awkwardly. Her concession to mourning was a huge black bow in her hair. She'd just come back from a memorial service for Shelly, an informal event that the people at Lame Duck had arranged. "I've never seen so many people crying at one time. Everybody loved her."

That brought back the tears but this time she was able to control the sobbing. Rune watched her wander through the living room. Nicole had started—obsessively, it seemed—to pack up Shelly's belongings. But since the actress had no close family she didn't know what to do with them. Moving cartons lay half-filled in the bedroom.

Sunlight streamed through the open-weave drapes and fell in bright patterns on the carpet. Rune squinted against it as she waited for Nicole to finish aligning the boxes, folding the lids over. Finally Nicole sighed and sat down.

And that was when Rune said to her: "I think Shelly was murdered."

Nicole gazed blankly for a minute. "Well, yeah. The Sword of Christ."

"Sword of Jesus."

"Whatever."

"Except that it's fake," Rune said. "It doesn't exist."

"But they left these notes about angels destroying the earth and everything."

"It's a cover-up."

"But I read it in *Newsweek*. It *has* to be true."

Rune looked at the centerpiece on the table, hungry and wondering if the apples were too ripe; she hated mushy apples. But if she started to eat one she couldn't very well put it back. She said, "Nobody's every heard of them. And I can't find any reference to the group anywhere. And think about it—you want to kill someone, okay? You make it look like a terrorist thing. It's a pretty good cover."

"But why would somebody want to kill Shelly?"

"That's what I'm going to find out. That's what my movie's going to be about. I'm going to find the killer."

Nicole asked, "What do the police think?"

"They don't. First of all, they don't care she was killed. They said . . . Well, they don't think much of people in your line of work. Second, I haven't told them my theory. And I'm not going to. If I do, and it's true, then everybody'll get the story. I want it for me. An exclusive . . ."

"Murder?"

"What do you think, Nicole? Was there anybody that would've wanted Shelly dead?"

Rune could sense the gears turning beneath the teased, sprayed hair that glittered with tiny silver flecks, a living Hallmark decoration.

Nicole shook her head.

"Was she going out with anybody?"

"Nobody serious. The thing is, in this business, it's real—what's the word?—incestuous, you know? You can't just meet some guy at a party like anybody else. Sooner or later he's gonna ask what you do for a living. Nowadays, with AIDS and Hep B and everything, that's a way for a girl to get dropped real fast. So what happens is, you tend to just hang out a lot with other people in the business.

Date a lot. Maybe move in with a guy and finally get married. But Shelly didn't do that. There was one guy she was seeing recently. Andy . . . somebody. A funny last name. I don't remember. He was never over to the apartment. It seemed pretty casual."

"Could you find out his name?"

Nicole walked into the kitchen and looked at the wall calendar. She traced a pencil-written note with her finger; it made a sad sweep as it followed Shelly's writing.

"Andy Llewellyn. Four l's in his name. That's why I thought it was weird."

Rune wrote down the name, then looked over the calendar. She pointed. "Who's that?" *A. Tucker* was penned in. His name appeared almost every Wednesday going back for months. "Doctor?"

Nicole blew her red nose with a paper towel. "That was her acting coach."

"Acting coach?"

"The movies we did, they paid the rent. But she loved real plays most of all. It was kind of a hobby of hers. Going to auditions. Doing small parts. But she never got any big roles. As soon as they found out what she did for a living it was, Don't call us, we'll call you. Come here. . . ." Nicole motioned Rune back into the living room and over to the bookcases. Her neck crooked sideways, Rune read some of the titles. They were all about acting. Balinese theater, Stanislavsky, Shakespeare, dialects, playwriting, history of theater. Nicole's hand strayed to a book. The astonishingly red nails tapped the spine. "That was the only time Shelly was happy. When she was rehearsing or reading about the theater."

"Yeah," Rune said, remembering something that Shelly'd told her. "She said she had some real parts. She made a little money at it." Rune pulled a book off the shelf. It was written by someone named Antonin Artaud. *The Theater and Its Double*. It was dog-eared and battered.

A lot of it was underlined. One chapter had an asterisk next to it. It was headed, "The Theater of Cruelty."

"Sometimes she'd take time off and do summer stock around the country. She said that regional theater was where most of the creative playwrights were being show-cased. It was all very brainy stuff. I tried to read some of the scripts. Gosh, I tell you, I can follow lines like, 'And then they take their clothes off and fuck.'" Nicole laughed. "But this stuff Shelly was interested in was way, way beyond me."

Rune put the book back on the shelf. She jotted Tucker's name next to Andy Llewellyn's.

"Shelly said what made her decide to do the film was that she had a fight with somebody she worked with. You know who that was?"

Nicole paused. "No."

Rune had seen Nicole in *Lusty Cousins*. She was a bad actress then and she was a bad actress now.

"Come on, Nicole."

"Well, don't make too much out of it—" .

"I won't."

"It's just, I don't want to get anybody in trouble."

"Tell me. Who?"

"Guy who runs the company."

"Lame Duck?" Rune asked.

"Yeah. Danny Traub. But him and Shelly fought all the time. They have since she's been working for them. A couple of years."

"What do they fight about?"

"Everything. Danny's, like, your nightmare boss."

Into the notebook. "Okay. Anybody else?"

"Nobody she worked with."

"But maybe somebody she didn't?"

"Well, there's this guy . . . Tommy Savorne. He was her ex."

"Husband?"

"Boyfriend. They lived together in California for a couple years."

"He still lives there?"

"He does, yeah. Only he's been in town for the past couple weeks. But I know he didn't have anything to do with the bomb. He's the sweetest guy you'd ever want to meet. He looks kind of like John Denver."

"What happened with them? Did they break up because of her business?"

"She didn't talk about Tommy much. He used to make porn. Did a ton of drugs too. Hey, who doesn't, right? But then he cleaned up his act. Got out of the business, dried out at some fancy clinic like Betty Ford, did the twelve steps or something. Then he started doing legit videos—exercise tapes, something like that. I think Shelly resented that he went legit. Kind of a slap at her. I think he kept needling her to leave the business, but she couldn't afford to. Finally she left him. I don't know why she wouldn't go back. He's cute. And he makes good money."

"And they were fighting?"

"Oh, not recently. They didn't have much contact. But they *used* to fight a lot. I heard her on the phone sometimes. He kept wanting to get back together and she kept saying she couldn't. One of *those* conversations—ex-boyfriend thing. You know, you've had those a hundred times."

Rune, whose romantic life had been nonexistent since Richard had left—and pretty damn bleak before him too—nodded with phony female conspiracy. "Hundreds, thousands."

"But that was months ago," Nicole added. "I'm sure he couldn't have hurt her. I see him from time to time. He's really sweet. And they were good friends. Seeing them together—there's no way he could look at Shelly and hurt a hair on her head."

"Why don't you tell me where he's staying anyway."

Hearing in her memory Sam Healy's voice: *I've been in ordnance disposal for fifteen years. The thing about explosives is that they're not like guns. You don't have to look the person in the eyes when you kill them. You don't have to be anywhere near.*

CHAPTER EIGHT

The hotel overlooked Gramercy Park, that trim private garden bordered in wrought iron at the end of Lexington Avenue.

The lobby of the place was all red and gold, with flecked fleur-de-lis wallpaper. Dozens of layers of paint coated the woodwork and the carpet smelled sour-sweet. One of the two elevators was broken—permanently, it seemed.

It was quiet as Rune waited for the elevator to descend to the ground floor. A woman in her fifties, wearing a green-and-gold dress, her face a smooth curve of foundation makeup, watched Rune from under jutting glossy eyelashes. A middle-aged musician with dirty brown hair sat with his foot up on a battered Ovation guitar case and read the *Post*.

Tommy Savorne's room was on the fourteenth floor, which, it occurred to Rune, was really the thirteenth, because when they built hotels in the thirties and forties they didn't label the thirteenth floor. That had a certain appeal for her. She felt that superstition was something people who were unliteral tended to believe in. And being too literal was a major sin in her bible.

She found the door and knocked.

Chains and latches jangled and the heavy door swung open. A man stood there, sunburned and cute—and looking, yeah, a bit like John Denver. More like a cowboy at a dude ranch. His face was somber. He wore blue jeans and a work shirt. He wore one crew sock; the other dangled from his hand. His hair was shaggy and blond. He was thin.

"Hi, what can I do for you?"

"You're Tommy Savorne?"

He nodded.

"I'm Rune. I knew Shelly. Nicole said you were in town and I just wanted to come by and say I was real sorry about what happened."

She hadn't been sure what she was going to say after that, but it didn't matter. Tommy gave a nod and motioned her inside.

The room was small, the walls off-white, the carpet gold. She got a whiff of a stale smell—what was it, old food? Aging plaster? Probably just the smell of a prewar hotel going to seed. But Tommy was burning incense—sandalwood—which helped. Two table lamps gave off a salmon glow. He'd been reading a cookbook, one of a dozen of them on the chipped brown-laminate desk.

"Sit down. You want something?" He looked around. "I don't have any liquor. Just soda. Mineral water. Oh, I have some babagounash."

"What's that, like sassafras? I had this ginseng cola one time. Yuck."

"It's eggplant dip. My own recipe." He held up a plastic container of brown-green mash.

Rune shook her head. "I just ate. But thanks. Nothing for me."

Savorne sat on the bed and Rune flopped into the Naugahyde chair with split sides; it bled dirty-white upholstery stuffing.

"You were Shelly's boyfriend?" Rune asked.

He was nodding, squinting slightly. Tommy said, "Shelly and I broke up over a year ago. But we were good friends. I still live in California where she and I used to live. I'm just in town now for a job."

"California," Rune mused. "I've never been. I'd like to go sometime. Sit under palm trees and watch movie stars all day long."

"I'm from the north. Monterey. It's about a hundred miles south of San Francisco. Hard to star-spot there. Except for Clint Eastwood."

"That's a pretty good exception."

Tommy was carefully pulling a sock over his large foot. Even his feet looked tanned and trim. She looked closely: Wild! He's got manicured toenails. She saw cowboy boots and several cowboy hats in the closet.

He sighed. "I can't believe it. I can't believe she's dead." He reached lethargically under the bed then snagged a black loafer. Slipped it on. Found the other one. It drooped in his hand. "How did you know her?"

"I was making a movie about her," Rune said.

Savorne said, "A movie?"

"A documentary."

"She didn't mention that."

"We just started the day she was killed. I was with her when it happened."

Savorne scanned her face. "That how you got those scratches?"

"I was outside when the bomb went off. It's nothing serious."

"You know, even though we weren't going out anymore we still talked a lot. I was thinking. . . . That's something I won't be able to do anymore. Not ever again . . ."

"How long've you known her?"

"Five, six years. I used to . . ." He looked away. "Well, I used to be in her line of work. The films, I mean."

"An actor?"

He laughed wanly. "Not really built for that." Laughed again; his red face turned redder. "I'm talking about physique, not equipment."

Rune smiled. He continued. "No. I was a cameraman and director. Did some editing too. I'd was in film school at UCLA for a couple of years, but that wasn't for me. I knew how to handle a camera. I didn't need to sit in classes full of these nerds. So I borrowed some money, bought an old Bolex and opened my own production company. I was going to be the next George Lucas or Spielberg. I didn't get to first base. I went under in about three months. Then this guy I knew called and told me about a job shooting an adult film. I thought, Hey, watching beautiful women and getting paid for it? Why not? I gotta admit I thought maybe I'd get a little of the action myself. Everybody in the crew thinks that but it never works out that way. But they paid me a hundred cash for two hours' work and I decided that was going to be my career."

"How'd you meet Shelly?"

"I moved to San Francisco and started making my own films. Shelly was auditioning at the theaters in North Beach—the legit theaters. Actually I picked her up in a bar is how we met. We started going out. When I told her what I did, well, most girls'd go, I'm outa here. But Shelly was interested. Something about it really turned her on. Something about the power . . . She was reluctant, sure, but since her theater career was going nowhere I talked her into working for me."

Or she let you *think* you talked her into it? Rune asked silently. Just how well did you know your girlfriend? She couldn't imagine talking Shelly into anything.

"I saw one of her films," Rune said. "I was surprised. She was good."

"Good? Man, forget about it! What it was, she was real. I mean, *real*. She played an eighteen-year-old cheerleader, man, she *was* a cheerleader. She played a thirty-five-year-old businesswoman, you believed her."

"Yeah, but with those kinds of movies, do the audiences care?" Rune asked.

"That's a good question. I didn't think so. But Shelly did. And that's all that mattered. We got into some wild fights over it. She'd insist on rehearsing. Christ, we'd shoot a film a day. There's no dialogue; there's a couple-page treatment is all. What's this rehearsal bullshit? Then she'd insist on setting up the lighting just right. I lost money on her. Cost overruns, missed delivery dates to the distributors . . . But she was right, I guess—in some kind of artistic sense. The films she made, some of them are fabulous. And a hell of a lot more erotic than anything else you'll see.

"See, her theory is that an artist has to know what the audience wants and give it to them, even if they don't *know* they want it. 'You make the movie for the audience, not yourself.' Shelly said that a million times."

"You're not in the business anymore?"

Tommy shook his head. "Nope. Porn used to be a classier crowd. And a smarter crowd. Real people. It was fun. Now, there's too many drugs. I started to lose friends to overdoses and AIDS. I said, Time for me to move on. I wanted Shelly to come with me but . . ." Another faint smile. "I couldn't exactly see her working for my new company."

"Which does what?"

"Health food how-to videos." He nodded at the baba-gounash. "You ever hear of infomercials?"

"Nope."

"You buy a half hour—usually on cable—and make it look like a real program, something informative. But you also sell the product it's about. They're fun."

"How's business?"

"Oh, not great compared with porn, but I'm not embarrassed to tell people what I do." His voice faded. He stood up and walked over to the window, pulled aside a stained orange drape. "Shelly," he whispered. "She'd still be alive if she'd quit too. But she didn't listen to me. So pigheaded."

Rune flashed back to her fiery blue eyes.

Tommy's lips were trembling. His thick, sunburned fingers rose to his face. He started to speak but his breath caught and he lowered his head for a moment in silent tears. Rune looked away.

Finally he calmed, shook his head.

Rune said, "She was quite a person. A lot of people'll miss her. I just met her and I do."

It was hard to watch him, a big man, a healthy, cheerful man overcome by grief.

But at least it answered the first of Rune's two questions: Tommy Savorne probably wasn't Shelly's killer. He didn't seem to be that good an actor.

So, Rune asked the second: "Do you know anyone who might have wanted to hurt her?"

Savorne looked up, a frown of curiosity on his face. "This religious group . . ."

"Assuming this Sword of Jesus doesn't exist."

"You think?"

"I don't know. Just consider it."

At first he shook his head at the foolishness of the question, at the craziness of anyone's wanting to hurt

Shelly. But then he stopped. "Well, I wouldn't make much out of it . . . but there was somebody. A guy she worked for."

"Danny Traub?"

"How did you know?"

■■■■■■

"Let me tell you, and I mean this sincerely, that I loved Shelly Lowe. I loved her as an artist and I loved her as a human being."

Danny Traub was short and thin, but muscular thin, tendony. His face was round and his hair was a cap of tight brown curls. He had jowl lines that enclosed his mouth like parentheses. He was wearing baggy black slacks, a white sweatshirt with a design like semaphores. His jewelry was heavy and gold: two chains, a bracelet, a ring with a sapphire in it and a Rolex Oyster Perpetual.

That watch cost more than my parents' first house, Rune guessed.

Traub continually looked around him as if there were a crowd of people nearby, an audience. An insincere smile kept curling into his face and he gestured constantly and arched his eyebrows. The phrase *class clown* came to mind.

They were in Traub's Greenwich Village town house. It was a duplex, done in blond wood and off-white walls and loaded with small trees and plants. "Like a jungle," she said when she'd arrived. He had her leave the Betacam and the battery packs in the front hall and walked her through the place. He showed her his collection of Indonesian fertility gods and sculpture. One, Rune loved: a four-foot-high rabbit with a mysterious smile on his face. "Hey, you're great!" she'd said, walking right up to it.

"Oh, she could have dicks and boobs but *she* wants to talk to the rabbit," Traub had said to his invisible audience, glancing over his shoulder.

They'd walked past blotchy paintings, glass and metal sculpture, huge stone pots, Indian baskets, brass Buddhas, more plants (the smell was heavy-duty greenhouse). Upstairs, one door was partially open. As they'd walked past, Traub'd shut it quickly, but not fast enough to keep Rune from seeing an assembly of sleeping limbs. There were at least three arms and she was pretty sure she saw two blonde hairdos.

The back of the apartment opened onto a courtyard around a green bronze fountain. This is where they were sitting when Rune told him that she was doing a film about Shelly Lowe.

And Danny Traub had looked to the side—into the eyes of his portable audience—and delivered his line about really, truly, loving Shelly Lowe.

He was stationary when he offered this, but he didn't stay still for long. As he talked about Shelly he bounced up, radiating energy, and rocked on his feet, swinging his arms back and forth. He dropped into the chair again and continued to shift positions and stretch out until he was nearly horizontal, then swung his legs over the arm.

"I was, the word that comes to mind is, *devastated.* I mean, like, fucking devastated about what happened. She and me were best buddies on the set. I'm not saying we didn't disagree—we both have strong personalities. But we were a team, we were. An example, always better if you have examples. Now, it's cheapest and most efficient to shoot direct to video."

"Betacam or Ikegami running one-inch tape through an Ampex."

Traub grinned and pointed Rune out to the audience. "Do we have a sharp kid or what? Yessir, ladies and gentlemen." Back to Rune. "Anyway, Shelly wanted to shoot on thirty-five millimeter fucking *film.* I mean, forget it. Your budget is ten thousand for the whole *flick.* How can you spend eight on film and processing alone—and even that's Jewing down the price at one of the labs. Then forget about postproduction. . . . Well, finally I get Shelly to agree no thirty-five millimeter. But right away she starts up on sixteen millimeter. It looks better, so can I argue? . . . Anyway, that was typical. Creative disputes, you know. But we respected each other."

"Who won? About the film, I mean?"

"I always win. Well, most of the time. A couple films we shot on sixteen. 'Course that was the one that got the AAAF Picture of the Year Award." He pointed to an Oscar-like statue on his mantel.

"What does a producer do exactly?"

"Hey, this kid is just like Mike Wallace—question, question, question. . . . Okay, a producer in this business? He tries out the actresses. Hey, just kidding. I do what all producers do. I finance a film, hire the cast and crew, contract with a postpro house. The business side, you know. I happen to direct some too. I'm pretty good at it."

"Can I tape you talking about Shelly?"

The smile flickered for a moment before it returned. "Tape? Me? I don't know."

"Or maybe you could recommend somebody else. I just need to talk to somebody who's pretty high up in the business. Somebody successful. So if you know anybody . . ."

Rune thought this was way too obvious but Traub snagged the bait greedily.

"Okay? She wonders if I've been successful. . . . I've done fucking astronomical. I've got a Ferrari sitting not thirty feet away from us right this moment. In my own garage. In New York. My own fucking garage."

"Wow."

" 'Wow,' she says. Yeah, wow. I own this town house and I could eat in any restaurant in Manhattan every night of the year, I wanted to. I own—not a share—I *own* a house in Killington. You like to ski? No? I could teach you."

"You own Lame Duck?"

"A controlling percentage. There are some other people involved."

"The Mafia?" Rune asked.

The smile stayed on Danny Traub's face. He said slowly, "You don't want to say that. Let's just say they're silent partners."

"You think they might have anything to do with the bombing?"

Again the fake smile. "Some calls were made. Some questions were asked. Nobody from . . . over the river, let's say, had anything to do with it. That information's gold."

She supposed that meant Brooklyn or New Jersey, headquarters of organized crime.

"So, yeah, I'll talk to you. I'll tell you my whole life story. I've been in the business for about eight, nine years. I started as a cameraman, and I did my share of acting too. You wanta see some tapes?"

"That's okay. I—"

"I'll give you one to take home."

A blonde woman—maybe last night's entertainment—appeared, groggy and sniffling. She was dressed in a red silk jumpsuit, unzipped to the navel. Traub raised his fingers as if he were signaling a waiter. The woman hesitated, then walked toward them, combing her long hair—it tumbled to her mid-back—with her fingers. Rune stared at the hair, a platinum-gold color. Neither God nor Nature could take credit for a shade like that.

Traub said to Rune, "So what would you like? Coke? I mean the real thing, of course." He held up a saltshaker. Rune shook her head.

The audience heard: "She's a Puritan. Oh, my God." Traub glanced back at Rune. "Scotch?"

Rune wrinkled her nose. "Tastes like Duz."

"Hey, I'm talking single-malt, aged twenty-one years."

"Old soap isn't any better than new soap."

"Well, just name your poison. Bourbon? Beer?"

Rune stared at the woman's hair. "A martini." It was the first thing that came into her mind.

Traub said, "Two martinis. Chop-chop."

The blonde wrinkled her tiny nose. "I'm not, like, a waitress."

"That's true," Traub said to Rune, who had apparently joined his audience. "She's not *like* a waitress at all. Waitresses are smart and efficient and they don't sleep until noon." He turned back to the woman. "What you're like is a lazy slut."

She stiffened. "Hey—"

He barked, "Just get the fucking drinks."

Rune shifted. "That's okay. I don't—"

Traub gave her a cool smile, the creases cut deep into his face. "You're a guest. It's no problem."

The blonde twisted her face in anemic protest and shuffled off to the kitchen. She muttered a few words Rune couldn't hear.

Traub's smile fell. He called, "You say something?"

But the woman was gone.

He turned back to Rune. "You buy them dinner, you buy them presents, you bring them home. They still don't behave."

Rune said coldly, "People just don't read Emily Post anymore."

He missed the dig completely. "You mean like the flier? Wasn't she the one tried to fly around the world? I did a movie about an airplane once. We called it *Love Plane*. Sort of a takeoff on *The Love Boat*—I loved that show, you ever see it? No? We rented a charter 737 for the day. Fucking expensive and a pain in the ass to shoot in. I mean, we're in this hangar in March, everybody's turning blue. You don't realize how small a plane is until you try to get three, four couples spread out on the seats. I'm talking wide-angle lenses. I mean, almost fish-eyes. Didn't work out too good. It looked like all the guys had dicks about an inch long and three inches wide."

The blonde returned. Rune said to Traub, "My film. Will you help me out? Please. Just a few minutes about Shelly."

He was hesitating. The blonde handed out the drinks and put an unopened jar of olives on the thick glass coffee table. Traub started to grimace. She turned to him and looked like she was going to cry. "I couldn't get it open!"

Traub's face softened. He rolled his eyes. "Hey, hey, honey, come here. Gimme a hug. Come on."

She hesitated and then bent down. He kissed her cheek.

"You got any?" she whined.

"Say please."

"Come on, Danny."

"Please," he prompted.

She said, "Please."

He fished into his pants pocket, then handed her the saltshaker—filled with coke, Rune assumed. She took it, then walked sullenly off.

She hadn't said one word to Rune, who asked Traub, "She's an actress?"

"Uh-huh. She wants to be a model. So does everyone else in this city. She'll make some movies for us. Get married, get divorced, have a breakdown, get married again and it'll take and she'll be out in Jersey in ten years, working for AT&T or Ciba-Geigy."

Rune felt Traub's eyes on her. The feeling reminded her of the time her first boyfriend, age ten, had put a big snail down the back of her blouse. Traub said, "There's something, I dunno, *refreshing* about you, you know. I see all these women all day long—beautiful blondes and red-heads to die for. Stunning, tall . . ."

Oooo, watch the tall, mister.

". . . big tits. But, hey, you're different."

She sighed.

"I mean that sincerely. You want to come down to Atlantic City with me? Meet some wild people?"

"I don't think so."

"One thing I am is talented. In the sack, you know."

"I'm sure."

"Plenty of recreational pharmaceuticals."

"Thanks anyway."

He looked at his watch. "Okay, tell you what, Uncle Danny'll help you out. You want to shoot me, so to speak, go ahead. But let's hurry. I got a busy day."

In ten minutes Rune had the equipment set up. She slipped a new tape into the camera. Traub sat back, popped his knuckles and grinned. He looked completely at ease.

"What do you want me to say?"

"Anything that comes to mind. Tell me about Shelly."

He glanced sideways, then looked into the camera and smiled sadly. "The first thing I have to say, and I mean this sincerely, is that I was wholly devastated by Shelly Lowe's death." The smile faded and his eyes went dull. "When she died, I lost more than my star actress. I lost one of my very dearest friends."

From somewhere, Rune had no idea where, Danny Traub produced what might pass for a tear.

CHAPTER NINE

The gruff man, in his sixties, with abundant white hair and cool eyes, looked down at Rune.

"So you think you can act?" he asked sternly.

Before she could say anything he turned and walked back into his office, leaving the door half-open. It was an old-fashioned office door, with a large window of mottled glass in it. The sign, in gold lettering, read: ARTHUR TUCKER, ACTING AND VOICE INSTRUCTION.

Rune stepped into the doorway, but stopped. She didn't know whether she'd been dismissed or invited in. When Tucker sat down at his desk she continued inside and closed the door behind her. He wore dark slacks and a white shirt and tie. His dress shoes were well worn. Tucker was slightly built, which made him seem younger. His legs were thin and his face chiseled and handsome. Bushy white eyebrows. And those piercing green eyes . . . It was hard to hold his gaze. If Tucker were a character actor he would've played a president or king. Or maybe God.

"I don't know whether I can act or not," Rune said, walking up to the desk he sat behind. "That's why I'm here."

The office on Broadway and Forty-seventh was a theater museum. The walls were covered with cheap-framed photos of actors and actresses. Some of them Rune had seen in films or heard of—but nobody was very famous. They seemed to be the sort of actor who plays the male lead's best friend or the old wacko woman who shows up three or four times during a movie for comic relief. Actors who do commercials and dinner theater.

Also on the walls were props, bits of framed fire curtains from famous theaters now gone, *Stagebill* covers pasted on posterboard. Hundreds of books. Rune recognized some titles; they were the same as Shelly Lowe had on her bookshelf. She saw the name Artaud and she remembered the phrase again: the Theater of Cruelty. It brought a jolt to her stomach.

Tucker went through an elaborate ritual of lighting a pipe and a moment later a cloud of smoke, smelling of cherry, filled the room.

He gestured to the chair, sat. Lifted an eyebrow, saying in effect, keep going.

"I want to be a famous actress."

"So does half of New York. The other half wants to be famous actors. Where have you studied?"

"Shaker Heights."

"Where?"

"Ohio. Outside of Cleveland."

"I don't know any academies or studios there."

"It was the middle school. I was in the Thanksgiving pageant."

He stared at her, waiting for her to go on.

No sense of humor, she noted. "That's a joke."

"Uh-huh."

"I was also a snowflake once. And in high school I painted backdrops for *South Pacific*. . . . That's another joke. Look, sir, I just want to act."

"I'm a coach," Tucker said. "That's all I am. I improve, I don't create. If you want to go to school, study drama, come back, I may be able to help you. But for now . . ." He motioned toward the door.

Rune said, "But my friend said you're the best in the city."

"You know one of my students?"

"Shelly Lowe," Rune said and pressed the button of the little JVC camcorder in her bag. The lens was pointed upward, toward Tucker. She knew she wouldn't get the whole angle, but she'd see enough. Also, she thought the little black border might give it a nice effect.

Tucker turned to look out the window. A pile driver in a nearby construction site slammed a girder down toward the rock that Manhattan rested on. Rune counted seven bangs before he spoke. "I heard what happened to her." Tucker's ruddy face gazed at Rune from under those bushy white eyebrows. Did he brush them out like that? Rune changed her mind: He'd be a much better wizard than a president. A Gandalf or Merlin.

Rune said, "Whatever else about her, she was a good actress."

After a long moment Tucker said, "Shelly Lowe was my best student." A faint, humorless smile. "And she was a whore."

Rune blinked at the viciousness in his voice.

Tucker continued. "That's what killed her. Because she sold herself."

Rune asked, "Had she been coming to see you long?"

Reluctantly Tucker answered her question. Shelly had been studying with him for two years. She'd had no formal training other than that, which was very unusual nowadays, when schools like Yale and Northwestern and UCLA were producing the bulk of the professional actors and actresses. Shelly had a superb memory. She was like a chameleon, slipping into parts like someone possessed by the character's spirit. She had a talent for dialects and accents. "She could be a barmaid from northeast of London, then change herself into a schoolteacher from Cotswold. The way Meryl Streep can."

Tucker spoke these words of admiration with troubled eyes.

"When did you find out about her film career?"

His voice was bitter again. "A month ago. She never said a word about it. I was stunned." He laughed with derision. "And the irony is that when it came to her legitimate auditions she wouldn't take just any job. She didn't do commercials or musical comedy. She didn't do dinner theater. She wouldn't go to Hollywood. She did only serious plays. I said to her, 'Shelly, why are you being so pigheaded? You could work full-time as an actress if you wanted to.' She said, no, she wasn't going to *prostitute* herself. . . . And all the while, she was doing those . . . films." He closed his eyes and moved his large head from side to side to shake off the unpleasantness. "I found out a month ago. Someone was returning a tape at the video store I go to. I glanced at it. There she was on the cover. And, what's more, it was under the name Shelly Lowe! She didn't even use a stage name! When I found out I can't tell you how betrayed I felt. That's the only way I can describe it. Betrayal. When she came in for the next lesson we had a terrible fight. I told her to get out, I never wanted to see her again."

He spun around to face out the window again. "Every generation has its candidates for genius. Shelly could have been one of those. All of my other students—" He waved his hand around the room, as if they were sitting behind Rune. "They're talented and I like to think that I helped them improve. But they're nothing compared with Shelly. When she acted you *believed* her."

Just what Tommy Savorne had said, Rune recalled.

"It wasn't Shelly Lowe on stage, it was the character. Tennessee Williams, Arthur Miller, the Greek classics, Ionesco, Ibsen . . . Why, she came this close to the lead in Michael Schmidt's new play." He held his fingers a millimeter apart.

Rune frowned. "The big producer? The guy gets written up in the newspapers?"

He nodded. "She went to his EPI—"

"What's that?"

"Equity Principal Interview. It's like an audition. She met with Schmidt himself twice."

"And she didn't get the part?"

"No, I guess not. That was just before our fight. I didn't keep up with her." Tucker ran the stem of his pipe along his front lower teeth. He was not speaking to Rune as he said, "My own acting career never went very far. My talent was for coaching and teaching. I thought that with Shelly I'd leave behind someone who was truly brilliant. I could make *that* contribution to theater. . . ."

He stared at a photo on the opposite wall. Rune wondered which one.

"Betrayal," he whispered bitterly. Then he turned his gaze to Rune. She felt naked under his deep eyes, shaded by the brush of his eyebrows. "You seem very young. Do you make those films too? The ones she did?"

"No," Rune said. She was going to make up something, the sort of job a girl her age should be doing, but with those strange currents shooting out from his eyes—a green version of Shelly's blue laser beams—she just repeated the denial in a whisper.

Tucker studied her for a long moment. "You have no business being an actress. Pardon my bluntness but you should look for another line of work."

"I just—"

But he was waving his hand. "I wouldn't do you a favor by being kind. Now if you'll excuse me."

He pulled a script toward him.

⬛

It wasn't much of a list.

Rune sat at her desk—Cathy's old battered gray government-issue. She'd pushed it right next to the cracked front panel of L&R's air conditioner, which was churning out about a tenth of the BTUs it once had. She closed the Manhattan phone book.

There were only two A. Llewellyns listed and neither of them was an Andy. That left only the remaining twenty million citizens to survey in the other boroughs, Westchester, New Jersey and Connecticut.

Shelly's most recent boyfriend would have to go un-questioned for the time being.

Larry walked into the office and glanced at Rune. "Whatcha doing, luv?"

"Looking up things."

"Things?"

"Important things."

"Well, if you could postpone your search for a bit *I've* got something important for you."

"Letters to type?"

"Yeah, well, I wasn't going to mention it but those last ones? They were 'ardly the best typing job I've ever seen."

"I told you I wasn't a typist."

"You spelled the man's name three different ways in the same bleedin' letter."

"Was that the Indian guy? He had a weird name. I—"

"But his first name was James and that's the one you misspelled."

"I'll try to do better. . . . . You have my distributor for me yet?"

"Not yet, luv, but what I do 'ave is the people for this advertising job, right? In the next room. Did the estimate go out yet?"

"I typed it."

"But did it go out yet?"

Rune said patiently, "It's going to go out."

"So it 'asn't gone out yet?"

"It's finished, though."

"Rune, they're 'ere. Now. We're going to talk concepts today. They should've 'ad the estimate before this meeting."

"Sorry. I'll bring it in."

He sighed. "All right, let's go meet everybody. If they ask we'll tell 'em we were 'olding on to the estimate till this meeting. It was intentional."

"Larry, you shouldn't do advertising. It—"

"Oh, one of your boyfriends called."

"Yeah, who?"

" 'ealy, something like that. Wants you to call."

"Sam called? Great. I'll just be—"

"Later."

"But—"

He held the door open and smiled threateningly. "After you, luv."

Rune heard the name but forgot it immediately.

Larry was droning on, looking impressed as he recited, ". . . the second biggest wallet and billfold manufacturer in the United States."

Rune said, "How interesting."

The man with the company and the unmemorable name—Rune called him Mr. Wallet—was about fifty, round and sharp-eyed. He wore a seersucker suit and sweated a lot. He stood with his arms crossed, hovering beside a doughy woman in her late twenties, who also crossed her arms, looking with flitting eyes at the lights and cameras and dollies. She worked for the company too and was his daughter. She was also, Rune found out, going to act in the commercial.

Larry pretended to miss Rune's eyes as they made a circuit of the ceiling at this news.

Another young woman, horsey, with a sensible page-boy haircut and an abrasive voice, said to Rune, "I'm Mary Jane Collins. I'm House O' Leather's advertising director. I'll be supervising the shoot."

"Rune."

Mary Jane extended her bony hand, the costume jewelry bracelets jingling. Rune gripped it briefly.

Daughter said, "I'm a little nervous. I've done voice-overs but I've never been on camera before."

Mr. Wallet: "You'll do fine, baby. Just forget that—" He looked at Mary Jane. "How many people are going to see her?"

"The media buy should put us at about fifteen million viewers."

He continued, "Fifteen million people are going to be watching your every mood . . . oops, I mean move." He laughed.

"Daddy." She smiled with a twisted mouth.

Mary Jane read some papers. To Larry she said, "The budgets. I haven't seen the revised budgets."

Larry looked at Rune, who said, "They're almost ready."

He mouthed, *Almost?*

Mary Jane's dark hair swiveled as she looked down at Rune. "Almost?"

"A problem with the typewriter."

"Oh." Mary Jane laughed with surprise. "Sure, I understand. It's just that . . . Well, I would've *thought* you'd have them for us before this. I mean, this is the logical time to review them. Even today is a little tardy, in terms of timing."

"Another couple hours. I glued the key back on."

Larry said, "Rune, maybe you could go work on them now."

Rune said, "I thought we were going to talk concepts."

"Oh," Mary Jane said, looking down at her, "I hadn't understood you were in a creative position here at the studio."

"I—"

"What do you do, exactly?"

Larry said, "Rune's our production assistant."

Looking her up and down, Mary Jane said, "Oh." And smiled like a fourth-grade teacher.

Mr. Wallet was looking at a huge roll of a backdrop, twenty feet across, mottled like a pastel Jackson Pollock painting. "Now, that's something else. You think we can use that for the shoot? Mary Jane, what do you think?"

She glanced toward it and said slowly, "Might just fly. We'll put our thinking caps on about it." She turned back to the desk and opened her briefcase. "I've done a memo with all the schedule deadlines." She handed the paper to Rune. "Could you run and make a copy of it?"

Larry took the paper and held it out to Rune. "Sure she will." His eyes narrowed and Rune took the sheet.

"I'll be back in just a minute. I'll run just like a bunny."

"Daddy, will they have a makeup person? I don't have to do my own makeup, do I?"

Rune vanished through the door into the office. Larry followed.

"I thought you said it was bleedin' finished."

"The *e* fell off your cheap-ass typewriter. That's the most-used letter in the English language."

"Well, go buy a new fuckin' typewriter. But I want those estimates in a half hour."

"You're a sellout."

I don't 'ave time for your bleedin' lectures, Rune. You work for me. Now get the copies made and get those estimates to us."

"You're going to let those people walk all over you. I'm looking out for your pride, Larry. Nobody else's going to."

"You gotta pay the rent, honey. Rule number one in business: Get the bucks. You don't have any money you don't get to do what you want."

"They're obnoxious."

"True."

"He smells bad."

"He does not."

"*Somebody* smells bad. And that woman, that Mary Jane, is a dweeb."

"What the 'ell's a dweeb?"

"Exactly what she is. She's—"

The door opened and Mary Jane's smiling face looked out, her eyes perching on Rune. "Are you the one who's in charge of lunch?"

Rune smiled. "You betcha."

"We should probably get a head start on it. . . . We were thinking in terms of salads. Oh, and how's that copying coming?"

Rune saluted with a smile. "It's on its way."

▬▬▬

The next day at eleven-thirty Sam Healy picked her up outside of L&R and they drove north.

"It's just a station wagon." Rune, looking around inside, was mildly disappointed.

Sam Healy said, "But it's blue and white, at least." It also had BOMB SQUAD stenciled in large white letters on the side. And a cage, empty at the moment, that he explained was for the dogs that sniffed out explosives. "You were expecting . . . ?"

"I don't know. High-tech stuff, like in the movies."

"Life is generally a lot lower-tech than Hollywood."

"True."

They drove out of Manhattan to the NYPD explosives disposal facility on Rodman's Neck in the Bronx.

"Oh, wow, check this place out. This is totally audacious."

It was essentially a junkyard without the junk. Her feet bounced up and down on the floorboards as they pulled through the gate in the chain-link fence, crowned with spirals of razor wire.

To their left was the police shooting range. Rune heard the short cracks from pistols. To their right were several small red sheds. "That's where we keep our own explosives," Healy explained.

"Your own?"

"Most of the time we don't dismantle devices. We bring them here and blow them up."

Rune picked up her camera and battery pack from the backseat. There was a green jumpsuit there. She hadn't noticed it before. She tried to pick it up. It was very heavy. The helmet had a green tube, probably for ventilation, coming out of the top and hanging down the back. It looked just like an alien's head.

"Wow, what's that?"

"Bomb suit. Kevlar panels in fireproof cloth."

"Is that what you wear when you disarm bombs?"

"You don't call them bombs."

"No?"

"They're IEDs. Improvised explosive devices. The Department's a lot like the military. We use initials a lot."

They walked into a low cinder-block building that reeked of city government budget. A single, overworked air conditioner groaned in the corner. Healy nodded at a couple uniformed officers. He carried a blue zipper bag.

She glanced at a poster. RULES FOR BOILING DYNAMITE.

·

There were dozens of others, all with bullet points of procedures on them. The clinical language was chilling.

In the event of consciousness after a detonation, attempt to retrieve any severed body parts. . . .

Jesus . . .

He noticed what she was reading and, maybe to distract her from the gruesome details, asked, "Hey, want to hear the basic lecture on explosive ordnance disposal?"

She looked away from the section on improvising tourniquets and said, "I guess."

"There are only two goals in dealing with explosives. First, to avoid human injury. Destroy or disarm by remote if at all possible. Goal number two is to avoid injury to property. Most of our work involves investigating suspicious packages and sweeps of consulates and airports and abortion clinics. Things like that."

"You make it sound, I don't know, routine."

"Most of it is. But we also got odd jobs, like a couple weeks ago—some kid buys a sixty-millimeter mortar shell from an army-navy store in Brooklyn and takes it home. He and his brother're in the backyard playing catch with it. Supposed to be a dummy—all the powder drained out. Only the kid's father was in Nam and he thinks it looks funny. Takes it to the local precinct station. Turns out it was live."

"Ouch."

"We got it taken care of. . . . Then we get a lot of false alarms, just like the Fire Department. But every once in a while, bingo. There's a suitcase at the airport or a bundle of dynamite or a pipe bomb and we've got to do something with it."

"So somebody crawls up and cuts the wires?"

Healy said, "What's the first goal?"

Rune grinned. "Don't get anybody's ass blown up."

"Mine included. First we evacuate the area and set up a frozen zone."

"Frozen?"

"We call it a frozen zone. Maybe a thousand yards wide. Then we'll put a command post behind armor or sandbags somewhere within that area. We have these remote-control robots with video cameras and X rays and stethoscopes and we send one up to take a look at the thing."

"To listen for the ticking?"

"Yep. Exactly." He nodded at her. "You'd think everybody'd be using battery-powered digital timer-detonators—Hollywood again. But ninety percent of the bombs we deal with are really crude, homemade. Pipe bombs, black or smokeless powder, dynamite, match heads in conduit. And most of these use good old-fashioned dime-store alarm clocks. You need two pieces of metal coming together to complete the circuit and set off the detonating cap. What's better for that than a windup alarm clock with a bell and clapper on top? So, we look and listen. Then if it really is an IED and we can disarm without any risk we do a render-safe. If it's a tricky circuit or we think it'll go off we get it into the containment vehicle." He nodded toward the field near the shack. "And bring it here and blow it up ourselves."

They walked outside. Two young men stood a hundred yards away from them in one of the three deep pits dug into the field. They wound what looked like plastic clothesline around a square, olive-drab box.

Rune looked around. She said, "This looks just like the Underworld."

Healy frowned. He asked her, "Eliot Ness?"

"No, like Hades, I mean. You know, hell."

"Oh, yeah—your analysis of the crime scene the other day." Healy looked back to the men in the pit. He said to Rune, "You have to understand something about explosives. In order to be effective, they have to be explosive only under certain conditions. If you make this stuff that blows up when you look at it cross-eyed, well, that's not going to be real useful now, is it? Hell, most explosives you can destroy by burning them. They don't blow up; they just burn. So to make it go bang, you need detonators. Those're powerful bits of explosive that set off the main charge. Remember the C-4 that they used in the second bombing? If you don't have the detonator surrounded by at least a half inch of C-4 you might not get a bang at all."

She heard enthusiasm in his voice. She thought how good it is when you've found the one thing in life that you're really good at and that you enjoy doing for a living.

"That's what we look for," Healy continued. "That's the weak point in bombs. Most detonators're triggered electrically. So, yeah, we cut the wires, and that's it. If somebody wants to get elaborate they could have a timed detonator and a rocker switch, so that even if you cut the timer, any movement will set off the bomb. Some have a shunt—a galvanometer hooked up to the circuit so that if you cut the wire the needle swings to zero because the current's been cut and *that* sets off the bomb. The most elaborate bomb I ever saw had a pressure switch. The whole thing was inside a sealed metal canister filled with pressurized air. We drilled a tiny hole to test for nitrate molecules—that's how bomb detectors at airports work. Sure enough, it was filled with explosives. There was a pressure switch inside. So if we'd open the canister the air would have escaped and set it off."

"God, what did you do?"

"We brought it up here and were just going to detonate it but the word came from downtown they wanted to check the components for fingerprints. So we put it in a hyperbaric chamber, equalized the pressure inside and outside, opened it up and rendered it safe. It had two pounds of Semtex in it. With steel shot all around.

Like shrapnel. Purely antipersonnel. Mean, son-of-a-bitch bomb."

"You got the robot into the chamber?"

"Well, no. Actually I dismantled it."

"You?"

He shrugged and nodded to the pit, where the two men had finished their wrapping exercise and were retreating to a bunker of concrete and sandbags.

"They're practicing setting off military charges. That's an M118 demolition block. About two pounds of C-4. For blowing bridges and buildings, trees. They've wrapped it with detonating cord and'll set it off by remote control."

Over the loudspeaker came a voice: "Pit number one, fire in the hole! Fire in the hole!"

"What do they mean?" Rune asked.

"That's what they used to yell in coal mines when they lit the fuse on the dynamite. Demolition people use it now to mean there's about to be an explosion."

Suddenly a huge orange flash filled the sky. Smoke appeared. And an instant later a clap of thunder slapped their ears.

"Boaters hate us," Healy explained. "City gets a lot of claims for broken windows."

Rune was laughing.

Healy looked at her. "What?"

She said, "It's just weird. You brought me all the way out here to give me a lesson on IEDs."

"Not really," he said, considering.

"Then why did you invite me?"

Healy looked away for a moment, cleared his throat. His face was ruddy to start with but it seemed he was blushing. He opened his attaché case and took out a couple of cans of diet Coke, two deli sandwiches, a bag of Fritos. "I guess it's a date."

CHAPTER TEN

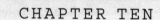 He may have looked like a cowboy but he wasn't the silent type.

Detective Sam Healy was thirty-eight. Nearly half of his fellow Bomb Squad detectives had gotten into demolition in the military but he'd gone a different route. First a portable—a foot patrolman—then working an RMP.

"Remote motor patrol. It means police car."

"Initials, I remember."

Healy smiled. "You're talking to an MOS."

"Moss?"

"Member of Service."

After a few years of that Healy'd gone into Emergency Services: New York's SWAT team. Then he'd signed up for the Bomb Squad. He'd taken the month-long course at the FBI's Hazardous Devices School in Huntsville, Alabama, and then was assigned to the Squad. Healy had majored in electrical engineering in college and was studying criminal justice at John Jay.

He talked with excitement about his workshop at home, inventions he'd made as a kid, his twenty-year, uninterrupted subscription to *Scientific American*. Once he had come up with a formula for a chemical solution to neutralize a particular high explosive and had almost gotten a patent. But a big military supplier beat him to it.

He'd never fired his gun, except on the range, and had only made four arrests. He carried a Brooklyn gun shop's business card, on the back of which was printed the *Miranda* recitation; he knew he'd never remember the words in a real arrest. He'd been called on the carpet several times for failing to wear his service revolver.

When the conversation turned personal he became quieter, though Rune sensed he wanted to talk. His wife had left him eight months before and she had informal custody of their son. "I want to fight it but I can't bring myself to. I don't want to put Adam through that. Anyway, what judge is going to award *me* custody of a ten-year-old kid? I deal with explosive devices all day."

"Is that why she left you?"

Healy pointed across the field. Rune heard the staticky warning again. Another huge flash, followed by a tower of smoke fifty feet high. Rune felt a concussion wave slap her face like a sudden summer wind. The cops watching lifted their fingers to their mouths and whistled. Rune jumped to her feet and applauded.

"Nitramon cratering charge," Healy said, studying the smoke.

"Fantastic!"

Healy was nodding, looking at her. She caught him and he looked away.

"The job, you mean?" he asked.

Rune had forgotten her question. Then she recalled. "The reason your wife left?"

"I don't know. I think the reason was I didn't ever get home. Mentally, I mean. I live in Queens. I've got a house with a lab in the basement. One night I'd been doing some work downstairs and I was kind of lost in it and my wife came down and said dinner was ready. I wasn't paying any attention and I told her about the experiment and I said, 'You know, this feels just like home.' And she said, 'This *is* your home.' "

Rune said, "Don't be too hard on yourself. Takes two."

He nodded.

"Still in love with her, huh?"

"No way," he said quickly.

"Uh-huh."

"No, really."

The sound of wind filled the range. He became silent, almost impenetrable.

Which would have been one of his wife's gripes. The difficulty of reaching him.

After a moment Healy said, "All of a sudden, out of the blue, she says she can't stand me. I'm just one big irritation. I don't understand her. I'm never there for her. I was floored. I really asked for it, in a way—I pushed her, I kept telling her how much I loved her, how sorry I was, how I'd do anything. . . . She said that was just torturing her. I went a little nuts."

"Lovers can do that to you," Rune said.

Healy continued. "For instance—when she left, Cheryl took the TV. So the next day all I can think about is getting a replacement. I went out and bought *Consumer Reports* and read all about the different kinds of sets. I mean, I had to buy the best TV there was. It became an obsession. Finally, I went to SaveMart and spent—God, I can't believe it—eleven hundred on this set. . . ."

"Whoa, that must be one hyper TV."

"Sure, but the thing is: I never watch television. I don't *like* TV. I'd do things like that. I was pretty depressed. Then one day we got a call on this pipe bomb. See, they're real dangerous because they're usually filled with gun-powder, which is awfully unstable. Thing weighed about thirty pounds. Turns out it's planted in front of a big bank downtown. In a stairwell. We can't get the robot in there so I get a bomb suit on and take a look at it. I could just carry it out to where the robot can pick it up, then put it in the containment vehicle. But I'm thinking, I don't care if I'm dead or not. So I decide to do a render-safe myself.

"I started twisting the end off the pipe. And what hap-pened was some of the powder got in the threads of the cap and the friction set off the charge."

"God, Sam . . ."

"Turned out it was black powder—not smokeless. That's the weakest explosive you can find. And most of it was wet and didn't go off. Didn't do anything more than knock me on my ass and blister my palms. But I said to myself, 'Healy, time to stop being an asshole.' That helped me get over her pretty well. And that's where I am now."

"Over her."

"Right."

After a moment Rune said, "Marriage is a very weird thing. I'm not sure it's healthy. My mother's always after me to get married. She has a list of people for me. Nice boys. Her friends' sons. She's nondenominational. Jewish, WASP . . . doesn't matter to her. Okay, they are sort of ranked by professions and, yeah, a doctor's first—but she doesn't really care as long as I end up rich and pregnant. Oh, and happy. She does want me to be happy. A rich, happy mother. I tell you, I have a great imagination but that's one thing I can't picture, me married."

Healy said, "Cheryl was real young when we got mar-ried. Twenty-two. I was twenty-six. We thought it was time to settle down. People change, I guess."

Silence. And Rune sensed he felt they'd gone too far into the personal. He shrugged in a dismissing way, then noticed a uniformed cop he recognized and asked what had happened to a live hand grenade someone had found in the Bronx.

"S'in the captain's office. On his chair."

"His chair?" Healy asked.

"Well, we took the TNT out first."

He turned back to Rune and to fill the silence she asked, "You ever happen to talk to that witness?"

Healy drank most of his soda but left half his sandwich. "What witness?"

"The guy who was hurt in the first bombing? The first angel?"

The wind came up and whipped smoke from a burning pit toward them.

"Yeah."

"Ah," Rune said. "Was he helpful?"

Healy hooked his thumbs into his thick belt, which really made him look a lot like a cowboy.

"Aren't you going to tell me what he said?"

"No."

"Why not?"

"Doesn't concern you."

"You just filed it away, what he said. And that's it?"

"No, that's not it." Healy debated for a moment. Finally he said, "The witness wasn't helpful."

"So there're no leads."

"There're leads."

"But nobody's following up on them," she said cynically. "Because of the word, right? From downtown."

"I'm following up," Healy said.

"What?" she asked quickly. "Tell me!" And she guessed he was wondering whether the date had been a good idea.

"I checked the fingerprints from the phone where the killer called her the night of the bombing."

"And—"

"Nothing. I'm also tracking the explosives. The wrapper I mentioned. I think we can trace the inventory."

"So, you going to get fired for doing all this? Because of the word from headquarters?"

"Way I figure it, the ops coordinator or precinct commander's got my phone number. They want me to stop, they can always give me a call."

Her hand closed on his shoulder. She felt a sizzle. Part of it was gratitude that he was going out on a limb to find out who'd killed Shelly. Part of it was something else.

But she concentrated on the detective part at the moment. "Look, Sam, how 'bout I help you?"

"Help me what?"

"Find the killer."

"No."

"Come on, we can be a team!"

"Rune."

"I can do stuff you can't. I mean, you have to do things legally, right?"

"Rune, this isn't a game."

"I'm not treating it like a game. You want to catch a perp." She emphasized the word to let him know she'd been around crime and criminals. Then added, "And I want to make a film." Her lips were taut. "That's not a game."

He saw that fire in her eyes. He didn't say anything else.

After a moment she asked, "Just tell me one thing."

"What?"

"Promise you'll answer."

"No."

"Please."

"Maybe," Healy said.

"What about the fingerprints?"

"I told you. They were negative."

"Not on the phone," Rune said. "On the letters? The ones from the Sword of Jesus, about the angels?"

He debated. Then said, "Whoever wrote them used gloves."

"Where was the paper from?"

"I said I'd answer one question."

"You said maybe you would. Which means you haven't ruled out answering two."

"I make the rules. I answered you. Now promise me you'll just make your movie and stay out of the investigation."

She brushed her bangs out of her eyes, then stuck her hand out. "Okay. But only if you give me exclusive press coverage."

"Deal." His large, tough hand enfolded hers. He didn't let go. For a moment the only sound was of the wind. She knew he wanted to kiss her and she was ready to kiss him back—in a certain noncommittal way. But the moment passed and he released her hand. They gazed at each other for a moment. Then he turned toward the pit.

"Come on," he said, "I'll let you throw a hand grenade, you want."

"Yeah?" she asked excitedly.

"Well, a practice one."

Rune said, "That's okay. I'll work my way up."

■

Through the huge backstage doorway Rune saw a construction site, not a theater.

The aroma was of sawn wood and the nose-pinching, sweet smell of paint and varnish. Lumber was in constant motion, carried by husky men in T-shirts printed with the names of long-gone Broadway plays. Cables snaked along the dusty, battered stage.

Shouts, the *boom, boom, boom* of hammers, the shrill screech of electric saws, routers, drills.

She walked into the wings of the stage. True, she'd painted backdrops for one high school play, as she'd told

Arthur Tucker. And she had been in several pageants. But she'd never been backstage at a real theater. And she didn't realize how much space there was behind the curtain.

And what an ugly, scuffed, beat-up space it was.

A huge cavern, a massive pit in the Underworld. She made her way unnoticed to the front of the stage. Three people sat in the front row, bent over a script. Two men and a woman. Their discussion was animated. They were having a disagreement.

Rune interrupted. "Excuse me. . . . Are you Michael Schmidt?"

A man about forty-five looked up and his first motion was to remove his reading glasses, which had half lenses in the bottom of the frames.

"Yes?"

The others—a heavy man in a work shirt and a woman inhaling greedily on a cigarette and looking grim—had not looked up. They stared at the script as if they were identifying a body in the morgue.

Rune said, "Your office told me I could find you here."

"Did they now? I'll have to talk to someone about that." Schmidt was short, very compact, and in good shape. Rune could see his biceps squeezed by the cuffs of his close-fitting short-sleeve shirt. Though he was muscular his face looked unhealthy; his eyes were red and watery. Maybe allergies.

Maybe, she thought, CS tear gas . . .

She looked around the seats near the producer for a red windbreaker and a hat. Didn't see any.

And he didn't seem to recognize her as the person he might've attacked on the pier. Still, his profession was creating the illusion of the theater. . . .

"What do you want?" he said curtly.

Rune said, "Can I have your autograph?"

Schmidt blinked. "How the fuck did you get past security?"

"Just walked in. Please, I've always wanted your autograph."

He sighed.

"Please."

He glanced at the others, who were still staring at the script and whispering darkly. He stood. Schmidt was limping and winced once as he climbed a stained set of plywood stairs onto the stage.

She stuck her hand out. He glanced at her without a bit of expression on his face and walked past. Went to the coffee machine and poured himself a large cup. He returned, glanced again at the arguing writers, or whoever they were, and said, "Okay."

"This is so neat. Thanks." She handed him a piece of paper and a Crayola.

"To who?"

"Mom."

He scrawled some illegible words. Handed it back. Rune took it, then gazed up at him. He sniffled, blew his nose with a linen handkerchief and asked, "Anything else I can do for you, Miss Rune?" He stood with a cocked hip, looking at her, waiting.

"Okay." She put the autograph away. "I lied."

"I figured that."

"Well, I did want your autograph. But I wanted to ask you a couple questions too."

"I don't do casting. Give your resume to the—"

"I don't want to be an actress either."

He blinked, then laughed. "Well, in that case you're the only woman under twenty-five in the whole city who doesn't."

"I'm doing a film about an actress who auditioned for you. Shelly Lowe?"

Did his eyes flutter like a startled squirrel's? So maybe had he recognized her now?

He said, "I don't recall a Shelly Lowe."

"You must. I heard you almost offered her a part in this play."

He laughed, startled. "I *must*? Well, young lady, I don't."

"She was going to be the lead."

"There were hundreds of actresses who hoped to be the lead in this play. We finally selected one. It wasn't a Ms. Lowe. Now, if you'll—"

"She was killed."

His attention wavered. He studied some of the construction. "I'm sorry to hear that."

Which he wasn't, Rune could see. She remained silent, staring up at him.

Schmidt finally said, "And you're doing her life story?"

"Something like that. Here's her picture." Rune handed him a publicity still that Nicole had given her. He studied it with the detached interest of a bored traffic cop reading a driver's license and handed it back to her. "Don't recall her. Why do you think she auditioned for us?"

"I heard she did."

"Ah," Schmidt said, smiling again. "Theatrical gossip. Never to be trusted."

"Then maybe you can set the record straight. You really don't remember her?"

"Miss Rune, you've got to understand. First of all, I do none of the preliminary casting myself. We have a casting director for that—"

"What's his—"

"—who is no longer with the company, and I don't know where he is. Second, most of the people who say they interview or audition with Michael Schmidt do nothing more than have their agent send a head shot and a copy of their resume to us or stand in line for an EPA or

EPI that lasts ten seconds. Did this Ms. Lowe ever really audition for us? I doubt it. Did she ever audition for *me*? No disrespect to the dead . . . but if your friend said she almost had the part"—he turned his palms upward—"she lied."

There was a loud crash nearby. A stagehand had knocked over a huge stack of two-by-fours. Schmidt turned to him, the producer's face twisted in fury. "*What* are you doing?"

"Sorry, Mr. Schmidt. I—"

"We're behind schedule because cretins like you don't know what on earth you're doing. One more mistake and you're out of here."

"I said I was sorry," the beefy young man said. "It was an accident."

Schmidt turned back to Rune. "Idiots all around me . . . Next time you want to talk to me, call my office. Make an appointment. Although"—he turned and walked toward the stairs—"I sincerely hope there won't be a next time."

Rune watched him for a moment. Saw that as far as Michael Schmidt was concerned she had ceased to exist. She slipped backstage and paused, watching the young stagehand angrily restack the lumber that had fallen to the floor.

She yawned so hard that her jaw shivered and from her eyes sprang thick tears.

It was ten p.m. Rune sat in the L&R studio, at the Moviola—an old flatbed film editing machine—rewinding the footage for the House O' Leather commercial. Larry'd shot about an hour of the homely daughter doing retakes against the pimply backdrop. Rune was editing together chunks of the film, following Bob's notes.

Mary Jane—who Rune decided would have made

someone a wonderful administrator—had left a note of
her own, a long list of corrections to the estimate. She
signed off with: *Please aim for 8:30-ish. And remember: big
day tomorrow. Let's all be bright-eyed. Ciao! M. J. C.*

The door opened. Bob came in and walked right over
to the gray machine, staring at the screen. He didn't say
anything to her for a moment. " 'Ow're they coming, luv?"

"I'll have them for you in the morning." He waved her
hand away from the crank and turned it himself, studying
the jerky scenes in the small screen. Rune watched his 18-
karat gold bracelet as she said, "I didn't know you did
daily rushes when it's just a commercial."

"We're being a little more—whatsa word?—diligent
with this one. The budget and all, you know."

"How was the client dinner?"

"Guy's an old fart and his daughter . . . Christ. She
'ad 'er foot up to no good, you know what I mean. On me
thigh. Wanted a drink after, just the two of us. I 'ad to
plead bloody exhaustion, get away from the crazy bird.
And then Mary bleedin' Jane—there's an iceberg for you."
He spun the knob. He frowned. "Add two more seconds
of 'er before the fade. Her old man thinks she's some
kinda Princess Di."

"I've already finished her sequence."

"Well, finish it again."

"Did you think about me, sitting here hungry, while
you were eating a gourmet meal?"

"Ah, brung you a present."

He handed her a paper bag with a grease spot on it.
"Yeah?"

She opened it. Inside was a foil swan.

"Hey, you brought me something to go."

"Well, yeah."

She opened the swan's back. She stared down at it.

"It's leftovers, isn't it, Bob? This isn't a swan bag. It's a
doggy bag."

"Thought you might like something."

Rune was poking at the contents with a pencil. "It's green beans and potatoes. That's all that's left. What went with it?"

"Dunno. May've been a steak." He stretched and for a moment looked like the cute, innocent boy he had never in his life been and walked out the door. "Eight-thirty for tomorrow, doll. 'E likes croissants, so pick up some on your way in, could you?"

The door shut behind him.

She wadded the cold potatoes up and was about to throw them out when she felt her stomach rumbling. Her hand hesitated.

"Double damn."

Rune opened the foil and then, with a glance out the window to make sure Bob had left, cued up her own videocassette on the Sony video editor next to the Moviola and started the tape. She watched it as she ate the potatoes and beans, using two pencils like chopsticks.

The shots of Danny Traub told her nothing other than that the porn producer was a stupid, egotistical, horny bastard. The shots of Michael Schmidt—taken with the hidden video camera—told her that he was a smart, insincere, egotistical bastard, who may or may not have been horny, but at least didn't let it get in the way of his job.

Rune replayed the flicker in his eye when she mentioned Shelly Lowe's name. A tiny motion. What was he thinking? What was he *remembering*?

She couldn't tell. As Larry had told her, "Cameras don't lie, luv, but that doesn't mean they tell the whole truth."

No, Schmidt's tape told her very little. But the tape of Arthur Tucker . . . that was different.

The first thing she noticed: Shelly's acting coach had spent several minutes casually covering up something on his desk as he talked to her. It might have been a pile of papers or a manuscript. He'd been very subtle; she hadn't even noticed him doing it in the office. What didn't he want her to see? Rune rewound the tape and freeze-framed the image. She couldn't make out anything.

But then she glanced at a plaque on the wall behind him. It held a set of medals. But not those mail-order medals that commemorate stupid events like Great Moments in the Industrial Revolution. Franklin Mint stuff. These were real-looking military medals, along with other mementos, including a gold cross.

She squinted as she studied them, recalling one of her favorite movies. A black-and-white film made by Metropolitan Studios in the fifties. *The Fighting Rangers*. A World War Two film. One of the main characters—the nice kid from a Midwestern town, played by somebody like Audie Murphy—is terrified of battle. He's never sure if his courage is going to break. But in the end, he sneaks up on an enemy bridge and blows it to bits all by himself to keep the enemy from sending reinforcements.

She remembered the little crescent name badge—the simple word RANGERS on the hero's shoulder—when he lay dying in the last scene of the movie. It looked just like the tag Arthur Tucker had in his plaque of medals. He'd been a Ranger too.

The other thing she remembered was the scene earlier in the movie when another soldier had asked the hero if he knew how to rig the explosives on the bridge.

And he'd answered, "Sure, Sarge. All Rangers know how to blow up things. It's what they teach us in training."

CHAPTER ELEVEN

Arthur Tucker was feeling old.

Sitting in his dusty Times Square office, he dropped a dull-white heater coil into a chipped cup of water. It sputtered fiercely. When the water boiled he removed the coil and dropped in a twice-used, crusty Lipton tea bag. The sunlight came through the curtains, which were faded in waves that marked the sun's passage over the year. Outside, the sounds of construction were like the noises of battle.

Feeling old.

Sometimes, watching one of his young protégés on stage, he felt anything but old. He almost believed he was still the twenty-five-year-old, dressed in the musty costume of Rosencrantz or Benvolio or young Prince Hal, waiting for his cue to enter from stage right.

But not today. Something had triggered this morbid feeling of antiquity as he'd climbed off the Eighth Avenue train at Fiftieth Street and walked in a slow zigzag to his office. Looking at the marquees of the theaters. Many of them were now on the ground floors of high-rise buildings; they weren't separate structures like the grand old Helen Hayes, the Martin Beck, the Majestic. He thought that said something—the theaters being parts of office buildings. When he remembered the old marquees—the huge, jutting trapezoids of dotted lights—he remembered mostly the logos of musical comedies. Why did he picture those (a form of theater he did not enjoy and rarely attended) more easily than the marquees announcing the plays of Miller and O'Neill and Ibsen and Strindberg and Mamet, all of whom he believed to be geniuses?

It must be because he was getting old, he figured.

He thought of his students. Where were they all? A dozen on or off Broadway. Six or seven on television sitcoms or adventure shows. Two dozen in Hollywood.

And hundreds and hundreds that had gone into accounting or law or carpentry or advertising or plumbing.

Hundreds and hundreds who were good but weren't good enough for the system: the star system, that goddamn inverted pyramid, with so little room for people at the top.

Arthur Tucker sipped the tea and wondered if his life had been a failure.

And now . . . the incident with Shelly Lowe. He wasn't sure if—

His phone rang, a jarring metallic blare. He picked it up, said, "Hello."

And heard some breathless young girl talking a mile a minute. Checks? She was saying something about a problem with the mail. She was on the first floor of the building and some checks addressed to him had been misdelivered to her office. Tucker didn't believe he was expecting any checks. Most of his students paid in cash at the end of their lessons, handing him the crisp, precious twenties straight from the Chase ATM.

"Well, they look like checks. I'm all alone here. I can't bring them up. You want me to leave them outside my door tonight."

In which case they'd vanish in five minutes, he knew.

"I'll come down. What office?"

"One-oh-three. If I don't answer right away I might be on the phone," she said. "I'll just be a minute."

Tucker pulled on his tweed jacket, with its leather elbow patches and torn satin lining. He forwent his hat. He walked into the dark corridor, locking the door after him. He pressed the big black button to summon the elevator and waited for three minutes until it arrived. He stepped inside and began the grinding journey down to the first floor.

████

Rune tried a dental pick.

She'd bought it at a pharmacy from a clerk who didn't seem particularly curious why someone wearing Day-Glo Keds and a miniskirt printed with pterodactyls would be interested in a dental tool. Then she'd gone back to the houseboat. She'd practiced on the locks to some of the interior doors and got them open pretty fast. She hadn't graduated to the front door, which had a doorknob cylinder and a Medeco, because she got impatient. Anyway, she figured, the theory was undoubtedly the same.

It wasn't.

Sweating, the panic growing, she worked at Arthur Tucker's door for five minutes. Nothing happened. She'd get the pick in and twist it and turn it and hear clicking and snapping and unlocking sounds, all of which was real satisfying.

But nothing happened. The door remained snugly locked.

She stood back. There was no time. Tucker'd be back in three or four minutes, she estimated.

She looked up and down the corridor. There were only two other tenants on this floor: a lawyer's office, with signs in English and Korean, and an import company. There were no lights under either door.

"Oh, hell."

Rune shoved her elbow through the glass. A large triangular piece fell inside. She reached in and turned the latch.

Four minutes . . . you've only got four minutes.

But it turned out she didn't need even that much time.

Because right in the middle of Tucker's desk was what she was looking for—the stack of papers he'd been going to great lengths to cover up. But it wasn't just any stack of papers; it was a play. The title was *Delivered Flowers.* Tucker, it seemed, had been making notes in the margin—additions, deletions, stage directions. Not many, a few words here and there. One change was pretty radical, though, Rune thought. Not in the play itself, but on the cover page: Tucker had crossed out *by Shelly Lowe* and written his own name in.

The copyright line had been changed too, his name substituted for hers.

On the cover was another note: *Haymarket Theater, Chicago—interested.*

Shelly's been dead a few days, Rune thought angrily, and this prick's already stolen her script and sold it to somebody.

Take it, she told herself. *It's evidence.*

But then Tucker would see it was gone. She looked behind the desk. There were piles of other plays, also loose-bound like this one, on his credenza. She rummaged through them and found another one on which Tucker had crossed off Shelly's name and put his own in its place.

She tossed it into her leopard-skin bag and left the office. There was a loud click behind her, up the corridor.

She'd been wrong. Tucker hadn't waited at the door downstairs for as long as she'd hoped. Or maybe someone had told him the company had moved months ago. In any event the elevator opened just as she got into the stairwell. She heard his footsteps, heard them stop, heard his muttered "Oh, no" as he saw the broken glass. She eased through the fire door and took the stairs two, then three at a time down to the ground floor.

Outside, she saw a cop up the street. Her first inclination was to bolt. But then she remembered that no way would Arthur Tucker call the police. At best he was a thief. At worst, a killer.

———

The lights were brilliant dots of pure sun.

Rune, thirty feet away, standing behind greasy pillars, felt the heat from the lights and wondered two things. Why had the lighting man decided to use four 800-watt Redhead lamps, which were way too big for the size of the set?

That was the first thing she wondered. The second was: What was going through the mind of Nicole D'Orleans, who was naked and grappling with a tall, thin, dark-haired man on a pink satin sheet, her long, perfect legs squeezing the guy's waist with all their strength?

"That's it baby yeah there there ooooo you know what I like you know what I want give it to me fuck me fuck me. . . ."

When she got tired of delivering dialogue like that Nicole would simply wail and mew. The man above her mostly grunted.

Sweating furiously, they changed position often—missionary seemed to be passé. Some of the poses were creative but seemed exhausting even to watch; it was good that Nicole and her partner were athletic.

Jesus, Rune thought, I couldn't get my legs up that high if you paid me. . . .

The sounds of their lovemaking sailed into the dark crevices of the Lame Duck studio.

The T-shirted cameraman moved in close, as if the probing lens of the Ikegami video camera was the third member of a ménage à trois. The rest of the crew was bored, leaning on light stands and tripods, sipping coffee. Outside the hot glow surrounding the mattress Danny Traub—today acting as director—gestured impatiently and ordered the cameraman around the set. "You miss the come shot, your ass is grass."

"I won't miss it."

"Yesterday, Sharon's leg was in the way. You couldn't see diddly."

"I won't miss it," the cameraman responded. And moved closer to the action.

Rune returned to her meditation. What would Nicole be thinking about? They'd been at it for half an hour. She seemed aroused. But was it fake? Was she concentrating on—

Then, a disturbance.

The actor had stopped his pumping and was standing up. Dazed, bleary, breathing heavily. Nicole glanced down at his crotch and saw the problem. She leaned forward and went to work with her mouth. She looked pretty skillful but the man didn't respond. He suddenly retreated out of the lights. Nicole sat back and took the bathrobe that a young woman, an assistant, offered her. The actor looked for a towel, found one and pulled it around his waist.

"That's it," the actor called. Gesturing, palms out, with a shrug.

Danny Traub sighed, then barked orders. The lights went out. The camera shut off. The grips and gaffers walked off the set.

"Third time this week, Johnny," Traub whispered.

The actor was deeply inhaling on a Camel. "It's too fucking hot in here. What's with the air conditioner?"

"The air conditioner?" Traub's head swiveled to his imaginary mezzanine. "He needs—what?—thirty-two degrees before he can get it up?"

Johnny was looking at the floor but focusing six inches beneath it. "I'm tired."

"I'm paying you a thousand dollars for a hard dick. This film shoulda been in the can a week ago."

"So shoot around me. Put in some stock inserts."

"Johnny"—like Traub was talking to a six-year-old—"people save up their pennies to rent tapes of you and your foot-long. They want to see the wand do its magic thing, you understand?"

"I'm *tired*."

"You're strung out is what you are. You know what coke does to your yin-yang. You can be a lawyer, a doctor, a musician, probably even a fucking airline pilot and do all the blow you want and it isn't going to fuck up your job. But a man who makes porn can't do as much as you're doing."

"Just give me a couple of hours."

"No, I'm giving you the fucking boot. Get out."

Nicole had been watching from the side of the bed. She stepped toward them. "Danny . . ."

Traub ignored her.

Johnny muttered something. He walked to the corner of the set. From a leather shoulder bag he took a blue glass vial. Traub stepped up and slapped it from his hand. It hit the wall and fell, spinning.

"Fuck, Danny, why—"

He shoved Johnny up against the wall hard. Gave a vicious smile, looking around. "He thinks I'm joking? Yeah, he does! The man thinks I'm joking. . . . I can't afford to carry you anymore."

"Cut it out."

"Shut up!" The words were jarring, pitched high, frantic. Everyone on the set must've heard. But they all looked away—at scheduling sheets or invoices or scripts. Or they stared at the coffee and tea they stirred compulsively.

Johnny pulled away. He sat on the bed, looking absently for his clothes.

Nicole walked to the fallen coke shaker, picked it up and offered it tentatively to Johnny. Traub stepped forward and pulled it from her hand.

"You dumb bitch. Didn't you hear what I just said?"

"I was just—"

Traub had turned back to Johnny. "I paid you up front for this week. I want half back."

Nicole said, "Danny, leave him alone, come on."

Traub turned on her. Said viciously, "A real actress'd know how to get him up. You're fucking useless."

Nicole was obviously frightened of him. She swallowed and looked away from his tiny piercing eyes. "Don't fire him, Danny. Come on. He's, you know, had trouble getting jobs."

Traub's face broke into a dark, simian grin. "An impotent porn star, having trouble getting work? You're shitting me."

"He's having a rough time is all."

Traub said to Johnny, "Fuck the money. Just get outa here."

Johnny turned abruptly and walked off the set.

"Asshole," Nicole whispered.

Traub spun around and grabbed her teased hair. He pulled her head close to his. "Don't . . . you . . . ever."

Nicole whimpered. "I'm sorry, I'm sorry, I'm sorry. . . ."

Anger swept through Traub. He drew his hand back in a fist. But he looked around. A beefy, T-shirted assistant stirred. The cameraman took a step toward them. Traub waited a moment and released her hair.

Nicole's hand rose to her head and massaged her scalp. Traub gave her a fake smile again and patted her cheek. She flinched, waiting for a slap. He laughed and slipped the vial of coke between her breasts. "There's my—"

She tossed her hair and walked away.

Traub called after her, "—good girl."

───

"Shoes," Nicole said to Rune. "A lot of times I think about shoes."

"Shoes? Like on your feet?"

"Yeah. You know. Just shoes."

Rune and Nicole were sitting in one of the dressing rooms at Lame Duck, which wasn't a room at all but just an area set off from the rest of the studio with cracked and mouse-gnawed Sheetrock. They were on the fourth floor, the floor above the bombing. Nicole had said the company had decided not to move, which she thought was real tacky, what with Shelly being killed just below them. "Danny says we're got a sweetheart deal with the landlord. Whatever that means."

Rune had snuck up to the dressing rooms after the incident with Traub. There she'd set up the camera and zoomed in for a close-up of Nicole's face. She'd lowered her voice to sound like Faye Dunaway's in *Network* and asked, "When you're on the set with the cameras rolling and you're with a man, doing it, what do you think about?"

"Just one man?"

"I mean, with anyone."

"Danny likes to shoot with two men a lot."

Rune said, "Okay, say you're on the set with two men."

Nicole nodded to show she understood the question and started talking about shoes.

"I think about Ferragamos a lot. Today, before that thing with Johnny I was picturing this great pair. It has a nifty bow on the side, real small and cute." Nicole was dressed in a shiny silver jumpsuit with a wide, white belt. She wore cowboy boots with metal rivets on the side. Her hair was teased up high. Rune noticed that her scalp was slightly red from where Traub had grabbed her.

"I love shoes. I have about sixty pairs. I don't know. They calm me down. For some reason."

"Sixty?" Rune whispered in astonishment.

"That was one difference between Shelly and me. I spend everything I make. She put it all in mutual funds and stocks, things like that. But, hey, I like clothes. What can I say?"

"I saw a couple of your films. You looked like you were really turned on, really into it. And you were just faking?"

Nicole shrugged. "I'm a woman; I've had lots of practice faking."

"You must think about something other than shoes."

"Well, there's technical stuff to worry about. Am I at the right angle, am I looking at the camera, did I shave my underarms, am I repeating the same words all the time?"

"Who writes the dialogue?"

Nicole glanced nervously at the camera. She cleared her throat. "We make up most of it. Only the thing is, you'd think it'd be easy. You just look at the camera and talk. But it isn't like that. You kind of freeze up. You know *what* to say, the words and all, but the *how to say it* part, that's what's so hard for me."

Rune said, "You sounded okay to me. And I've seen a couple of your films."

"Yeah?" Nicole turned her face, glowing with purple and beige makeup, toward Rune. "Which ones?"

"*Bottoms Up*. And *Sex Wars*. Oh, and *Lusty Cousins*."

"That was an old one, *Lusty Cousins*. Kind of a classic. I got mentioned in *Hustler*. I have to say I was kinda happy with the way it worked out. I rehearsed that one for a week. Shelly made us."

Rune glanced outside into the empty corridor.

"Did Shelly ever write plays?"

"Plays? Yeah. That was another one of her hobbies. She'd send them out and they'd come back with a rejection letter."

"Did she ever have anything produced?"

"Naw, I don't think so. But one she wrote a few months ago was supposed to be real good. Some theater was interested in it."

The Haymarket Theater, Chicago, Rune bet, recalling the note on the copy of the play in Tucker's office.

"*Delivered Flowers*?"

"Yeah. I think so. That might have been it."

"You know what it was about?"

"Naw."

Rune said, "I interviewed Danny Traub. I was talking to him about Shelly."

"Uh-huh."

"And he said that he really loved her. That they were this like team."

"Danny said that?"

"Yep."

"He's lying," Nicole said.

"That's sort of what I thought too."

"He didn't give a shit for Shelly. Or for anybody else except himself. Did he, like, tell you about the times he propositioned her—which was every other day?"

"No. Why don't *you*?"

Nicole looked at the camera. "Maybe if you could shut that off."

Rune clicked the switch.

"He was always . . ."

"Harassing her?"

Nicole shrugged as if there was a fine line between

coming on to some woman and harassing her. "It wasn't like he was stalking her. But he was pretty hung up. She thought he was a little toad. She hated him. He'd come parading onto the set and start putting everybody down. Wisecracking and insulting everyone. You know how he does that? Talking *about* you, not to you, even when you're right in front of him. And since he pays them—and, man, he pays good—they all put up with it."

"But not Shelly."

"Oh, no way. Not Shelly. Hell, she laughed at him. A couple weeks ago Danny was ordering the director around on the set and Shelly called him a pissant. I don't know what that is exactly—you ever hear of it? Anyway she called him that, then walked off the set. Boy, was he mad. All these veins and stuff stood out on his face. I thought he was going to have a heart attack."

"I saw the fight you guys just had."

"Me and Danny? You saw that? That's not even a fight hardly." She took a brush and started working on her hair. It was hard work—there was a lot of spray. "Johnny's a sweetheart. He's just not doing too well right now. He's an alcoholic and he does way too much coke. He oughta retire. He was really a star in the seventies. He's kind of big, you know."

Rune said, "I saw."

"But Danny's right. He's no good anymore. Lame Duck's the only place he can work. Nobody else'll hire him. I guess even Danny's lost patience. I mean, that's pretty much one thing you need with a guy—they've got to get it up." Nicole shrugged. "Sort of in the job description, you know?"

Rune paused. Water dripped somewhere. Outside, a motorcycle driver ran through his gears in a tenor roar. She leaned forward and whispered, "Do you think he could have killed Shelly?"

"Danny?" Nicole laughed, started to shake her head.

Then she stopped. The smile faded and she rummaged around in her purse. "You want some blow?" The blue vial appeared. "Johnny always has good stuff."

Rune shook her head.

Nicole inhaled a line, sniffed. After a moment, she said, "Why would he do that?"

Rune was studying the Sheetrock, the uneven angles, the bent nails, the ragged sawing job. After a moment she asked, "You know what's kind of odd?"

"What?"

"That, when I said that—about Danny killing Shelly— you didn't seem really shocked."

Nicole considered that for a moment. "I don't like Danny. He's obnoxious and all he thinks about is women and coke and his cars. But, I'm like, all *I* think about is clothes and coke. So I can't really, you know, cast stones." Her eyes darted. She was debating.

"Go on," Rune said, keeping her voice low. "I have this feeling there's something you want to tell me."

She looked at her watch, then leaned close. Rune smelled perfume and Ponds cold cream and Listerine. "Don't tell anyone, but I want to show you something."

Nicole rose and shoved open the warped paneling that served as the door. They stepped into the gritty hallway and walked to a service elevator. "We're going to the basement," Nicole said, closing the accordion grate. She pressed the first-floor button.

They got out in a filthy lobby and walked to a door that opened onto a flight of stairs descending into the dark.

Rune said, "Looks like it goes down to a pit, like a dungeon."

Nicole gave a cold laugh. "That's *exactly* what it is."

She stared into the dark for a few seconds, then started down the stairs. "I don't think anyone's down here. I hope not."

It was a long descent. They walked a full minute, with just a rickety wooden handrail for support. The only light came from two dim bulbs screwed into huge, wire-cage fixtures meant for lamps much larger. The steps were spongy from rot.

From the foot of the stairs a corridor led to a dark, low tunnel made of rock and uneven smears of concrete. Pools of greasy water mottled the floor. Iron rods stuck out of the stone at various points. Someone years ago had poured red paint, like blood, around the rods—probably as warnings. Cobwebs and the feathery carcasses of insects filled the corners. Rune coughed several times; the air stank of fuel oil and mold.

They continued down the tunnel.

"This used to be a boiler room or storeroom," Nicole said, stepping through a doorway and clicking on a light switch. Fluorescent tubes flickered overhead, then burst into light. The two women squinted in the brilliance. It was a square room, twenty by twenty. The walls were the same stained, sloppy concrete and stone as the tunnel. Rings hung from the ceiling on chains. Stained leather vaulting horses sat in the corner and there was a complicated wooden rack covering one wall.

"A gym?" Rune asked. She walked over to a trapeze made of wood and chromed steel. "I keep thinking I should work out but I don't really feel motivated. I think basically exercise should have a purpose—like running from somebody who wants to beat the hell out of you."

"This isn't a workout room, Rune," Nicole said softly.

"No?"

The actress walked to a tall, battered metal locker and opened it. Took a long, thin stick from it. It looked like the sort of pointer a teacher would use.

"See, in the movies I make sometimes we do a little fake S and M. We take a cat-o'-nine-tails made out of yarn or a riding crop that's wrapped in foam rubber. Some guys get off watching girls in leather bras and garters and black stockings making men lick their high heels. But that's all silly stuff. Somebody really into S and M'd take a tape like that back and ask for a refund. Real S and M uses things like this."

Nicole whipped the thin stick down onto a vault. It whistled and bounced with a slap like a gunshot. Rune blinked.

"Hickory," Nicole said. "Doesn't look bad, but it raises welts. It'll break the skin. You could kill somebody with this if you hit them enough times. I've heard about it happening."

"And you're telling me that Danny's into that?"

"I came down here one time and saw him making one of those flicks. He sells them privately. I don't think the regular tapes Lame Duck makes do it for him anymore. He needs something like this to get it up."

"What was he doing?"

"It was terrible. He was beating this girl and using needles—I mean, they're sterile and everything but, still, Jesus. And what happened was she started begging him to stop. But he just went crazier when he heard that. He was, like, totally out of control. I think he wanted to kill her. She passed out and a couple assistants grabbed Danny and took the girl to the hospital. She was going to go to the cops but he paid her off."

Nicole looked around the room. "So you like asked if he'd kill Shelly? I don't know. But I can tell you he likes to hurt people."

Rune picked up a thin chain with sharp alligator clips on each end. The clips were crusted with blood. She set them down.

Nicole shut off the lights, and they walked down the corridor to the stairs.

Which is when Rune heard the noise.

She whispered, "There, what was that?"

Nicole paused on the second step. "What?"

"I heard something, back there. Are there other rooms like that?"

"A couple of them. In the back. But they were dark, remember? We didn't see any lights."

They waited a moment.

"Nothing." Nicole was halfway up the stairs before Rune put her foot on the lower step. Then she heard it again, the noise.

No, she decided, it was actually two noises. One was similar to what she'd heard before: the ominous swishing of the hickory stick as it swung down on the leather bench.

The second was maybe just the sound of air escaping from a pipe or steam or distant traffic.

Or maybe it was what Rune thought it sounded like— the sound of a man's restrained laugh.

CHAPTER TWELVE

 The watering can leaked but aside from that, Rune decided, it was a pretty good idea.

She rang the bell at Danny Traub's town house and wasn't surprised to find a stunning brunette in a silk teddy opening the door. She had breasts so high and jutting that Rune could have walked underneath them.

Bimbos from the Amazon . . . Lord help us.

Rune walked past her. The woman blinked and stepped aside.

"Sorry we couldn't make it yesterday. Had a load of rhododendraniums to deliver to an office in Midtown, one of Trump's buildings, and the whole crew was busy."

"You mean rhododendrons?"

Rune nodded. "Yeah."

She'd have to be careful. A bimbo with some intelligence.

"Careful," the woman said. "Your can leaks. You don't want to, you know, hurt the wood."

"Got it." Rune started to work, watering Traub's plants and trimming the leaves with a pair of scissors. She carefully stuffed them into her pocket. The green jacket she wore had said MOBIL on it when she'd bought the thing at a secondhand store. But she'd cut the logo off and replaced it with a U.S. Department of Forestry patch.

She'd called Lame Duck and the studio receptionist had reported that Traub would be on the set for a couple of hours and couldn't be disturbed. Her only concern had been running into the woman who'd brought them the martinis the other day.

Well, it was a risk coming here. But what in life isn't?

Traub's only guest, however, appeared to be this brunette basketball player.

The woman didn't seem too suspicious; she was more *interested* in what Rune was doing. Watching everything she did, which—as far as Rune knew—was to murder every plant she touched. She didn't know zip about gardening.

"Did it take you a long time to learn all that stuff? About plants?" the Amazon asked.

"Not too long."

"Oh," she said and watched Rune cut through the roots of an African violet.

Rune said, "You want to give them *some* water but not too much. And *some* light. But—"

"Not too much of that either."

"Right."

The woman nodded and recorded that fact somewhere beneath her shiny, henna-enriched mass of hair.

"Never cut too many leaves off. And always make sure you use the proper type of scissors. That is extremely important. Sharp ones."

A nod; the woman's mental computer disk whirred.

"You make a living doing that?"

Rune said, "You'd be surprised."

"Is it hard to learn?"

"You need some talent but if you work hard . . ."

"I'm an actress," Amazon said, then did a line of cocaine and sat down in front of the TV to watch a soap opera.

Ten minutes later Rune had defoliated half of Traub's plants and had worked her way upstairs into his office.

It was empty. She looked up and down the corridor and saw nobody. She stepped inside and swung the door shut. There was no file cabinet inside but Traub did have a big desk and it wasn't locked.

Inside she found bills, catalogs from glitzy gadget companies, a dildo missing its batteries, dozens of German S & M photo magazines, roach clips and parts of water pipes, matchbooks, pens, casino chips. Nothing that could help her—

"Want another martini?" the voice asked, coldly.

Rune froze, then turned slowly. The blonde, the same woman who had served her and Traub the other day—the one she'd been hoping she didn't run into—stood in the doorway.

Well, it was a risk coming here. . . .

"I—"

The woman walked sullenly past her and pulled open another drawer. It held maybe a thousand in crumpled tens and twenties. "Help yourself." She turned and walked out of the office.

Rune closed the drawer. "Wait, can I talk to you?"

The blonde kept walking. When Rune caught up to her in the corridor she said, "I'm Crystal. You're . . . ?"

"Rune."

"You want to get into films or just robbing my boyfriend?"

"Is he really your boyfriend?"

She didn't answer.

Crystal led the way to the roof. Outside, she took off

her bathrobe and bikini top and stretched out on a lawn recliner covered with thick pink towels. She rubbed aloe vera sunscreen on her chest and arms and legs and lay back, closing her eyes.

Rune looked around. "Nifty place."

Crystal shrugged, wondering, it seemed, what was nifty about a gray sundeck. She said, "He's not." She pulled on sunglasses with dark blue lenses. Looked at Rune. "My boyfriend, I mean." She didn't speak for a moment, then she said, "Every once in a while you see these big cruise ships come down the river. I wonder where they're going sometimes. Have you ever been on a cruise?"

Rune said, "I took this neat cruise around the city once. The Circle Line. I pretended I was a Viking."

"A Viking. With the helmets?"

"Right."

"I mean a real cruise."

"No."

"I never have either. I'd like to go sometime."

Rune said, "You have a wonderful figure."

"Thank you," she said as if no one had ever told her. "You want some blow?"

"No thanks."

Crystal's head lolled toward the sun. Her arms draped over the edges of the recliner. Even her breathing was lethargic. "I'd like to live in the Caribbean, I think. I was in St. Bart's once. And I've been to Club Med a couple times, Paradise Island. I met a guy, only he was married and was separated and after we got back to New York he went back to his wife. Funny, he had a kid and he didn't even tell me about it. I saw him on the street. You don't want to get into movies."

"I know I don't."

"I could do exotic dancing—I don't have to make films. But the thing is, with the dancing . . . You stand in a little room and guys look at you and, well, you know what they're doing. It's not really disgusting, it's more . . . what's the word? . . ." She searched for a while but couldn't find it. She gave up. Put on more lotion. "What were you looking for upstairs?"

"Did you know Shelly Lowe?"

The head turned but where the eyes might be looking under the gunmetal-blue reflections Rune couldn't tell. She saw only two identical, fish-eye images of herself. Crystal said, "I met her once or twice. I never worked with her."

"Did she and Danny get along?"

Crystal eased onto her stomach. "Not too bad, not too good. He's a, you know, asshole. Nobody gets along with Danny very much. Are you, like, a private detective or something?"

"Just between you and me?"

"Sure" was the response, so lazy that Rune believed her.

"I'm doing a film about Shelly Lowe. She was a real actress, you know."

"We're all real actresses," Crystal said quickly as if she'd been conditioned to respond this way. But she didn't sound defensive or angry.

"I want to do a film about her career. She wasn't happy. She didn't like the business, you know."

"What business?"

"Adult films."

Crystal seemed surprised. "Didn't she? Why not? She could have anything she wanted. I make fifty a year cash for working two times a week. And Shelly could get twice that. Only . . ."

"What?"

"People're scared now though. With this AIDS thing. I keep getting tested; everybody does. But you never know. . . . John Holmes died of AIDS. He said he slept with ten thousand women." She rolled onto her back again, the glasses tilted toward the hot disk of a sun.

Crystal finally continued. "She was good. Shelly was. We get a lot of fan letters. Some are kind of weird—like, men'll mail us their underwear—but mostly it's just, I love you, I think about you, I rent all your movies. I get asked for a lot of dates. Danny told me that Shelly used to get things like airline tickets and checks so she could come visit guys who watched her movies. She was one of the company's big stars."

Rune watched the Circle Line *Dayliner* chugging along in the Hudson. "Hey, that's my Viking ship. You gotta ride it sometime."

Crystal glanced quickly. "Danny doesn't talk to me much about business stuff. He thinks I'm not real, you know, bright." The glasses lifted. "I went to college."

"Did you?"

"Community college. I was going to be a dental technician. And look what I've got now. . . . Everything I could want."

Rune said, "You won't mention that I was . . ."

Crystal took off the sunglasses and shook her head. "You still haven't told me what you were looking for."

Rune couldn't see past the blue lenses but she had an odd feeling that this was someone she could trust. "Could Danny've hurt Shelly?"

"Killed her, you mean?"

A hesitation. "That's what I mean."

Her answer was as drowsy as the rest of her conversation. "I don't know. Even if I did I wouldn't, like, testify against him. You know what he'd do to me, I did that?"

She knew something.

A long moment passed as Crystal rubbed more sunscreen on. Finally she dropped the tube on the roof. "You were looking in the wrong place."

"What do you mean?"

"He's not stupid."

"Traub?"

"He's not. He doesn't keep the important things in his desk. He doesn't keep important papers there, for instance."

"Why would I be interested in his papers?"

"He keeps them where he keeps his stash. There's a safe in the kitchen, under the sink. He doesn't think I know the combination. But I figured it out. Want to know what it is?"

"What?"

"It's forty right. Twenty-nine left. Back around to thirty-four. See, that's his idea of a perfect woman. Her measurements. He tells us girls that all the time. The perfect woman."

"What's in the safe?" Rune asked.

"You know, I have to tan my back now. And when I do that I fall asleep. Good-bye."

"Thanks," Rune said. But the woman didn't respond.

She hurried downstairs and found the safe. The combination worked. Inside were dozens of ounce bags of coke. Some crack too. But that didn't interest Rune very much—she already knew about Traub's likes.

What interested her was the insurance policy.

A thin binder from New York Accident & Indemnity. Rune opened it up. There were a lot of strange words, all capitalized, like *Double Indemnity* and *Key Man* and *Named Insured* and *Owner of the Policy*. She couldn't figure out what they meant. But it didn't take her long at all to figure out that the policy was on Shelly Lowe's life and that because of her death Danny Traub was going to be $500,000 richer.

■

Rune had called Sam Healy and asked him to meet her. She was going to tell him about Tucker and Traub. But

before they could get together she got a phone call at
L&R. And that was why she was now in a coffee shop on
West Forty-sixth Street—Restaurant Row, in the heart of
the Theater District.

"I'm one of a very unelite corps," the man said. "Theater people who've been betrayed, fired or assaulted by
Michael Schmidt. I don't know why you want to do a film
about *him*. There're so many decent people in the business."

"It's not really about him."

"Good." Franklin Becker poured another sugar into his
coffee, stirred. He was a former casting director for
Michael Schmidt. After she'd had her talk with the producer at the theater she'd approached the stagehand
Schmidt had dressed down about dropping the load of
lumber. She'd bought the poor man a cup of coffee and
delicately extracted from him the names of several people
who might be willing to dish on Schmidt. Becker was the
first one who'd called her back.

Rune explained, "It's about Shelly Lowe."

"The actress who was killed in that bombing. And you
know about her connection with Schmidt?"

"Right."

Becker reminded her somewhat of Sam Healy. Tall,
thinning hair. Unlike the cop's stone face, though,
Becker's broke frequently into curls of emotion. Her impression too was that he wouldn't have any wives in his
past, only boyfriends.

"What can you tell me about them—Shelly and
Schmidt."

He laughed. "Well, I can tell you quite a story. What
she did . . . it was astonishing. I've been casting on
Broadway for almost twenty years but I've never seen anything like it.

"We had a number of EPIs. . . . Michael preferred
interviews to EPAs—auditions. He's a funny fellow. You

ever talk to him, you know he's got very definite ideas. Usually the producer couldn't care less about the hired help—the actors, I mean. He leaves that to the director. As long as the principals get good reviews and pull in a crowd that's enough for them. But not for Michael. He rides herd on everybody: director, principals, walk-ons, arrangers, musicians, everybody."

Rune wasn't sure where this was going but she let the casting director continue at his own pace.

"So when it came time for casting, Michael kept his beady little eyes over my shoulder. We read resumes, we saw tapes, we talked to talent agencies." He shook his head. "Everybody went through the standard interview—everybody but Shelly. That's the astonishing part.

"Somehow she'd gotten her hands on a copy of the script for the new play. I can't guess how. Michael treated them like gold ingots. There just weren't any copies floating around. But she'd gotten one and had memorized the leading role. So it's time for her interview. She walks into Michael's office and doesn't say anything. She just starts walking around. What's she doing? I don't know. He doesn't know.

"But then I catch on. I've cross-read the play enough during auditions. . . . She's doing one of the crucial scenes, following the stage directions for the beginning of Act Three. Then she gives the first line of dialogue in that act and looks at me—like a prima donna looking at a conductor who's dropped the beat. So I start feeding her the lines. I thought Michael was going to be royally pissed. He doesn't like people to do clever things he hasn't thought of. But after a minute he's impressed. My God, he's beside himself. And so was I. Shelly was amazingly good. We tell her, Great, thank you, we'll be in touch, which is what we always say. And Michael was his typical noncommittal Michael. Only she's got this look in her eye because she knows she's blown everybody else out of the water.

"After she leaves we read her resume again. Strange, you know: She doesn't have any formal training. Some respectable off-Broadway productions, some LORT—that's regional theater. Some summer stock and some performance pieces at Brooklyn Academy and local repertory groups. Either she shouldn't be as good as she is or we should've heard of her. Something was fishy."

Rune said, "And he did some investigating?"

"Right. Michael found out what kind of movies Shelly made. And that was it for her."

"He's got a thing about dirty movies?"

"Oh, yes. See, he's very religious."

"What?" She laughed.

"I'm not kidding. The pornography thing—it was a moral issue. And the funny thing is he was furious. Because she was perfect for the part. But he wouldn't let himself hire her. He was quite, um, vocal when he found out."

"But the way he behaved . . . This poor stagehand, the one who gave me your name . . . I thought he was going to kill the guy."

"Ah, but not one foul word passed his lips, did it?"

"I don't remember."

"He's very active in his church. He prays before each performance."

Rune said, "Well, so what? The Bible's full of begatting, isn't it?"

"Hell, there're actresses on Broadway've slept with as many men—and women—off camera as Shelly Lowe did on film. But Michael's a deacon of his church. A newspaper story—oh, the *Post* would love it—about Michael Schmidt's leading lady being a porn queen?" Becker's eyes brightened. "As appealing as that thought is to those of us who'd like to scuttle the bastard . . . So, you see why he couldn't let that happen."

"She must have been heartbroken."

Becker shrugged. "She was an adult and she made a choice to make those films. Nobody forced her to. But she didn't give up without a fight. And what a fight it was."

"What happened?"

"After I called her to give her the bad news—I felt I owed her that—Shelly made an appointment to see him. We'd already cast somebody else by then but I guess it half-crossed my mind that she was going to try to *charm*, if you want to be euphemistic, Michael into giving her the part after all."

"Shelly wouldn't do that."

Becker looked at her with his eyebrow raised.

"Not to get a part," Rune said. "She wasn't like that. It doesn't make sense but I know that about her now. There were some lines she wouldn't cross."

"In any case that's what occurred to me. But that wasn't what happened. . . ." His voice faded. "I probably shouldn't be telling you this."

Rune squinted. "Just pretend it's gossip. I love gossip."

"A terrible fight. Really vicious."

"What could you hear?"

"Not much. You read poetry, Robert Frost?"

Rune thought. "Something about horses standing around in the snow when they should be going some-where?"

Becker said, "Ah, does anybody read anymore? . . . Well, Frost coined this term called the *sound of sense*. It refers to the way we can understand words even though we can't hear them distinctly. Like through closed doors. I got a real *sense* of their conversation. I've never heard Michael so mad. I've never heard him so scared, either."

"Scared?"

"Scared. He comes out of the meeting, then paces

around. A few minutes later he calms down. Then he asks me about the new lead for the play and whether the Equity contract has been signed and I tell him it was. And I can tell he's thinking about casting Shelly again even though he doesn't want to."

"What happened, do you think?"

"I noticed something interesting about Shelly," Becker said. "She really did her homework—getting the script in the first place, for instance. See, we get a lot of young, intense hopefuls in here. They know Chekhov and Ibsen and Mamet cold. But they don't have a clue about the *business* of the theater. They think producers are gods. But as creative as Shelly was she also had a foot in the real world. She was a strategist. For the first EPI, she'd found out everything there was to know about Michael. Personal things as well as professional." Becker gave Rune a meaningful smile and when she didn't respond he frowned. "Don't you get it?"

"Uh, not exactly."

"Blackmail."

"Blackmail? Shelly was blackmailing him?"

"Nobody here knows for certain but there're rumors about Michael. A few years ago he was traveling through some small town in, I don't know, Colorado, Nevada, and we think he got arrested. For picking up a high school boy—the story was that he was just seventeen."

"Ouch."

"Uh-huh. Also around that time there was an announcement that Michael had paid two hundred thousand for the rights to a play. *Nobody* pays that kind of money for a straight, nonmusical play. It had to've been a phony transaction—I'm sure he used company money to pay off locals and keep out of jail."

"I thought he was a deacon in his church?"

"This was before he saw the light."

"You think Shelly found out about it?"

"Like I say, she did her homework."

Rune said, "He fired you. You're a little prejudiced against him."

Becker laughed. "I respect Medea's strength. Can I forgive her for killing her children? I respect Michael for what he's done for New York theater. Personally, I think he's a pompous ass. Draw your own conclusions about what I tell you."

"One last question. Was he in Vietnam? Or was he ever a soldier?"

"Michael?" Becker laughed again. "That would have been a delightful sight. When you're in the army I understand you have to do what other people tell you. That doesn't sound very much like the Michael Schmidt we all know and love, now does it?"

CHAPTER THIRTEEN

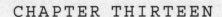 *His eyes squint, picking up golden light from the sun, as he gazes over the sagebrush and arroyos for signs of Indians or buffalo or strays. His .45 is always on his hip. . . .*

Rune was using her fingers as an impromptu camera viewfinder to frame Sam Healy. She waved to him and he ambled slowly toward her.

He'd be great in her film.

There was something different about him today. Two things, in fact. One, he wasn't somber anymore.

And, two, he gave off some kind of quiet strength she hadn't seen before in his face.

Then Rune looked past him and she realized why the change. The ten-year-old boy, who Rune had thought just happened to be walking beside him, was undoubtedly Adam, his son. Healy's face revealed the protective, authoritative, aware nature of a parent.

Sam seemed to stop just short of a hug and a kiss and nodded to her. "Thanks for meeting me. Well, us."

"Sure," she answered, wondering why he hadn't told her he was bringing the boy. Maybe because he'd been afraid she wouldn't show up.

Healy introduced them and they shook hands. Rune said, "Nice to meet you, Adam."

The boy said nothing, just looked at Rune critically. Healy said, "Come on, son, what do you say?"

The boy shrugged. "They're getting younger all the time?"

Rune laughed and Healy, blushing a bit, did too. The successful joke had been delivered so smoothly she knew he'd used it before.

They started down the sidewalk in lower Manhattan.

"You like U2?" Adam asked Rune as they walked along Broadway past the Federal Building. "They're so totally awesome."

"Love that guitar! Chunga, chunga, chunga . . ."

"Oh, yeah."

Rune said, "But I'm mostly into older music. Like Bowie, Adam Ant, Sex Pistols, Talking Heads."

"David Byrne, yeah, he's like your megagenius. Even if he's old."

"I still listen to the Police a lot," Rune said. "I kinda grew up with them."

Adam nodded. "I heard about them. My mom used to listen to them. Sting's still around."

Healy said, "Um . . . Crosby, Stills and Nash?"

Rune and Adam looked at him blankly.

"Jimi Hendrix? The Jefferson Airplane?"

When he got a stare in response to "The Doors?" Healy said quickly, "Hey, how 'bout some lunch?"

They sat across from the ornate Woolworth Building, Rune and Healy. Adam, replenished by two hot dogs and a Yoo-Hoo chocolate soda, chased squirrels and shadows and scraps of windblown paper.

"Sam," she began, "say you have a couple different suspects and you know one of them did it but you don't know who."

"In a bombing?"

"Say, any crime. Like you're an ordinary movable investigating something."

"Portable, not movable. But it'd probably be a detective evaluating suspects."

"Okay, a detective with three suspects. What would you do to figure out who the perp is?"

"Perp," he said. "See, I said you were a born cop."

In a thick Slavic accent: "I learned English from *Kojak* reruns." She grew serious. "Come on, Sam. What would you do?"

"In order to make an arrest you need probable cause."

"What's that?"

"Something that shows your suspect is more likely than not to've committed the crime. A witness, conflicting alibis, physical evidence at the scene connecting the suspect and the crime, fingerprints, genetic marker test . . . A confession's always good."

"How do you get confessions?"

"We put the suspect in a room, turn the camera on and ask them questions. You don't arrest them because then their lawyers show up and tell them not to say anything. They can leave at any time but we . . . encourage them to stay."

"You ever trick somebody into a confession?"

"Sure. That's part of the game. But no more answers till you tell why you're curious about police procedures."

"Okay, I've got three suspects."

"What suspects?"

"In the Shelly Lowe killing."

"Three suspects? You mean, you know three people in

the Sword of Jesus? Why didn't you tell Begley or somebody in Homicide?"

"Oh, there is no Sword of Jesus. It's a cover-up. Somebody's making it look like it's a religious thing but it's
not."

"But—"

She continued before he could ask what would undoubtedly be some questions that would result in either
awkward answers or outright lies. "See, Shelly didn't just
do those movies. There's this guy named Arthur Tucker.
He was Shelly's acting coach. Only you know what's interesting?" Her voice faded and she looked at him.
"What's the matter?"

"Rune, you weren't going to do this."

"I was just interviewing people about her, for my film,
and I found some funny things." She grew quiet, looking
up at the gargoyles two-thirds of the way up the sky-
scraper. She wondered if she and Healy were about to
have their first fight. That was really a bad sign—to have a
fight before you'd spent some time seriously kissing someone.

Healy glanced at Adam, stalking a mangy pigeon
twenty feet away, and rested his large hand tentatively on
her knee.

Rune stared at the gargoyles. They were smiling, not
leering, she thought. It seemed that was an important
omen but she couldn't tell what it meant.

Healy didn't speak for a second. He clicked his tongue.
"Okay. Funny things. Go ahead and tell me."

"Shelly was a legitimate actress and she wrote plays,
okay? She and her coach, this Arthur Tucker, had a big
fight when he found out about her movie career. Oh,
oh—he also was a commando in the war. So he knows
about bombs."

"But you need a motive to—"

"I've got one. He stole a play that Shelly wrote. He took

it and put his name on it. He told me he'd never gotten anywhere with his career and I think he could've killed her and stolen that play."

"Pretty damn speculative. Who else is a suspect?"

"Michael Schmidt."

Healy was frowning. "It's familiar. Who's he?"

"The Broadway producer. The famous one."

"*Him?*"

"Right. He told me he didn't remember Shelly but he was lying. It turns out he'd almost offered her a role in one of his plays. Then he found out she did porn and withdrew the offer. She was going to blackmail him into getting the part."

"You don't kill someone—"

"He's a deacon in the church. She could've brought down his whole career. He's also an obnoxious son of a bitch."

"That doesn't violate the Penal Code of the State of New York, being obnoxious. Who else is on the list?"

"Another asshole. Danny Traub. He's part owner of Lame Duck. Shelly's company."

"And you heard about an insurance policy on the building?"

"No. On *her.*"

This got Healy's attention. "Go on."

"Shelly told me that she had a terrible fight with some-one she worked with. I think it might've been him. He was always flirting with her and she was rejecting him. And he's really into S and M; he gets off on beating women. So I broke into his town house—"

Healy put his face in his hands. "Rune, no, no, no. You can't do these things."

"It's okay. One of his girlfriends said it was all right. She also let me go through his safe."

Healy sighed. "At least you didn't steal anything." He looked at her. "Tell me you didn't steal anything."

"What, I look like a thief?" Rune asked. "Anyway, what I found was this insurance policy on Shelly. Almost a half-million dollars."

"No exclusion for murder?"

"Nope. His girlfriend made a copy of it for me."

"You've got three suspects. Could any of them been the one who attacked you?"

"They're all about the same build. Oh, and Schmidt's eyes were all red. Like he'd been teargassed recently."

"Teargassed? What does that have to do with anything?"

"The man in the windbreaker?" she said sheepishly. "I sort of teargassed him."

"Sort of?"

"Self-defense," she pointed out in a lame voice.

But Healy didn't lecture her about illegal weapons in the city of New York. He just shrugged. "I don't know. Tear gas burns disappear within twelve hours or so. How 'bout the other two?"

"They're all built about the same. Not muscle builders."

"Did any of them look really shocked to see you? I mean, if they'd tried to kill you, there would've been some recognition in their faces."

"I don't think so," she said, frowning in disappointment.

"Of course," Healy added, "the smart thing would be to hire a strong-arm."

"A hit man?"

Healy was nodding absently. "That's good. . . . It's not enough for probable cause but . . ." Then he laughed and shook his head as if coming out of a daydream. "Hey, forget this whole thing." He held up his hand—not the one that was still resting on her knee. "I'm not even in Homicide. . . . I don't want to know any of this."

"Just tell me about the explosives. From the second bombing."

"No."

"I thought you were having them traced."

"I am."

"Well?"

"No results yet, and when I get them I'm writing them in my report and sending it upstairs. And that'll be that."

She said defiantly, "*I'll* just have to keep looking, I guess."

"Rune." Healy was debating. "Tell you what. I'll steer a couple guys from Homicide over to check out—what was his name?—the acting coach. He's the only one seems to know anything about explosives."

"Really? Only promise you won't arrest him till I'm there. I want to film the bust."

"I think you know we can't make any promises like that."

"Well, just try. Please!" Rune wrote Tucker's name on a mustard-stained napkin and handed it to Healy. She asked, "What about the other two?"

"You want my opinion? The insurance angle with, what's his name, Traub. That's too obvious. And Michael Schmidt? Doesn't seem a celeb like him'd risk a murder conviction because of a blackmail threat."

"Oh, but he's got an ego like the Grand Canyon."

Healy looked at the napkin. "Let's do one at a time. No rush. There's no statute of limitations on murder."

"See, I told you we'd make a great team."

"Team," he was saying, only in a softer voice. He leaned toward her. His head tilted slightly. His eyes darted to where Adam had been just a moment before; the boy wasn't visible. Quickly Healy bent closer to her. "You're very pretty. You know that?"

She didn't know it at all. But it didn't matter. She was perfectly happy to know that *he* felt that way. Rune found her eyes closing, her head tilting back, lifting up to meet his lips. He reached over and took her hand and she was surprised that his was shaking slightly.

"Don't do it," Adam said, scaring the hell out of them both as he climbed on top of the bench from behind it, where he'd been stalking them. "You'll scar me for life."

Healy jerked back.

The boy grinned and motioned for Rune to help him chase pigeons. She squeezed Healy's knee and ran into the park.

———

"Where do I apply?"

The receptionist on the fourth floor of the Lame Duck studio looked up at Rune, scanned her figure, and went back to her occult paperback. "We don't need no secretaries."

"I want to be in films," she said.

"You know what kind of films we make here?"

"I figured *The Erotic Adventures of Bunny Blue* isn't an army training film," Rune said.

Today—after another phone call—Rune had found that Danny Traub was at home, entertaining some prospective actresses, if that verb worked with Traub. The woman who'd blown the whistle on the insurance policy had assured her that the producer would be busy for hours.

The Lame Duck receptionist marked her place and looked up from underneath a sheen of brown eye makeup.

Rune had decided she wasn't as content as Sam Healy was to forget about the other two suspects. So she was going to find more evidence—either for or against Danny Traub and Michael Schmidt.

The receptionist continued. "The thing is, the people they hire are a certain kind of person."

"Certain kind?"

"A little, well . . ."

"What?" Rune was frowning. The girl glanced at her chest.

"More . . ."

"Are you trying to tell me something?"

". . . voluptuous, like."

Rune's eyes went wide. "Don't you know about the *Constitution*?"

The horror novel was a loss. The girl folded it over without marking her place. "Like the ship? That was a ship in the Civil War? What's that got to do with—"

Rune said, "You can't discriminate against anyone just because they aren't Dolly Parton."

"Dolly Parton?"

"All I want to do is audition. If you don't want me because I can't act, okay. But you can't deny me a chance to try out because I don't have big boobs. That's, like, a federal lawsuit."

"Federal?"

There was a pause. The woman debated within herself, rifling pages of the paperback.

Rune asked, "Can I have an application?"

"They don't have applications. All they do is, like, they look at a reel you bring in of yourself. Or else you go into the studio here and, you know, do it. They tape it and if they like it, they call you back. Let me see if there's anybody around."

The girl stood up and walked into the back part of the office, swaying her independently connected hips. "Wait here."

She returned a minute later. "Go on back, the second office on the right." She looked at her novel with disappointment, realizing she'd have to find her place again.

The rooms were divided off with the same clumsily cut Sheetrock rectangles that she remembered from Nicole's so-called dressing room. The walls had been recently painted but the surfaces were already scuffed and dirty. The posters and shades were from discount import stores, the sort where newlyweds and NYU students buy wicker, bamboo and plastic to furnish first apartments. There was no carpet.

The Second Office on the Right contained more or less what she'd been expecting. A fat, bearded man in a T-shirt and black baggy slacks.

He looked up and smiled in a curious way. It wasn't lecherous, wasn't provocative, wasn't friendly. The odd thing about this smile was that the face it was etched into didn't seem to understand he was looking at another human being.

"I'm Gutman. Ralph Gutman. You're who?"

"Uh, Dawn."

"Yah. Dawn what?"

"Dawn Felicidad."

"I like that. Are you, what? Hispanic or something? You don't look it. Well, doesn't matter. So you want a job. I'm a tough guy to work for. I'm a ballbuster. But I'm the best producer in the business."

"I think I may've heard of you."

His Second Office on the Right glance said, Well, of *course* you've heard of me.

"Where you from?" Gutman asked. "Jersey, right?"

"Ohio."

"You're from Ohio? I don't think we've ever had any porn stars from Ohio. I like it. Ohio. Hey, lose the *Dawn*. I like *Akron* better. Akron Felicidad."

"But I—"

"Yah. The girls work for me get four hundred a day. Also, a discount from my supplier. We shoot on location two months a year. Used to be Europe but with the budgets and so on now it's usually Florida. I'm the one did *Triangle Trap*."

"No kidding. You did that?"

"Yah, sure did. I got nominated for a Golden Stallion. So, you want a job, huh?" He looked her over. "No tits but your face isn't too bad."

He's going to die and they'll never find all the pieces again.

"Nice ass. Why're you waiting to get your boobs done?"

"I like 'em just the way they are."

He shrugged. "Suit yourself. You look young. Maybe you could play somebody's teenage niece. Get it on with her aunt and uncle. Your typical incest."

"I could do that, sure."

"You have a reel?"

"All I know about reels is they go on fishing rods."

"Ha. Rods." He laughed, and it seemed that she'd made some kind of joke. Then he explained, "Samples of your work."

"I've never been in film before. But I do this little act. Kind of a strip. Do you have a place where I can change?"

"Change? You'll be taking your clothes off in front of twenty people every day you shoot. You want to go someplace and change?"

"No, I want you to get the full effect." She nodded toward her bag. "I've got this outfit. I think you'll like it. Just an office or something? It'll take five minutes."

Gutman was moderately interested. He looked her over again, then waved his arm. "Find an office, change. I'll be here."

She found Danny Traub's office right up the hallway. She walked in, closed the door behind her. She glanced around quickly—at the walls done in Ace Home Center wood paneling, the big fake-ebony desk, more plants, a leather couch.

And two file cabinets.

Rune started through the first one.

She was looking for evidence. A piece of wire. A book

on explosives. A letter from Shelly telling him he was a son of a bitch. A *Bible,* where Traub might've gotten the quote about the angels destroying the earth . . . Anything that might link him to the bombing.

Physical evidence. That's what Healy'd said she needed for probable cause.

She didn't find any. Just contracts, correspondence. Just like any other businessman would keep in his office.

She turned to the second cabinet and started through it. This one contained more contracts and legal documents. She didn't find anything significant until she got to the *L*'s and saw the file labeled *Shelly Lowe.*

But she didn't have a chance to read it because just then the door swung open and Danny Traub walked inside.

He froze. Then recovered. He swung the door shut and, never one to neglect his invisible audience, said, "Well, this kiddo's looking in my drawers. Wonder if she's found anything interesting."

CHAPTER FOURTEEN

■■■■■■ Rune closed the file cabinet, checking distances, checking exits. She was on the fourth floor. That was forty feet. Would a jump through the window kill her? Might.

Traub stepped toward her, shaking his head. "Gosh, here we are in New York, crime capital of the world. . . . I mean, there are people from Iowa hold on to their wallets when they fly *over* New York in an airplane. This city's got such a bad rep, I can't believe it."

"I was just—"

"And what do we have here? A young lady stealing *files*! My God! Does she realize that those manila folders cost a couple cents each? Steal a hundred thousand of them—"

"I was—"

"—and she could buy herself a set of Tupperware. Or a Big Mac feast for her and her friends. Trying to fence them though's a little tricky. . . ." The smile faded. The audience was gone. "Okay. What the fuck you doing here?"

He walked over to where she was standing and lifted the file out of her hands. Glanced at the name on the folder.

He nodded knowingly. Tossed it back into the cabinet.

As he was turning to her Rune dropped to her knees and pulled the tear gas canister out of her purse.

But Traub moved faster. He grabbed the cylinder, ripped it out of her hand and shoved her into the couch. He looked at it closely, amused, it seemed. Rune sat up.

"What's this all about? And don't gimme this cute Nancy Drew shit. I had a fucking bomb take out my star and a floor of my company. I'm not in the mood."

Rune didn't say anything. Traub pointed the tear gas spray at her face.

Remembering the terrible sting, she cringed, looked away.

"Answer me."

Breathlessly she said, "You didn't tell me you had a policy on Shelly Lowe."

He frowned. "A policy?"

"An insurance policy."

"That's right. I didn't. But you didn't ask me if I had one, now, did you?"

"It seems like that'd be a pretty normal thing to mention, I tell you I'm doing a film about one of your stars."

Traub glanced again at the tear gas, weighed it in his hand. "You're asking all this shit for your film? Is that it?" He leaned up against the door. Rune saw his muscles stand out, sinewy and pale. He reminded her of one of the flying monkeys in *The Wizard of Oz*—the characters that scared her the most, even more than the Wicked Witch.

"The police know I'm here."

Traub laughed. "That's like on D-Day, yelling to the Germans: 'Ike knows I'm here.'" He looked her over and the motion of his eyes was like his tongue coursing over her body. She pulled away from him, crossed her arms, glanced down at the desk for paperweights. There was a letter opener she might go for.

"So, you think I killed Shelly, do you? That I planted a bomb so I'd get the insurance money."

"I didn't say that."

Traub paced. Intermission was over; he was looking around once more. "That's pretty good detective work this cookie's done, don't you think? She's a star, she's a regular little Sherlock Holmes. Well, you got me, honey. Yep, yep. The insurance company paid off. I got myself a check for five hundred thousand dollars."

Rune didn't answer.

Traub set the tear gas down. He looked at Rune, then took a key out of his pocket and walked behind his desk. Rune leaned forward, putting her weight on the balls of her feet. He was going for a gun. He could just shoot her like a burglar and the police wouldn't do anything.

Traub glanced at her. "On your mark, get set . . . I don't think she can make it in time."

He grinned and pulled out the black pistol.

Enjoyed the sight of her eyes widening.

"Here's a present for our little Ms. Detective."

Rune winced. When it looked like he was going to pull the trigger she'd just dive forward, grab the tear gas and hope for the best.

Then Traub's other hand emerged with a piece of paper.

Neither of them moved for a moment.

"I don't know about her but the suspense is killing me. Is she going to read it? Is she going to make a paper airplane?"

Rune took the sheet of paper and read:

Dear Mr. Traub:

With intense, heartfelt gratitude, we acknowledge receipt of your check in the amount of $400,000. Your generosity will go very far in supporting research to find a cure for this terrible *affliction and in easing the burden of those whose lives have been affected by it. . . . .*

The letter was signed by the director of the New York AIDS Coalition.

"Oh."

Traub dropped the gun in the drawer. " 'Oh,' she says. 'Oh . . .' Well, you know, there's still a hundred of the insurance proceeds unaccounted for. But since I personally take home a hundred fifty a year cash, off the books, you can probably deduce that I ain't gonna kill my biggest star to pick up fucking chicken feed. Oh, by the way, my personal property insurance has a hundred thousand deductible so with the repairs to the floor downstairs this whole thing was a wash for me."

"I'm sorry."

He tossed the tear gas to her. "I think it's time for our little detective to leave. Let's give her a big round of applause."

███████

Throughout the interview Arthur Tucker never quite got over the shock that two police officers were questioning him as a suspect in a murder case.

They were polite as they asked him questions about Shelly Lowe. They tried to make it seem casual but there was something they were trying to get at. Something they knew.

What? he thought desperately. He felt vulnerable—as if they could see into his mind but he had no clue as to what they were thinking.

One of the officers glanced up at Tucker's medals. "You in the service, sir?"

"I was in the Rangers."

"You ever do demolition?"

He shrugged. "We all knew how to use bangalore torpedoes, grenades. But that was forty years ago. . . . Are you suggesting that I had anything to do with those bombs?"

"Nosir. We're just looking into what happened to Ms. Lowe."

Tucker looked perplexed, confused, and asked them about the Sword of Jesus.

They continued to be evasive.

But it was more than evasion. They were grasping at straws and even then they came away holding nothing at all. He wondered how on earth they had come to think he might be the killer. He supposed that Shelly had written his name in a Day-Timer or a wall calendar. Maybe she kept a diary—he told all of his students to keep one—and she'd written about one of their lessons. Maybe about one of their fights.

That could have brought them here.

But as he thought about Shelly, his mind wandered, and with his strong will and talents at concentration he brought his attention back to the policemen.

"She was a fascinating person, Officer," Tucker explained, with the sorrow and reverence one should have in his voice when speaking of a fascinating person who had just died. "I hope you're close to catching these people. I can't condone her career—you know how she made her living, I suppose—but violence like this." He closed his eyes and shuddered. "Inexcusable. It makes us all barbarians."

Tucker was a good actor. But they didn't buy it. They looked at him blankly, as if he hadn't said a word. Then one officer said, "I understand you write plays too, sir. Is that correct?"

He believed his heart stopped beating for a moment. "I've done just about everything there is to do in the theater. I started out as a—"

"But about the writing. You do write plays?"

"Yes."

"And Ms. Lowe did too. Isn't that correct?"

"She may have."

"But she was your student. Isn't that something you'd talk about with her?"

"I think she did, yes. We were more concerned with acting than writing in our—"

"But let's stick with the writing for a minute. Do you have in your possession any plays that she wrote?"

"No," Tucker answered, managing to keep his voice rock-firm.

"Can you account for your whereabouts the night Ms. Lowe was killed? At around eight p.m.?"

"I was attending a play."

"So I guess there'd be witnesses."

"About fifteen hundred of them. Do you want me to give you some names?" Tucker asked.

"That won't be necessary."

The other cop added, "Not at this time."

"You mind if we look around the office?"

"Yes, I do. You'll have to get a warrant for that."

"You're not cooperating?"

"I have been cooperating. But if you want to search my office you'll have to get a warrant. Simple as that."

This didn't evoke any emotion at all in their faces. "Okay. Thank you for your time."

When they were gone Tucker stood at his window for five minutes—making sure they'd left the building. He turned back to his desk and with unsteady hands found the script for *Delivered Flowers*. He put this into his battered briefcase. He then began looking through the manuscripts on his credenza. Throwing the ones Shelly had written into the briefcase too.

But wait. . . .

One was missing. He searched again. No, it wasn't there. He was sure he'd left it there. Jesus . . . What had happened to it?

Then he looked up and saw the glass door to his office, the replacement for the one that was broken the other day in that abortive robbery. He'd *thought* nothing had been stolen in the break-in.

Tucker sat down slowly in his chair.

The House O' Leather filming had been arduous.

Larry had taken Rune off catering detail for the time being and actually let her operate the camera during one session.

It had been a long shoot. Daughter had needed eighteen takes before she could get two lines of dialogue in the can. But Rune didn't care—the camera was a real Arriflex 35, a beautiful piece of precision machinery, and feeling the mechanism whir beneath her fingers made up for a lot of the recent grief she'd been put through at the company.

Mr. Wallet—she just *couldn't* remember his name—had turned out to be not so bad. He thanked Rune whenever she brought him something to eat or drink and, on a break, they'd shared a few words about recent movies. He had pretty good taste.

Ad director Mary Jane, though, was a different story. She hovered over the set, wearing a distracting blue-and-red suit with shoulder pads like a linebacker's. Wanting to correct the light, wanting to look through the Arri's eyepiece. And when Rune wasn't behind the camera the woman would ask her to make copies and retype memos. She *wondered* a lot (her favorite phrase seemed to be "I wonder if it might not be better to . . ."; the second was "I would have thought you . . ."). Her saving grace was that, unlike Mr. Wallet, she didn't ask Rune to fetch coffee—which told her that in her pre–Ann Taylor incarnation Mary Jane had been a put-upon secretary (the resentments of servitude run deep, Rune knew).

The shoot was finished and Rune was in the office late,

checking props for the dramatic logo scene, to be shot in a day or two. This was Bob's idea; it would be a tracking CU—a moving close-up shot—of dominoes falling over, followed by a pullback to reveal that the dominoes had formed the company's name and logo. It had been Rune's job to find and rent thousands of white, dot-free dominoes.

Rune heard a noise. She looked up and saw Sam Healy standing in the doorway.

She said, "If you're here in a, like, official capacity I'm hauling ass outa this building right now," she said.

"So you really *do* have a job."

"That's a real liberal use of the word *job,* Sam."

He walked inside and she opened the massive refrigerator and gave him a beer.

"We've got one more shot for this stupid commercial. Then the boys collect a nifty two hundred G's. And that's profit."

"Phew," Healy whistled. "Not a bad line of work. Beats civil-servant pay grades."

"At least you have your dignity, Sam."

She showed him the studio, then ran some of the rushes from the House O' Leather shoots on the Moviola.

"I can set you up with the daughter, you want."

"That's all right. Think I'll pass."

They walked back to the office and sat down.

He said, "A couple buddies from the Sixth Precinct checked up on Tucker. He looked guilty, they said. But so do most people when they're being interviewed by two cops."

He continued: "But here's the gist of it. They checked out his military history. He hardly ever saw combat and once he was discharged never had anything to do with the military again. Was in theater all his life. No criminal record, no apparent contact with criminals. Attends church regularly. He—"

"But he still knows how—"

"Hey, hey, let me finish. They also checked out what an original play by an unknown playwright is worth. You're talking in the thousands, tops, unless a miracle happens and it takes off—like *Cats* or something like that. And that's a one-in-a-million chance. Believe me, nobody's going to risk a murder conviction for a couple of thousand dollars."

"But the play . . . I *saw* he'd changed the name."

"Sure he did. She was killed and he figured he'd steal them and make a little money. Her estate wouldn't even know about it. That's larceny. But who cares?" Healy looked into one of the hundred of boxes of dominoes that surrounded Rune. "So?"

"So?"

"You out of the detective business?"

"Totally and completely."

"I'm really glad to hear that."

"I have some information," the young woman's voice said.

Sitting at his oak desk, Michael Schmidt held the phone receiver in one hand and with his other tapped on the unopened lid of the carton of clam chowder.

The voice, a woman's and disguised somehow, continued. "It links you to Shelly Lowe's death."

He poked his finger listlessly against the cello packet of saltines until each cracker popped into crumbs. "Who is this?"

"I think it's information you'd be interested in."

"Tell me who you are."

"You'll meet me soon enough. If you're not afraid to."

"What do you want? You want money? Are you trying to blackmail me?"

"Blackmail? It's funny you should mention that word.

Maybe I am. But I want to meet you in person. Face-to-face."

"Come to my office."

"No way. Where there are plenty of people around."

"Okay. Where?"

"Meet me at noon at Lincoln Center. You know the tables they have set up there?"

"The restaurant outside?"

"Yeah, there. Meet me there. And don't bring anybody with you. Got it?"

"I—"

The line went dead.

Schmidt sat staring at the glossy black-and-gray phone for a full minute before he realized he was still holding the silent receiver. He hung it up angrily.

He felt like swearing, though he knew that if he did he'd immediately regret saying the cuss word. He was proud of the fact that he was both a tough, moneymaking businessman and a deeply religious man who abhorred the use of obscenities. With his thumb he continued to crush the crackers into dust.

His appetite for the soup was gone and he pitched it into his wastebasket. The lid came off and the soup spilled into the plastic bag lining the garbage can. The smell of fish and onions wafted up, which made him even more angry.

But he remained completely still as he folded his hands together and prayed until he was calm. That was one thing he had learned to do—he never made a decision when he was in what he called a secular state.

In five minutes the spirit of the Lord had calmed him. His decision was to do exactly what he'd thought of doing when he'd hung up after speaking to the girl. He picked up the phone and gently pressed out a number.

CHAPTER FIFTEEN

■■■■■ "You can use L&R's camera. It's got a telephoto built in."

Stu, the cook-editor-food stylist from Belvedere Post-Production, said, "Why exactly do you want to film this guy?"

"I'm going to get a confession. I'm going to trick him."

"Isn't it illegal to film people if they don't know about it?"

"No. Not if they're in a public place. That's what public dominion means."

"Public domain. And that's something different. The copyright law."

"Oh." Rune was frowning. "Well, I don't know. But I'm sure it's okay and I'm doing it."

"What kind of camera is it?"

"Betacam. Have you—?"

"I know how to use one. Ampex deck?"

"Right," Rune said. "You'll be up on the balcony at

Lincoln Center, shooting down. That's all you have to do. Just tape me talking to this guy."

"You still haven't told me why. What kind of confession?"

"I'll have a tape recorder," she said quickly. "You don't even have to worry about audio."

"I'm not going to do it, you don't tell me what you're up to."

"Trust me, Stu."

"I hate that phrase."

"Don't you like adventures?"

"No. I like cooking, I like eating. I'd like money if I had any. But one thing I definitely don't like is adventures."

"I'll give you a credit on my film."

"Great. Just be sure to put my prison number after my name."

"It's not illegal. That's not the problem."

"So there *is* a problem. . . . What is it, getting beat up? Or killed? Will you dedicate the film to my memory?"

"You aren't going to get killed."

"You didn't say anything about not being beat up."

"You won't get beat up."

"It sounded to me," Stu said, "that there was a tacit *probably* attached to that last sentence. Was there?"

"Look, you *definitely* won't get beat up. I promise. Feel better?"

"No . . . Lincoln Center? Why there?"

Rune slung the battery pack over her shoulder. "So that if you do get beat up there'll be plenty of witnesses."

━━━━━

Rune had flashed an ID to the security guard of Avery Fischer Hall. His eyes went wide for a moment, then he let her into the quiet hall.

"We're doing some surveillance," she told him.

"Yes, ma'am," he answered and returned to his station. "You need any more help you give me a call."

"What's that?" Stu asked. "That you just showed him?"

"An identification card."

"I *know* that. What kind?"

"Sort of FBI."

He said, "What? How did you get that?"

"I kind of made it. On L&R's word processor. Then I had it laminated."

"Wait—why did you tell me? I don't want to know things like that. Forget I asked."

They continued up the stairs. On the walls were dozens of posters of operas and plays that had been performed at Lincoln Center. Rune pointed at one. "Wild. Look." It was for Offenbach's *Orpheus in the Underworld.*

Stu glanced at it. "I prefer easy listening. What's the significance?"

Rune was quiet for a moment; she felt like crying. "That's Eurydice. That woman. She reminds me of someone I used to know."

They climbed the top floor and stepped out on the roof. Rune set up the camera.

"Now, don't pan. I'm worried about strobing. Don't get fancy. Keep the camera on me and the guy I'm going to be talking to. I want a two-shot most of the time but you can zoom in on his face if I give you the signal. I'll scratch my head. How's that? To zoom you just—"

"I've used a Betacam before."

"Good. You got an hour's worth of tape, two hours of batteries. And this'll probably be over in fifteen minutes."

"About the length of time of an execution. Any final words?"

Rune smiled nervously. "My first starring role."

"Break a leg," Stu said.

She'd thought that maybe he wouldn't show. And she'd thought that even if he did show, he'd sit way off to the side, where he could pull out a gun with a silencer on it and shoot her in the heart and get away and it would be half an hour before anybody noticed her, thinking that she'd just fallen asleep in the hot sun. She'd seen that in an old film—a Peter Lorre film, she thought.

But Michael Schmidt was obliging. He sat in the center of the outdoor restaurant around the huge fountain in the middle of Lincoln Center.

He was scanning the crowd nervously and when he saw Rune he glued his eyes on her. Recognition preceded fury by a millisecond. She paused, slipped her hand into her jacket and started the tape recorder. He noticed the gesture and leaned back, probably thinking she had a gun. He was clearly afraid. Rune continued to the table.

"You!" he whispered. "You're the one in the theater."

Rune sat down. "You lied to me. You didn't tell me you offered Shelly the part, then broke the deal."

"So? Why should I tell you anything? You interrupted me in the middle of a very important meeting. My mind doesn't work like other people's. I don't have little mundane facts at my beck and call."

"I know all about the fight you had with her."

"I fight with a lot of people. I'm a perfectionist. . . . What do you want? Money?" His eyes scanned the crowds once again. He was still nervous as a deer.

"Just answer—," she began.

"How much? Just tell me. Please."

"Why did you have to kill her?" Rune asked viciously.

Schmidt leaned forward. "Why do you think I killed her?"

"Because she tried to blackmail you into giving her the part."

Schmidt muttered angrily, "And you're going to do what? Go to the police with that story?"

There was something about the sweep of his skittish eyes that warned her. Twice now he'd glanced at an adjoining table. Rune followed his eyes and saw that two men were sitting in front of plates of fancy sandwiches that neither had touched.

Jesus, they were hit men!

Schmidt'd hired hit men. Maybe the skinnier of them was the man in the red windbreaker. They didn't give a shit about being in public or not; they were going to rub her out right here. Or follow her and kill her in an alley. Blasting away at her as if she were Marlon Brando in *The Godfather*.

Schmidt swung his eyes, forced them back to her face. The two men shifted slightly.

"Now, tell me how much you want."

Oh, hell. No more games, time to leave.

Rune stood up.

Schmidt glanced at her pocket, the tape recorder. His eyes were wide.

The heads of the two hit men swiveled toward her.

Then: Schmidt pushing back, sliding to the ground, yelling, "Get her, get her!"

The diners gasped and pushed back from their tables. Some ducked to the pavement.

The hit men stood quickly, the metal chairs bouncing to the stone ground. She saw guns in their hands.

Screams, people diving to the pavement, drinks falling, salads spinning. Lettuce and tomatoes and croissants flew to the ground.

Rune sprinted to Columbus Avenue and ran north. She glanced behind her. The hit men were closing in. They were in great shape.

You two assholes are surrounded by witnesses! What the hell are you doing?

Her chest was screaming, her feet stung. Rune lowered her head and ran full out.

At Seventy-second Street she looked behind her and couldn't see them any longer. She stopped running and pressed against a chain-link fence around a vacant lot, trying to fill her lungs, her fingers curled tight in the mesh.

A bus pulled into the stop. She stepped toward it.

And the hit men, waiting behind a truck, ran toward her.

She screamed and rolled to the ground, then crawled under a gap in the chain link. She staggered to her feet and sped toward the building across the lot. A school.

A vacant school.

She ran to the door.

Locked.

She turned. They were coming at her again, trotting, now looking nonchalant, trying to be inconspicuous. The guns in their hands at their sides.

Nowhere to go except down a long alley. There'd have to be an exit to the street. A door, a window, *something*.

Rune ran to the end of it. It was a dead end. But there was a rickety door. She threw herself against it. The wood was much more solid than it seemed. She bounced off the thick oak and fell to the ground.

And she knew it was over. The hit men, guns in the open now, looked around cautiously and walked toward her.

Rune got up on her knees and looked for a brick, a rock, a stick. There was nothing. She fell forward, sobbing. "No, no, no . . ." They were on top of her. She felt the muzzle of the gun at her neck.

Rune whimpered and covered her head. "No . . ."

That was when one of the hit men said, "You're under arrest. You have the right to remain silent. You have the right to an attorney and to have the attorney present during questioning. If you give up the right to remain silent, anything you say can and will be used against you in court."

The 20th Precinct looked a lot like the New York State unemployment office, except there weren't so many—or *as* many—writers and actors here. A lot of scuffed Lucite, a lot of typed announcements pinned up on bulletin boards, cheap linoleum, overhead fluorescents. Civilians milling about.

And cops. A lot of big cops.

Handcuffs were heavier than she'd thought. They weren't like bracelets at all. She rested her hands in her lap and wondered if she'd be out of prison in a year.

One of the hit men, a Detective Yalkowsky, deposited her in an orange fiberglass chair, one of six bolted together into a bench.

A woman officer in a ponytail like Rune's, the desk sergeant, asked him, "What've you got here?"

"Attempted grand larceny. Extortion, attempted assault, fleeing, resisting arrest, criminal trespassing—"

"Hey, I didn't assault anyone! And I was only trespassing to get away from *him*. I thought he was a hit man."

Yalkowsky ignored her. "She hasn't made a statement, doesn't want a lawyer. She wants to talk to somebody named Healy."

Rune said, "*Detective* Healy. He's a policeman."

"Why do you want to see him?"

"He's a friend."

The detective said, "Honey, the mayor could be a friend of yours and you'd still be in deep shit. You tried to extort Michael Schmidt. That's big stuff. You're gonna be potato chips for the newspapers."

"Just give him a call, please?"

The detective hesitated, then said, "Put her in a holding cell until we talk to him."

"A holding cell?" The desk sergeant looked Rune over and frowned. "We don't want to do that."

Rune looked at her concerned face. "She's right, you don't want to do that."

Yalkowsky shrugged. "Yeah, I think we do."

CHAPTER SIXTEEN

 Rune and Sam Healy made their way along Central Park West, past the knoll where dog-walkers gathered. Poodles and retrievers and Akitas and mutts tangled leashes and pranced on the dusty ground.

Healy was silent.

Rune kept looking up at him.

He turned and walked into the park. They climbed to the top of a huge rock thirty feet high and sat down.

"Sam?"

"Rune, it isn't that they could've prosecuted you—"

"Sam, I—"

"—they couldn't have made the extortion case, and, yeah, they didn't identify themselves as cops. And somebody found a fake FBI ID, but nobody's connected it to you yet. But what they could have done is shot you. Fleeing felon. If they thought you were dangerous they could have shot."

"I'm sorry."

"I do something risky for a living, Rune. But there are procedures and backup and a lot of things we do to make it less dangerous. But you, you get these crazy ideas about killers and blackmail and you dive right in."

They watched a softball game in the meadow for a minute. The heat was bad and the players were lethargic. Puffs of dust rose up from the yellow grass as the ball skipped into the outfield.

"There were some rumors about Schmidt and this teen-age boy in Colorado. I thought Shelly found out about it and was blackmailing him to get the part."

"Did the facts lead you to that conclusion? Or did you *imagine* that's what happened and shoehorn the facts into your idea?"

"I . . . I shoehorned."

"Okay."

Rune said, "Sam, I have this notebook at home. I write all kinds of stuff in it. It's sort of like a diary. You know what I have written on the first page?"

" 'I won't grow up'?"

"If I'd thought about it, yeah, it probably would say that. But what I wrote is: 'Believe in what isn't as if it were until it becomes.' "

Crack. A home run. The pitcher watched the ball sail toward the portable toilet a hundred feet from home plate.

"Sam, this movie is important to me. I didn't go to college. I worked in a video store. I did store-window design. I worked in restaurants. I've sold stuff on the streets. I don't want to keep doing that forever."

He laughed. "You've got a few years' worth of false starts ahead of you."

"At the film company they treat me like a kid. . . . Well, okay, sometimes I *act* like a kid. But I mean, they don't think I'm capable of anything more. I know this film about Shelly is going to work. I can feel it."

"What you did back there, with Schmidt, that wasn't bright."

"He was the last of my suspects. I thought he was the one."

"A suspect doesn't call the cops to—"

"I know. I was wrong. . . . It's just that, well, I can't point to anything in particular. I just had a, I don't know . . ."

"Hunch?"

"Yeah. That somebody killed her. And it wasn't this stupid Sword of Jesus."

"I believe in hunches too. But do us both a favor, forget about this movie of yours. Or just tell the story about a girl who got killed and let it go at that. Forget about trying to find the killer. Leave a little mystery in it. People like mystery."

"That's what my name means. In Celtic."

"Your real name?"

"Reality," she said, "is highly overrated. No, I mean 'Rune'."

He nodded and she couldn't tell whether he was sad or angry with her or whether he was just being a silent cowboy.

"I don't think you're going to see any more bombings," Healy said. "The profile is they get tired after a while. Too risky to be a serial criminal nowadays. Forensics are too good. You'll get nailed."

Rune was silent. Healy said, "I've got watch in a couple of minutes. I was thinking, you want, maybe you could stop by the Bomb Squad. See what it's like."

"Really? Oh, yeah. But I've got to get to work now. Today's the last shot for this stupid commercial."

Healy nodded. "I'll be there all night." He gave her directions to the 6th Precinct.

Dominoes. All she could see was dominoes.

"Come on, luv," Larry was cajoling, "you get to be the one to knock 'em over."

Rune was still setting them up. "I thought you were going to hire another couple of P.A.'s for the shoot."

"You're all the assistant we need for this one, luv. You can do it." Rune was working from a piece of paper on which he'd drawn the pattern. She reluctantly admitted to herself that it was probably going to be a hell of a shot.

" 'Ow many we have?"

"Four thousand, three hundred and twelve, Larry. I checked them all."

"Good for you."

Once, halfway through the assembly, two hours into the process, she set them off accidentally. The rows of rectangles clicked against one another with the sound of chips around a Las Vegas roulette wheel.

Double shit . . .

"I would've thought you'd've started from the other side," Mary Jane contributed. "That way you probably wouldn't've bumped into them as easily."

"Doing good," Larry said quickly.

"Is this art?" a fuming Rune asked him as she crawled over the twenty-foot sweep of gray seamless backdrop paper to set them up again.

"Don't start."

Finally, hours later, she got the little army of dominoes arranged and backed off the paper without breathing. She crawled to the first one and nodded to Larry.

Rune glanced at the camera operator, a nerdish, bearded guy who sat in the seat of the Luma crane boom. It looked like earthmoving equipment. "Make sure you got film," Rune said to him. "I'm not doing this again."

"Lights." Larry liked playing director. The lighting man turned the lamps on. The set was suddenly bathed in oven-hot white light. "Roll."

"We're rolling."

Then Larry nodded to Rune. She reached toward the first domino.

The dominoes fell and clicked as they spread over the paper, the camera swept over the set like a carnival ride and Larry murmured with the preoccupation of a man who was getting paid two hundred thousand dollars for five days' work.

Click. The last one fell.

The camera backed off for a longer angle shot of the entire logo: a cow wearing a top hat.

"Cut," Larry yelled sternly. "Save the lights."

The lights went out.

Rune closed her eyes, thinking that she'd still have to get all the little rectangles packed up and returned to the prop rental store before six; Larry and Bob wouldn't want to pay another day's fee.

Then the voice came from somewhere above them. "One thing . . ."

It was Mary Jane, who'd watched the whole event from a tall ladder on the edge of the set.

"What's that?" Mr. Wallet asked.

"I'm just wondering. . . . Do you think the logo's a little lopsided?" She climbed down from the ladder.

Mr. Wallet climbed up, surveyed the set.

"It does look a little that way," he said.

Mary Jane said, "The cow's horns aren't even. The left one and the right one."

Mr. Wallet looked at the fallen dominoes. "We can't have a lopsided logo."

Mary Jane walked forward and adjusted the design. She stood back. "See, that's what it should be like. I would've thought you'd tried a test first."

As Rune took a breath to speak the words that would send her straight to Unemployment, Larry squeezed her arm. " 'Ey, Rune, could you come out here for a minute, please?"

In the hall she turned to him. "Lopsided? *She's* lopsided. What does she think it is, oil paint? It's not the Sistine Chapel, Larry. It's a cow with a fucking top hat. Sure it's going to be lopsided. She's on some kind of a power trip—"

"Rune—"

"We do it again the horns'll be fine but the hat'll be wrong. I want to knock her—"

"I've got a distributor for your film."

"—buck teeth out. I—"

Larry repeated patiently, "A distributor."

She paused for a minute. "You *what*?"

"I found somebody who said 'e might want to handle your film. Looking for gritty, noirish stuff. It's not a big outfit but they've placed at public TV stations and some of the bigger locals. We're not talking network. But sometimes good films, you know, they get picked up in syndication."

"Oh, Larry." She hugged him. "I don't believe it."

"Right. Now then, we're going to go back in there and make nice with the ice lady, okay?"

Rune said, "That woman is a totally airborne bitch."

"But they're our clients, Rune, and in this business the customer is always what?" He raised an eyebrow.

She walked toward the door. "Don't ask me questions you don't want to hear the answers to."

■

Rune's favorite part was the dogs.

The rest was pretty neat—the artillery shells, the hand grenades, the sticks of dynamite wired to clocks, silver cylinders of detonators, which all turned out to be phony. But the really audacious part was the three Labrador retrievers that nosed their way up to her and rested their big

snouts on her knees when she crouched down to pet
them. They wheezed as she scratched their heads.

Healy and Rune stood in the Bomb Squad headquarters
upstairs at the 6th Precinct on Tenth Street. It wasn't easy
to miss the office: In the corridor, over the door, hung a
bright red army practice bomb, stenciled with BOMB SQUAD
in gothic lettering.

In the main room were eight battered desks. The walls
were light green, the floor linoleum. One woman, in a
dark sweater, sat at a desk, intently reading a technical
manual. She was pretty, with long, brunette hair and still
eyes. She was the only woman in the unit. The others
were men, mostly in their thirties and forties, wearing
white shirts and ties. Trim guns rested in hip holsters.
They read, talked among themselves, stretched back,
spoke quietly on the phone. A few acknowledged Healy
with waves or raised eyebrows.

No one looked at Rune.

"We've got the biggest civilian bomb disposal unit in
the world. Thirty-two officers. Mostly detectives. A few
waiting for the rank."

On the wall was an old wooden board mounted with
formal portraits of policemen. Rune caught the words "In
memory of . . ."

The board was the largest display in the room.

She bent down and patted a dog's head.

"EDC," Healy said.

"That's a weird name," Rune said, standing up.

"That what he *is*. An Explosive Detection Canine."

"The initials again."

"Saves time," Healy said. "You'd run out of breath, you
had to say, 'I'm taking the Explosive Detection Canine for
a walk.' "

"You could try *dog*." One rolled onto his back. Rune
scratched his stomach. "They sniff out explosives?"

"Labradors've got the best noses in the business. We've

used computerized nitrate vapor detectors. But the dogs work faster. They can sniff out plastic, dynamite, TNT, Tovex, Semtex."

"Computers don't pee, though," one cop offered.

"Or lick their balls in public," another one said.

Healy sat down at a tiny desk.

One detective said to him, "How'd you rate, missing the abortion clinic detail?"

"Lucky, I guess." Healy turned to Rune. "You want some coffee?"

"Sure."

Healy walked into the locker room. Three officers sat at a fiberboard table eating Chinese food. He rinsed out a china mug and poured coffee.

Rune stood at the bulletin board, looking at color snapshots of explosions. She pointed to a photo of a red truck that looked like a huge basket. "What's that?"

"The Pike-La Guardia truck. We don't use it much anymore. It was built in the forties. Got its name because it was built when a guy named Pike was C.O. of the Bomb Squad and La Guardia was mayor. See that mesh there? That's cable left over from the Triborough Bridge. They used to put IEDs in there and take them to the disposal grounds. If it went off the mesh stopped the shrapnel. Still a lot of flame escaped, though. Now we use a total-containment vehicle."

Rune said, "A TCV, right?"

Healy nodded.

Rune picked up a thick plastic tube about a foot long filled with a blue gelatin printed with the words DuPont. She squeezed it. Grinned. "This is kinda kinky, Sam."

He glanced at it. "You're holding enough Tovex to turn a pretty good-size boulder into gravel."

She set it down carefully.

"If it were live . . . That's just for training. So's everything else in here."

"That too?" She pointed to an artillery shell about two and a half feet long.

"Well, it's not live. But we picked that up a year or so ago. What happened was a woman calls 911 and says she got hit by a bullet. So Emergency Services shows up and they go into the apartment. They find her on the floor. They ask, 'Where's the shooter, where's the gun?' She says, 'There's no gun—just the bullet.' She points to the shell. Then says, 'I opened the closet door and it fell out.' It broke her toe. Her husband collected artillery shells and—"

· A voice shouted, "Sam."

He stepped into the main room. A heavy, square-jawed man with trim blond hair was leaning out of the commander's office. He glanced at Rune briefly, then looked at Healy. "Sam, ESU just got a Ten-thirty-three at a porn theater in Times Square. Somebody found a box, looked inside. Saw a timer in there and maybe a wad of something might be plastic. Seventh Avenue, near Forty-ninth. Rubin, you go with him."

No more bombings, he'd said? But before she could comment to him Healy and another cop, a thin man of about forty-five who looked like he belonged more in an insurance office circa 1950 than in the Bomb Squad, were racing to the locker room. They opened their lockers and pulled out battered canvas bags, then ran for the door. Healy snagged his attaché case as he disappeared into the corridor.

"Hey . . . ," Rune was saying. Healy didn't even glance back.

Where does he get off? Rune thought, speeding into the dark green corridor. Downstairs, the men disappeared into the station house. An officer in a blue turtleneck stopped her, wouldn't let her follow. By the time she went outside, their blue-and-white van was disappearing down Eleventh Street, the roof lights playing crack the whip.

The vehicle gave a bubble of electronic siren, then sailed north on Hudson Street.

She ran to the corner, waving for cabs that failed to materialize.

———

Sam Healy had the procedure down. That was one talent he had: the ability to memorize. He'd look at a list or circuit schematic once or twice and that would be it—it was in the mental vault.

Which was a good thing. Because there was a lot to remember when you were a Bomb Squad cop. He wondered if that had anything to do with why he'd chosen bomb detail in the first place. It was different from being a beat cop or an ESU cop. In Emergency Services you had to make fast decisions. They improvised.

Healy preferred to plan every detail out, then work step by step. Slowly.

The van clattered north. Hudson became Eighth Avenue and they passed Fourteenth Street.

The procedure: Set up a frozen zone for a thousand feet around the theater and evacuate everybody as best you can. Easy in a Long Island strip mall; impossible in densely populated Manhattan. Then you get the robot, with its gripping claws and TV-camera eyes, to stroll up to the damn thing and take a look at it. Then you pick it up in the claws . . .

The van rocked to a stop in the showroom of emergency vehicles on Seventh Avenue. They jumped out of the van.

. . . and wheel it out nice and easy because the cable on the robot is only fifty feet long and you can get killed as fast by chunks of robot as you can by IED shrapnel. Then you go up the ramp and into the containment vehicle. . . .

And pray that the damn thing goes off in the vessel so

you don't have to go inside and pick it up when you get to Rodman's Neck.

But also pray that if it *does* go off in the vessel it doesn't have such a high brisance and isn't so big that it turns the containment truck into a huge hand grenade.

And then you just pray. . . .

That's *if* you can use the robot, of course. Assuming the bomb wasn't in some place the bulky crawler, looking like a moon-lander car, couldn't go.

Under a theater seat, for instance.

Which is, of course, where the bomb turned out to be, they learned as they deployed at the scene.

Healy looked at his partner, Jim Rubin, and nodded. "I'll do a hand entry. Let's get the suit."

"I'll do it, you want," Rubin said.

And he would have. Because that was the way they all were. If Healy'd said, "Yeah, you take this one," Rubin would've done it. But Healy didn't. The game didn't quite work that way. It was who was there first, who took the call, who said "I'll go" before anybody else. Any of them *would* go, it came down to it. But Healy'd claimed this one. He didn't know why but he felt it was his. You just did that sometimes. For the same reason you sometimes didn't say "I'll go" quite as fast as somebody else.

Tonight Healy felt about as invincible as anybody picking up a box that could destroy the average house could possible feel.

"Sam!" Rune called as she climbed out of the cab. He looked at her only for an instant. She glanced at his eyes and fell silent. He understood that she was looking at someone she didn't know at all.

He whispered to Rubin, "Keep her the hell away. Cuff her, you have to, but I don't want her close."

"Sam . . ." He glanced at her once more. She put the camera on the ground, which was a message, he thought.

Telling him she wasn't here for the movie or because of Shelly Lowe or for any reason other than that she was worried about him. But he still turned away from her.

As Rubin drove the robot out of the van—they'd drive it as far as they could—Healy put on the heavy green bomb suit, thick with Kevlar panels and steel plates. He put the helmet on and started the circulator pump to get air into the helmet.

Rubin stopped just inside the theater doors and drove the robot down the aisle the supervisor had marked with yellow plastic tape. He wore a headset and a microphone on the tip of a thin armature that ended in front of his mouth. His eyes were distorted behind thick goggles. Healy walked past him, then past the robot. He said into the helmet's mike, "How you reading me, homes?"

"Good, Sam. Lucky you got the hat—this place fucking stinks."

Healy walked farther into the theater, his feet shuffling aside empty crack vials and Kleenex wads and liquor bottles.

"Talk to me, Sam, talk to me."

But Healy was counting on his fingers. The manager had said the bomb was in Aisle M. Was that the fifteenth letter of the alphabet? Man, he hoped not. Fifteen wasn't a good number for him. Cheryl had left on the fifteenth of March. Wasn't that the ides of March? His only car crash had been a rear-ender on the Merritt Parkway—Route 15.

J, K, L, M . . . Good. M was the *thirteenth* letter of the alphabet. He felt unreasonably cheered at this news.

"Okay, I see it," he said, smelling the stale air, sweating terribly already, feeling breathless. "Cardboard box, shoe box, lid off."

He knelt for stability—the suit was very heavy; if you fell over you sometimes couldn't get up by yourself. He leaned over the box. Said into the radio, "I'm looking at

C-3 or C-4, maybe six ounces, timer face up. If it's accurate, we got ten leisurely minutes. Don't see any rocker switches."

Rocker switches were the problem. Little switches that set off the bomb if it's moved.

But not seeing them didn't mean there weren't any.

He probed into the box with a pencil.

"You going to render safe?" Rubin asked.

"No, looks like the timer's pretty fancy. I'm betting there's a shunt, but I can see the circuitry. I'm not going to cut anything. I'm going to bring it out.

"Okay, here we go." He reached down. The gloves were plated, but Healy knew he was looking at enough plastic to snap a steel beam. The theory was that there wasn't much you could do about your hands anyway. At least, if anything happened, you'd be alive afterward to retire on disability, even if somebody else had to endorse the checks for you.

Healy squinted—pointlessly—and lifted the box off the ground. You had to be careful—you tended to think that explosives were going to be heavy as iron weights. They weren't. The whole thing didn't weigh more than a pound.

"No rocker," he said to the microphone. The smell of his own sweat was strong. He breathed slowly. "Or maybe I've got steady hands."

"Doing good, Sam."

The timer on the clock showed seven minutes until detonation.

Healy backed out into the aisle, sliding his feet behind slowly to feel the way. He set the box into the arms of the robot.

"This place is gross," Healy said.

"Okay, we'll take over," Rubin told him.

Healy didn't argue. He dropped his hands to his side

and walked backward until he felt Rubin tap him on the shoulder.

Rubin drove the robot out of the theater and up the ramp to the containment chamber, which fellow Bomb Squad officers had driven up from the garage connected to the 6th Precinct. It looked like a small diving bell on a platform. He gingerly manipulated the remote controls to get the box inside. The robot backed away and Healy approached the open door from the side. He pulled a wire to close the door most of the way, then quickly stepped in front and spun the lever. He stepped back.

Rubin helped him out of the suit.

"Whatsa time?" Rubin asked.

"I make it about a minute to go."

Rune broke through the police line and ran up to Healy. She squeezed his arm.

He pushed her around behind him.

"Sam, are you all right?"

"Shh. Listen."

"I—"

"Shhhh," Healy said.

Suddenly, a loud ping—it sounded like a hammer on a muffled bell. Smoke and fumes began to hiss out of the side of the changer. A sour, tear-gassy smell filled the air.

"C-3," Healy said. "I'd know that smell anywhere."

"What happened?" Rune asked.

"It just exploded."

"You mean that thing you were bringing out? It just blew up? Oh, Sam, you could have been killed."

For some reason Rubin was laughing at that. Healy himself was fighting down a grin.

He looked at her. "I'm going to be here for a while."

"Sure. I understand." She didn't like the glazed, wild look on his face. It scared her.

"I'll call you tomorrow." He turned and began speaking to a man in a dark suit.

She started back to the sidewalk and then glanced at the tailgate of the Bomb Squad station wagon. Sam Healy's briefcase was resting on it.

She wasn't exactly sure why she did it. Maybe because he'd scared her, looking the way he did. Maybe because she'd spent the day setting up little squares of plastic and enduring small-minded people.

Maybe because it was just in her nature never to give up a quest—just like it was in Sam Healy's to go into buildings like this and find bombs.

In any case Rune quickly flipped open Healy's briefcase and examined the contents until she found his small notebook. This she thumbed through until she found what she was looking for. She memorized a name and address.

She glanced toward Healy, standing in a cluster of other officers. No one noticed her. Their attention was on a clear plastic envelope Healy held. A moment later Rune's voice, theatrical and low, filled the theater. " 'The third angel blew his trumpet and a great star fell from heaven, blazing like a torch, and it fell on a third of the rivers and on the fountains of water.' "

CHAPTER SEVENTEEN

████████ "Look, I'll talk to you. But you can't use my name."

They sat on the deck of Rune's houseboat that night, drinking Michelob Light. The skinny young man continued, "I mean, my mother thinks I was in a car crash. If she ever found out . . ."

Warren Hathaway was the witness whose name she'd found in Sam Healy's notebook. He'd been in the Velvet Venus Theater when the first bomb blew. Rune had called him and asked if she could interview him.

"I'm the only person in the world who got blown up my first time in a porno theater. . . ." Then he caught her amused look. "Well, okay, maybe not my first. But I don't go all that often."

Hathaway was about five six, early thirties, pudgy. He had bandages on his neck and his arm was taped. He spoke loudly too—just like Rune after she'd witnessed the bombing—and she guessed the explosion in the Velvet

Venus had temporarily deafened him. "How did you find me?"

"The policeman who interviewed you? Detective Healy? I got your name from him."

The camera was set up. Hathaway looked at it uneasily. "You can mask my face out, can't you? So nobody'll recognize me?"

"Sure. Don't worry."

She started the camera. "Just tell me what you remember."

"Okay, I was doing an audit at a publishing company on Forty-seventh. I'm an accountant and financial advisor. And, what happened was I had a couple hours off and I walked to Eighth Avenue to this deli I'd seen. They had great-looking fruit cups—they seemed nice and fresh, you know, lots of watermelon—and there was this theater right in front of me and I thought, Hell, why not?" He took a sip of the beer. "So I walked in."

"What was your impression?"

"Filthy, first of all. It smelled like, you know, urine and disinfectant. And there were these tough-looking guys. They were . . . well, black mostly, and they looked me over like I was, I don't know, dessert. So I hurried down to a seat. There were about ten people in the whole place is all and some of them were asleep. I sat down. The picture was awful. It wasn't a movie at all but this video-tape. You could hardly see anything it was so fuzzy. After a while I decided to leave. I stood up. There was a big flash and this incredible roar and the next thing I know I'm in the hospital and I can't hear."

"How long were you in the theater?"

"Total? Maybe a half hour."

"Did you get much of a look at the other people in there?"

"Sure. I was looking around. You know, to make sure I

didn't get mugged. There were some folks there. Some dockworker sorts. And transvestites—you know, prostitutes." He looked away from both Rune and the camera.

Rune nodded sympathetically and it crossed her mind that Warren Hathaway might know more about transvestite prostitutes than he wanted to admit.

"Did you maybe see somebody in a red windbreaker?"

Hathaway thought for a moment. "Well, there was somebody in a red jacket, I think. And a hat."

"With a wide brim?"

"Yeah. It looked funny. He moved kind of slow. I got the impression he was older."

Older? Rune wondered. She asked, "He was leaving the theater?"

"Maybe. I couldn't swear to it."

"Any idea how old?"

"Sorry. Couldn't say."

"Could you describe him at all?"

Hathaway shook his head. "Sorry. I wasn't paying attention. What're you exactly, a newspaper reporter?"

"I'm doing a film about that girl who was killed in the second bombing. Shelly Lowe."

A motorboat went past and they both watched it.

Hathaway asked, "But she wasn't in a movie theater, was she?"

"No, it was in a studio that made adult films."

"It's terrible what people do to make a point, isn't it? That they feel lives are less important than politics or a statement . . ."

His voice faded and Hathaway smiled, then said, "I get too serious. My mother tells me all the time I get too serious. I should loosen up. Imagine your mother telling you that."

"Mine sure doesn't."

He looked at the camera. "So you're going to be a film

maker?" Squinted in curiosity. "You have any idea what the average ROI is in that industry?"

"ROI?"

"Return on investment."

Accountants might have been as bad as cops when it came to initials. Rune said, "I sort of do the creative part and leave the money stuff to other people."

"What's the market for a film like yours?"

And she told him about the independent circuit and art film houses and public TV and the new but growing cable TV market.

"And it wouldn't be a large investment," Hathaway considered, "for films like this. You can probably control costs pretty easily. Indirect overhead would probably be pretty low. I mean, look at fixed assets. Virtually nonexistent in your case. You can lease equipment, wouldn't have to amortize much, only the more expensive items. . . . If you were smart, the net-net could be great." Hathaway gazed off into the evening sky, seeing a huge balance sheet in the stars. "If you've got a success you're looking at pretty much pure profit."

They finished their beers and Rune got up to get more. She shut the camera off. He said, "I wasn't much help, was I?"

An older man in a red windbreaker . . .

"No, you were real helpful," Rune said.

As she returned with the beers she felt his eyes on her. And she knew the Question was coming. She didn't know exactly what form it would take but, as a single woman in New York, she'd have bet a thousand dollars that Hathaway was about to ask her the Question.

He took a sip of beer and asked, "So. Hey. You want to get a pizza or something?"

The Pizza version of the Question. A pretty common one.

"I'm really beat tonight. . . ."

Which was one of the classic Answers. But she added, "I really *am* exhausted. But how 'bout a rain check?"

He smiled a little bashfully, which she liked. "Got it. You, uh, going with anybody?"

She thought for a moment, then said, "I have absolutely no idea."

He stood up, shook her hand like the gentleman his mother had probably always instructed him to be. He said, "I'm going to check out some numbers about documentary films." He considered something and smiled. "You know, even if it's a flop, hell, you've got a great tax write-off."

"I'm not much help, I'm afraid," Nicole D'Orleans said to Rune the next morning.

"Somebody wearing a red windbreaker or jacket. Anybody at all. Wearing a hat. Like a cowboy hat maybe. Hanging around the set. Maybe a fan of Shelly's or something. Maybe somebody she knew."

Nicole shook her head.

"He attacked me at my loft, just after I first interviewed Shelly. Then I saw him just after Shelly was killed, outside Lame Duck. And I talked to a witness in the first bombing. He thinks he saw him leaving the theater just before the bomb went off. He could be young or old. You have any idea?"

"Sorry. I—"

The front buzzer rang and Nicole went to answer the door.

She returned with Tommy Savorne, Shelly's former boyfriend.

The first thing Rune noticed was a belt buckle in the shape of Texas.

She thought of Sam Healy.

Who still hadn't called.

No, don't think about him now.

Tommy absently polished the buckle with his thumb. The metal tongue went right through Dallas.

"Hey." He smiled. He squinted, meaning: Sorry, I've forgotten your name.

She stuck her hand out and as they shook she said, "Rune."

"Right, sure. How's your film coming?"

"Slow, but moving along."

Then he said to Nicole, "You're looking pretty good today."

There was silence for a moment.

Odd woman out. Rune stood up.

"I better be going. I'm late for work."

"Naw, stay, stay," Tommy said. "I only stopped by for a minute. I wanted to ask Nicole something. But maybe you're interested too, Rune. Want a job?"

"I better not take on another one. I'm not doing too well with the one I've got," Rune said.

"Like, doing what?" Nicole asked Tommy.

"I'm doing a tape on how to make vegetarian appetizers. I need a chef."

Rune shook her head. "Unless they come in a boil-pouch you're talking to the wrong person."

"I don't know," Nicole said. "Would I have to, you know, talk?"

"Not on camera. All you've got to do is mix up stuff. Garlic and avocado and sprouts and peanut butter . . . Well, not all together. I mean, they're great recipes. Come on, honey. It'll be a snap. It's for one of my infomercials."

She said, "You're sure I wouldn't have to, like, memorize dialogue?"

Tommy said, "Naw, it's all voice-over. You just make the food, then we record the vocal track after. Do as many takes as you want."

Nicole looked at Rune. "You're sure you don't want to?"

Tommy said to her, "I really could use two."

"Full plate right at the moment."

Nicole asked, "And I'd get paid?"

"Oh, sure. We aren't talking union. But the client'll cough up a hundred bucks an hour for talent. Should be about three hours tops, with the prep time and any reshoots."

"What about my fingernails?" She held them up—an inch-long and glossy burnt-umber.

"Come on," he chided, grinning. "You're looking for excuses."

"Go for it, Nicole," Rune encouraged.

A smile spread across her glossy lips. "A movie with my clothes on . . . My mother's been after me for years to try that." She shoved her hand, with its lethal nails, toward Tommy.

"Deal," she said, and they shook as if they'd just signed a million-dollar contract.

"Tomorrow night?" he said. "And the next day?"

"Well, sure. As long as it's at night. I'm shooting in the day. Where's your studio?"

"I don't rent studios. It's all location. We can do it right here. You've got a great kitchen." He looked at Rune. "Come on, can't we talk you into it?"

"Some other time."

"All right . . . See you then," he said to Nicole and kissed her on the cheek. He waved to Rune and let himself out.

Rune said, "He's cute. He's available. He cooks. That's a combination you can't beat."

But Nicole was looking off.

Rune said, "What's the matter?"

"Nothing."

"What?"

She hesitated. Then said, "This job. The one Tommy's doing?"

"Yeah?"

"I hope it works out. I hope I don't blow it."

"You'll do fine."

"I'd give anything to get out of the business."

"I thought you liked it."

Nicole walked to the couch and sat down. "Did you watch *Current Events* last night? That TV program? There were these women protesting porn theaters, picketing some of the theaters. They said some terrible things. My name was on the marquee. I mean, they didn't say anything about me specifically but you could see my name. And this lady is like, all this porn makes women get raped and children get molested. And this other woman goes, 'They've set back the women's movement twenty years.' Yada, yada, yada . . . I felt so guilty."

Suddenly she was crying.

Rune debated for a second or two. Her hand slipped to the trigger of the video camera. The lens was pointed directly at Nicole.

Looking off, Nicole said, "I don't mean to do anything bad. I don't want to hurt people. But, I mean, people came to see me and got killed in that theater. And maybe after one of my films some guy goes out and picks up a hooker and gets AIDS. That's terrible."

She looked at Rune, and the tears were coming steadily now. "These movies, the thing is, it's all I can do. I make love good. But I'm such a failure at anything else. I've tried. It doesn't work. . . . It's such a hard feeling, to hate the one thing you're good at."

Rune touched Nicole's arm, but she did so carefully. She wanted to make sure her own hand didn't slip into the field of view of the whirring Sony.

The owner of the theater on Forty-seventh Street between Broadway and Eighth was a fifty-two-year-old Indian immigrant from Bombay who had come to this country twelve years earlier.

He and his wife and children had worked hard at the small businesses he'd owned—first a newsstand, then a fast-food stand, then a shoe store in Queens. He'd made a bad investment, an electronics store in Brooklyn, and had lost most of the family nest egg. A year ago a friend had told him about a movie theater that was for sale. After some introductions and cumbersome negotiations and paying amazing sums to an attorney and an accountant, he'd bought out the lease and acquired the fixtures and what the lawyer called the theater's "goodwill," an asset he was completely unable to comprehend.

The diminutive man became the owner of the Pink Pussycat—an eight-hundred-seat movie theater in Times Square. Although at one time the theater used typical industry-standard 35mm dual projectors, all the movies were presently shown via a video projector, which was never quite in focus and gave the actors and actresses auras like fuzzy rainbows.

He had experimented with pricing, finding that the most he could charge during the day was $2.99, although after ten p.m. the price went up to $4.99. Since the theater, which was open twenty-four hours, doubled as an impromptu hotel for the homeless, he found that men were willing to cough up the extra two dollars so they could sleep to the earthy lullaby of *Sex Kittens* or *Lust at First Bite*.

There were no tickets. Patrons paid their money, refused the offered penny change and were clicked through a turnstile. They walked into the theater proper past a soda machine that had stopped working in 1978.

There was some cruising, despite warning signs about illegality and AIDS, but liaisons were discreet and the transvestites and the mostly black and Hispanic female hookers, who picked up twenty bucks for their half-hearted services, would usually take their clients up to the balcony, where even the vice cops didn't like to go.

Despite the unpleasant conditions the theater did make money. Rent was the highest expense. The owner and his wife (and an occasional cousin from the huge inventory of relatives overseas) took turns in the box office, thus keeping salary expenses down. And because of the video system they didn't need a union projectionist.

The owner also bypassed the largest expenses of movie theaters. Under the copyright laws he was supposed to pay license fees for each theatrical showing of a film—yes, even porn. This, however, he didn't do. He would buy three VHS cassettes for $14.95 each from an adult book-store on Eighth Avenue, show the films for one week, then return them. The owner of the store, who happened to be a Pakistani immigrant, gave him a five-dollar credit for each film and then resold them for the full $14.95.

This was, of course, a violation of federal law, both civil and criminal, but neither the FBI nor the producers of the films had much inclination to go after a small business like his.

When the man considered the type of films that his theater showed, he was not particularly proud, but he wasn't much ashamed either. The *Kama Sutra,* after all, had been written in his native country. And personally he was no stranger to sex; he'd come from a family of twelve children and he and his wife had seven. No, his major embarrassment about the business was the low profit margin of the theater. He would have been much happier if his return on investment had been five or six percent higher.

Today the owner was sitting in the ticket booth, smoking and thinking of the lamb kurma that his wife would be making in their Queens apartment for dinner. He heard angry words coming from the theater. That was one thing that scared him—his patrons. There were a lot of crack smokers, a lot of men working on their third or fourth Foster's. These were big men and could have broken his neck before they even thought about it. He called the cops occasionally but he'd gotten their message: Unless somebody had a knife or a gun the police didn't want to be bothered.

Now, when the dispute didn't seem to be vanishing, he rummaged under the ticket booth and found a foot-long pipe, capped at both ends and filled with BBs. A homemade cudgel. He walked into the theater.

The blonde on the screen was saying something about there being one kind of love she hadn't tried and would the actor please accommodate her. He seemed agreeable but no one could tell exactly what he was saying to the woman. The voices from the front row were louder.

"The fuck you think you're doing? S'mine, man."

"Fuck that shit. I lef' it here."

"An' fuck that! Wha' you mean, you lef' it, man? You sitting three seats over, maybe four, man. *I* seen it."

The owner said, "You must be quiet. What is it? I call police, you don't sit down."

There were two of them, both black. One was homeless, wearing layers of tattered clothes, matted with dirt. The other was in a brown deliveryman's uniform. He was holding a paper-wrapped box, about the size of a shoe box. They looked at the Indian—they both towered over him—and pled their cases as if he were a judge.

The homeless man said, "He be stealing mah package. I lef' it, I wenta take a leak, and—"

"Fuck, man. He din't leave no box. I seen some guy come in, watcha movie for ten minutes and leave. It was there when he left, man. I seen it. He left it and it's mine. That's the law."

The homeless man grabbed for the box, a shoe box.

The deliveryman's long arms kept it out of reach. "Get the fuck outa here."

The owner said, "Somebody leave it? He'll be back. Give it to me. Who was it left it?"

The deliveryman said, "How'm I supposed to know who the fuck he was? Some white guy. I found it. S'what the law say, man. I find it, I get to keep it."

The owner reached out. "No, no. Give it to me."

The homeless man said, "I said I lef' it. Give it—"

They were in that pose, all three sets of arms extended and gesturing angrily, when the fourteen ounces of C-3 plastic explosive inside the box detonated. Exploding outward at a speed of almost three thousand miles an hour, the bomb instantly turned the men into fragments weighing no more than several pounds. The theater screen vanished, the first four rows of seats shredded into splinters and shrapnel, the floor rocked with a thud that was felt a mile away.

Mixed with the roar of the explosion was the whistle of wood and metal splinters firing through the air as fast as bullets.

Then, almost as quickly, silence returned, accompanied by darkness filled with smoke.

No lightbulbs remained in the theater. But from the ceiling came a tiny green light, swinging back and forth. It was an indicator light on the videotape player, a large black box dangling from a thick wire where the projection booth had been. It blinked out and a second light, a yellow one, flickered on, indicating that *Caught from Behind, Part III* had finished, and *High School Cheerleaders* was now playing.

CHAPTER EIGHTEEN

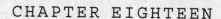 Detective Sam Healy, lying on his couch, was thinking about the women he'd had in his life.

There hadn't been a lot.

A couple of typical college romances.

Then he'd lived with one woman before he met Cheryl and had one affair just before they'd gotten engaged.

A little flirtation after he'd been married—a few drinks was all—and only after Cheryl had mentioned for probably the hundredth time what a nice sensitive man the contractor doing the addition to the bedroom was.

Though Cheryl hadn't been unfaithful. He was sure about that. In a way he wished that she had been. That would've given him an excuse to do a John Wayne number: kick in the door, slap her around, and in the aftermath give them a chance to pour out their hearts and express their fiery love for each other.

Nowadays, that wouldn't work. Think about *The Quiet Man*—Maureen O'Hara'd call the cops the minute John

Wayne touched her and he'd be booked on second-degree assault, first-degree menacing.

Times were different now.

Ah, Cheryl . . .

He stopped the VCR when he realized he hadn't been watching the tape for the past ten minutes.

The problem was that *Lusty Cousins* was just plain and simple boring.

He found the other remote control—the one for the TV—and turned on the ball game. Time for lunch. He walked into the kitchen and opened the refrigerator. He took out one of the thirty-six Rolling Rocks it contained and popped it. On a piece of Arnold's whole wheat bread he laid four slices of Kraft American cheese (four of the hundred and twenty-eight) and added mayonnaise from a quart jar. Then topped it with another slice of bread.

Sam Healy had been grocery-shopping that morning.

He walked back to the living room. He gazed out the window at quiet Queens. Silhouettes showed on window shades in the houses across the street. Seeing them depressed him. He couldn't concentrate on the game either. The Mets were having less luck than both of the lusty cousins.

He looked at the cover to the cassette of the film and decided he didn't like adult films in the first place. They were as interesting as watching a film about someone eating a steak dinner. He also didn't like the weird, slutty makeup and lingerie contraptions the actresses wore. They looked prosthetic and artificial: the fingerless lace gloves, the garters, the black leather bras, the orange fishnet stockings.

And he didn't like silicone boobs.

He liked women like Cheryl.

He liked women like Rune.

Were they similar? He didn't think so. Why would he be so interested in both of them?

He liked innocence, he liked pretty. . . . (But how innocent was Rune? She'd loaned him *Lusty Cousins*. And what was the message for him *there*?)

But whatever he liked, Sam Healy didn't think he had any business being involved with somebody like Rune. When he'd seen her the other night he'd promised to call her. But each of the dozen times he'd thought about picking up the phone he'd resisted. It seemed like the better thing to do. The more stoic. And safer for him. It was ridiculous. The weird clothes she wore. The three wristwatches. She only had one name and it was fake, of course, like a stage name. On top of that, she was probably fifteen years younger than he was.

Oh, no—that damn number fifteen again.

No business at all.

Add to that, she was playing detective, which really upset him. Good citizens, wound up to the excitement of police work by the cotton candy of TV, often tried to play cop. And ended up getting themselves, or someone close to them, killed in the process.

So why was he thinking about Rune so much? Why was he seeing her?

Because he wanted to make Cheryl, the soon-to-be ex-wife who dated regularly, jealous?

Because she was sexy?

Because he liked younger women?

Because he—

The phone rang.

He answered it.

" 'Lo?"

"Sam." It was the 6th Precinct's ops coordinator, the second in command at the station.

"Brad. What's up?"

"We got another one."

"Sword of Jesus?"

"Yep. Forty-seventh near Eighth. Blew just a while ago."

Christ. They were coming more quickly now. Only a day apart on these. "How bad?"

"Nobody outside the theater but inside it's a fucking mess."

"MO the same?"

"Seems to be. You get on it. Get on it big."

Healy hesitated. Didn't feel like he wanted to mince words. "I thought you wanted low-profile."

There was a second of silence. The ops coordinator hadn't anticipated that question. "It's kind of . . . What it is, it's kind of embarrassing now."

"Embarrassing."

"You know. We need a perp in custody. That's from the mayor."

"You got it," Healy said. "Any witnesses?"

The response was a bitter laugh. "Parts of 'em, yeah. Those pricks must've used a pound of plastic this time."

Sam Healy hung up the phone and pulled his blue-jean jacket on. He was all the way out to the elevator when he remembered his pistol. He went back and got it and had to wait three long minutes for the elevator. The door opened. He got in. He looked at his watch. At least the timing was right. Rune would be at work and wouldn't hear about the bombing until later. He'd have time to finish the postblast and seal the site before she found out.

It was one problem he'd never had with a girlfriend before: intruding at a crime scene.

███████

Rune, sitting on the subway, thought about men.

Older men, younger men.

Her most recent boyfriend, Richard, had been close to her age, just a few years older. Tall, skinny, with that narrow, dark, French face that you found everywhere in

straight and gay New York City. (She'd leave him alone in
bars to go to the john and come back and find bartender-
ettes leaning forward, dreamily pouring him free drinks.)

They were together about six months. She'd enjoyed
the time but toward the end she knew it wasn't going to
work. He'd gotten tired of her ideas for dates: picnicking
next to the huge air conditioner vents on the roof of a
Midtown office building, playing with the Dobermans in
her favorite Queens junkyard, wandering through the city
looking for the sites of famous gangland rubouts. They
talked about getting married. But neither of them was
real serious about it. Richard had said, "The thing is, I
think I'm changing. I'm not into weird anymore. And
you're . . ."

"Becoming weirder?"

"No, it isn't that. I think I'd say, you're becoming more
you."

Which she took as a compliment. But they still broke
up not long afterward. They still talked some on the
phone, had a beer now and then. She wished him well
though she'd also decided that if he married the tall,
blonde advertising account executive he'd been dating
their wedding present was going to be the four-foot
stuffed iguana she'd seen in a resale shop on Bleecker
Street.

Young, old . . .

But, naw, it isn't the age. It's the state of mind.

Her mother had told her—during one of the woman's
pretty much incoherent facts-of-life lectures that ran from
ages twelve to eighteen—that there was only one thing
that older men would want from her. Rune's experience,
though, was that it was pretty much *all* men who wanted
that one thing and older men were a lot safer because you
usually could stay up later than them and, if worse came
to worst, you usually could scare them into submission by

talking about your recent twenty-year-old lover who kept you up all night with sexual acrobatics.

Not that she was inclined to scare off Healy. Hell, she thought he was totally sexy. She just wished he'd hurry up and get the preliminary pass over with, then get down to some serious moves. Maybe it was out of line, loaning him *Lusty Cousins*. There was a lot of gentleman in him, though, and she wanted to see what was underneath that.

But what do you do with a sexy gentleman who doesn't call you?

The train pulled into the station, and she got off, climbed the steep stairs and began walking west.

Wondering if there was maybe something weird or Freudian about what she felt for him. Father image, something like that. That Oedipus thing.

Okay, he was older.

Okay, he was a cop.

Okay, her mother would shit a brick when she heard. Still . . .

At a deli she bought a chocolate milk and a package of Oreos—lunch—then walked up the street a half block and sat on a fire hydrant, sipping the milk out of the carton through a bent straw.

Healy's wife, she reflected. That was probably the problem. Why he hadn't called.

He was attracted to Rune—oh, she could tell that—but he was still in love with this wife.

That was a weird thing about men: Love was like a business to them. They get it into their heads that they invest so much time in somebody, it's like a total bummer to give it up too fast. The wife, what was her name, Cheryl? She'd be a bitch, of course. She'd eat him alive. Oh, already the shifty lawyers were working on gouging him for alimony, while she dressed up in silky oriental dresses and had affairs. She neglected Adam, locked him in the basement while she had sex with her lovers on the rec-room floor. . . .

Vampire, vampire!

He should dump her fast.

The last of the milk was slurping through the straw when she saw the station wagon turn the corner and cruise past, slowing down. It stopped fast and screeched backward, stopping quickly in front of her.

The engine idled for a moment, then went silent. Sam Healy got out. He looked at Rune, then at the smoldering front of the Pink Pussycat, then back to Rune. She picked up the video camera and walked over to him.

"How—," he began.

Rune held up a small black box. "These guys are great. Police radio receiver. Reporters use them to get the scoop. I heard the call. Code Ten-thirty-three."

The smile began low and wouldn't stay down. "You shouldn't be here. But I'm getting tired of telling you that so I don't think I will."

"Sorry to hear about the trouble at home."

He frowned, shook his head. "What trouble?"

"About your phone breaking. So you couldn't make calls."

Maybe he was blushing but if so he didn't look embarrassed. "I'm sorry. I should have."

No excuses. She liked that. "I'd be mad," she said, "except you actually look kind of glad to see me."

"Maybe I am."

A voice called from beside the shattered box office. "Hey, Sam."

They turned. Rune was glad to see it wasn't Brown Suit. A uniformed cop waved lazily. He shouted, "The battalion commander says it's okay to go in. We've rigged lights for you. Not much to see, though."

"Can I?" Rune asked.

Healy kept his face on the front of the building.

"Please?"

He said, "You get hurt in there, I could lose my job."

"I won't get hurt. I'm tough. I bounce."

His lips twisted slightly, Sam Healy's concession to a sigh, and he nodded his head in a way that might have meant anything but that Rune knew meant: *Shut up and get your ass inside.*

"No taping."

"Aw."

"No."

"Okay, you win."

Together, for an hour, they sifted through the debris. Rune kept running to Healy every few minutes with bits of metal and wire and screws in her hand and he'd explain they were chair hardware or wires from the wall or the plumbing.

"But they're all burnt. I thought—"

"Everything's burnt."

"That's true," she said and went back to sifting.

Healy's own pile of Significant Junk, which is how Rune thought of it, was growing, nestling in a stack of plastic bags under the exit sign.

"Zip is what I've got. Zip."

"No note this time," Rune pointed out.

He said, "The MO's the same as the first."

"Modus operandi," Rune said.

"The bomb was C-3. Timed detonator. You know, these last two bombs don't help your theory about someone covering up Shelly's murder. Nobody's going to keep bombing just to cover up a crime."

"Sure they are. If they're smart."

They'd both begun to cough; the fumes were thick. Healy motioned her to follow him outside.

As they stepped into the air, breathing deeply, Rune looked up at the crowd.

She saw a flash of color.

Red. It looked like a red jacket.

"Look! It's him!"

She couldn't see his face but it seemed that he saw her; the man turned and disappeared east down Forty-seventh.

"I'm going after him!"

"Rune!" Healy called but she ducked under the yellow tape and ran through the mass of spectators pressing forward to get a look at the disaster.

By the time she broke through them, though, he was two blocks away. Still, she could see that hat. She started across Broadway but the light was against her and she couldn't get through the traffic—there were small gaps between cars but the drivers were accelerating fast and she couldn't squeeze through. No one let her by. It was as frustrating as a toothache.

The man in the red windbreaker stopped, looked back, resting against a building. He seemed winded. Then he crossed the street and vanished into a crowd of pedestrians. Rune noticed that he was walking stiffly—and Rune remembered Warren Hathaway's observation that the man who planted the bomb seemed to be older.

She returned to Healy, panting. "It was him."

"The guy in the jacket?"

She nodded. Healy seemed somewhat skeptical and she thought about telling him that Hathaway had confirmed that he'd been in the Velvet Venus. But that would involve a confession about rifling Healy's attaché case and she wasn't prepared for what the fallout from *that* might be.

He was debating. He walked to a uniformed cop and whispered something to him. The cop trotted off toward his cruiser, hit the lights and drove off.

Healy returned to Rune. He said, "Go on home."

"Sam."

"Home."

Tight-lipped, she looked at him, making him see—
trying to make him see—that, goddamn it, this really
wasn't a game to her. Not at all.

He must have seen some of this; he breathed out a sigh
and looked around for an invisible audience like the kind
Danny Traub carried around with him. Healy said, "All
right, come on." He turned and walked quickly back inside the theater, Rune trotting to keep up with him.

Suddenly he stopped and turned. He spoke as if the
words were lines in a high school play and he was an
actor of Nicole's ability. "I know I didn't call like I said I
would. And you don't have to, if you don't want to. But I
was thinking, tomorrow night—it's my day off—maybe
we could go out."

What a place to ask her out on a date! A bombed-out
porno theater.

She didn't give him time to be embarrassed about his
delivery. She smiled and said, "Ah graciously accept yo
chahming invitation. Nahn, shall we say?"

He stared at her, totally lost.

Rune said, "Nine?"

"Oh, sure. Good."

And smiling while he tried not to, he walked back into
the theater, banging a plastic evidence bag against his leg.

CHAPTER NINETEEN

Rune spent the day assembling the reels of exposed footage for the House O' Leather commercial and stuffed it, along with the editing instructions, into a big white envelope.

Sam picked her up at L&R and drove to a postproduction house, where the technicians would edit the raw footage into a rough cut. Rune dropped it off with instructions to deliver cassettes to L&R and the client as soon as possible, even if it meant overtime.

Then she said, "Okay . . . work's done. Time to party. Let's go to the club." And she gave him directions to the West Side piers.

"Where?" Healy asked dubiously. "I don't think there's anything there."

"Oh, you'd be surprised."

She gave him credit—he was a sport.

Healy put up with the place for a couple of hours before he managed to shout, "I don't feel quite at home here."

"How come?" Rune shouted.

He didn't seem sure. Maybe it was the decor: black foam mounds that looked like lava. Flashing purple overhead lights. A six-foot Plexiglas bubble of an aquarium.

Or the music. (He asked her if the sound system was broken and she had to tell him that the effect was intentional.)

Also he wasn't dressed quite right. Rune had said casual and so she'd dressed in yellow tights, a black miniskirt and—on top of a purple tank top—a black T-shirt as holey as Jarlsberg.

Sam Healy was in blue jeans and a plaid shirt. The one thing he shared with most of the other clubbies was a pair of black boots. His, however, were cowboy boots.

"I think I got it wrong," he said.

"Well, you may start a trend."

Maybe not but he wasn't being eyed like a geek, either, Rune noticed. Two pageboy blonds lifted their sleek faces and fired some serious "Wanna get laid?" vibrations his way. Rune took his arm. "Sunken cheeks like that, you see them? They're a sign of mental instability." She grinned. "Let's dance some more." And began to gyrate in time to the music.

"Dancing," Healy said and mimicked her. Ten minutes later, he said, "I've got an idea."

"I know that tone. You're not having a good time."

Healy wiped his forehead and scalp with a wad of bar napkins. "Anybody ever dehydrate in here?"

"That's part of the fun."

"You sure like to dance."

"Dancing is the best! I'm free! I'm a bird."

"Well, if you're really into dancing, let's try this place I know."

"You're pretty good doing this stuff." Rune drank down half of her third Amstel as she continued to move in time to the music.

"Oh, you think this is good, try my place."

"I know all the clubs. What's this one called?"

"You've never heard of it. It's real exclusive."

"Yeah? You need a special pass to get in?"

"You need to know the password."

"All right! Let's go."

The password was "Howdy" and the girl at the door checking IDs and stamping hands with a tiny map of Texas responded with the countersign—"How y'all doing tonight?"

They were shown into the club—which for having a four-piece swing band was incredibly quiet. Or maybe it just seemed that way after the deafening roar of Rune's place. They were seated at a small table with a gingham plastic tablecloth.

"Two Lone Stars," Healy ordered.

Rune looked at a girl sitting next to them. A tight white sweater, a blue denim skirt, stockings and white cowboy boots.

"Very, very weird," she said.

"You hungry?"

"You mean this's a restaurant too? What, you get to pick your own cow out of the pen in the back?"

"The ribs are great."

"Very weird."

"I liked that other place," he said. "But I kind of have to watch the noise." Pointing to his ears. She remembered that bomb blasts had affected his hearing.

They drank the beers and were still thirsty so they ordered a pitcher.

"You come here much?" Rune asked.

"Used to."

"With your wife?"

Healy didn't answer for a minute. "Some. It's not like it was a special place for us."

"You still see her at all?"

"Mostly just when I pick up Adam."

Mostly, she noticed.

Healy continued. "There're books she left she comes by to pick up. Kitchen things. Stuff like that . . . I never asked you if you're going with anybody."

Rune said, "I'm sort of between boyfriends."

"Really? I'm surprised."

"Yeah? It's not as unbelievable as some things, like talking dogs or aliens."

"I'd think you'd have them lined up."

"Men have these strange feelings about me. Mostly, they ignore me. The ones who don't ignore me, a lot of them just want sex and then the chance to ignore me afterward. Sometimes they want to adopt me. You see people in Laundromats Saturday night doing their underwear and reading two-week-old *People* magazines? That's me. From what I've learned during the rinse cycle I could write a biography of Cher or Vanna White or Tom Cruise."

"Let's dance," he said.

Rune frowned and looked out over the dance floor.

Healy said, "It's called the two-step. Best dance in the world."

"Let me get this straight?" she said. "You hold on to each other and you dance at the same time?"

Healy smiled. "It's a whole new idea."

Tommy Savorne pressed the buzzer of Nicole D'Orleans's apartment and thought of how strange it was going to be to see *her* standing there and not Shelly.

He had tried—often, lately—to remember the first time he saw Shelly. He couldn't. That was another odd thing. He had a good memory and there didn't seem to be any reason why he shouldn't remember Shelly. She'd been a person you could picture clearly. Maybe it was the poses she struck. She was never—what was the word?—random about anything she did. She was never careless in the way she stood or sat or spoke.

Or in what she decided to do.

He had recent images: Shelly on Asilomar Beach in Pacific Grove or at Point Lobos, on the bluffs where the park rangers were always telling you to stay away from the edge. Man, he could picture her clearly there.

He pictured her in bed.

But the first time they met, no, he couldn't see that at all.

He'd tried a lot lately.

Nicole opened the door.

"Hey there," she said.

"Hi, babe." He took off his cowboy hat, kissed her cheek and hugged her and felt that wonderful presence of a voluptuous woman against your body. She looked good: a pale blue silk dress with a high neckline, high heels, hair teased up and back. The makeup—well, she was a little over-the-line there, but he could tone it down with some gels on the lights. He picked up his camera bags and carried them inside.

He noticed her dangling zirconia earrings. They were pretty but he'd get lens flare off of them. They'd have to go.

"You look nice," he said.

"Thanks, come on in. You want a drink?"

"Sure. Juice. Mineral water."

"So you've, like, completely stopped drinking?"

"Yep," he said.

"Good for you. You mind if I . . ."

"Oh, God, no. Go right ahead."

Nicole poured two orange juices. Added vodka to hers. The bottle vibrated slightly in her hand as she poured. He smiled. "What, you nervous?"

"A little I guess. Isn't that weird? I do a sex film and no big deal. I'm on camera with my clothes on and I get butterflies in my tummy."

"Ah, it'll be a piece of cake." They clinked glasses. "To your new career."

She sipped the drink, then set the glass down. Her eyes swiveled; she'd been thinking about something, it seemed. She decided to say it. "If this works out, Tommy, you think there'll maybe be others I could do?"

Tommy drank down half the juice. "I don't see why not." Then: "I ought to start getting set up. Can you show me the kitchen?"

She led him into the large, tiled room. It was chrome and white. In the center of the ceiling was a large steel rack hanging from chains. Dozens of heavy copper pans and bowls hung from it.

"This'll work just fine."

"We had it redone last year."

He looked over the room. "We can use those pans. Copper looks good on camera."

Together they began assembling the camera and lights.

Nicole asked, "Was it hard for you to, you know, get out of the business?"

"Out of porn? Yeah, financially it was a pain. What I did was assist at some film companies for a while."

"Like what Rune's doing?"

"Rune? Oh, that girl. Yeah, like her. And eventually I started getting some jobs as a cameraman, then I directed some documentaries."

"I'd like to act. I keep thinking I could take lessons. I mean, how hard can it be? Shelly had a good coach. Arthur Tucker. She said he helped her a lot. I don't know why he hasn't been around. He didn't go to the memorial service. I thought he would've called."

"The coach?"

"Yeah."

"I don't know," Tommy said. "When somebody dies it makes people feel funny. They can't deal with it." He turned to her, examined her closely. "You *should* act. You should be always in front of the camera. You're very beautiful."

Their eyes met for a moment. A copper bowl paused in Nicole's hand. She looked away.

He finished assembling the camera and lights. Nicole watched him, the smooth, efficient way he handled the equipment. She leaned against the island, absently spinning the round-bottomed copper bowl. She looked down at its hypnotizing motion.

"I know Shelly got some kind of kick out of the porn films she made but, all in all, I don't see why she didn't give it up."

"Because," Tommy said, stepping next to her, "she was a whore. Just like you." And he brought the long, lead pipe down on the back of Nicole's head.

CHAPTER TWENTY

■■■■■ They ended up at her houseboat.

First, after the country-western club they were drenched with sweat so they decided it'd make sense to go for a walk. Then a cool night breeze came up as they were walking in the West Village and that made Healy suggest coffee nearby and they went to a cappuccino place on Hudson Street with a fountain where water spit out of a goat's head into a trough filled with coins.

One of the coins was an Indian head nickel and Rune spent a couple minutes nonchalantly fishing the coin out while Healy tried to distract the waitress.

"Hmm," Healy muttered. "Petty larceny. And I'm an accessory."

She retrieved the coin and then wrung the slimy fountain water out of her sleeve. "It was in deeper than I'd thought."

After that they'd walked another five or six blocks and found themselves not far from her boat.

"I only live three blocks away."

"Where?" he asked.

"In the river."

He looked at her for the standard five seconds before asking the standard question. "*In* the river?"

"I have a houseboat."

"I don't believe you. Nobody's got a houseboat in New York. This I've got to see."

Which was a line that'd been tried on her before.

Not that it mattered. She was going to invite him home anyway.

After the tour of the houseboat Rune looked for something to offer him. Beer didn't seem right after coffee and her only bottle of brandy had been capped with foil a year or two ago and a dark residue floated in the bottom.

"Sorry." She held up the bottle.

"Bud's fine."

They stood on the deck, looking over at New Jersey, feeling the nerves in their legs click from all the dancing and feeling tired and energized at the same time.

She wasn't quite sure what started it. She remembered saying something about the stars, which you couldn't see very well because of the city lights, but they were both looking up, and then there was his face filling the sky as it moved toward her and they were kissing, pretty serious kissing too.

She felt the slight prickle of his mustache, then his lips, and she felt his arms going around her. She'd expected he'd maybe be more cautious, like feeling his way along a pipe bomb, ready to jump back at any moment.

But he wasn't that way at all. No reluctance, no hesitation. She guessed maybe she was the first girl he'd kissed like this since Cheryl had left. She knew he wanted her. Her arms went tight around his neck.

She maneuvered them into the bedroom.

A huge stuffed dragon sat in the middle of the bed.

"A monster," he said.

"A friendly monster."

"What's his name?"

"*Her* name is Persephone."

"My apologies."

Rune picked up the dragon and held the mouth up to her ear.

"She forgives you. She even likes you."

For a moment nothing moved, neither of them spoke. Then he knelt on the bed.

Her arms went around him, kissing hard, pressing, hands hungry. The dragon was still in between them. She considered making a joke about it. About something coming between them, ha, ha, but he was kissing her fast, urgently.

Rune grabbed the toy and dropped it on the floor.

■

When Nicole D'Orleans opened her eyes—gasping, gulping in air, mouth wide—when she came to, she was naked. Her arms were over her head, her wrists tied to the ends of the pot and pan rack. Her feet just touched the ground.

Good. He was worried that he'd hit her too hard.

He looked at the knots. Tied expertly, not cutting off circulation, but no way could she pull free from the binding.

"No! What're you doing?" She was crying.

Tommy was wearing a black ski mask. He was naked to the waist, bending down under her, tying her feet the same way—with precision, care, devotion. He tied one ankle to a chromium rack on the bottom of the island.

"Noooo!" A long wail, rising at the end. She kicked at him with her free foot. He dodged away easily.

"Why are you doing this, Tommy? Why? . . ."

The camcorder was trained on her and was running. The camera lights were hot and she was sweating from the heat as well as the fear.

Patiently he bound her other foot. He was irritated, though, that there was nothing to tie it to. He had to wrap it around a cabinet hinge. "Doesn't look right." He stepped back and adjusted the camera upward, to avoid shooting the clumsy jerry-rigged job.

"What are you going to do?"

He had his hands on his hips. With his chest naked, his tight blue jeans, the mask, he was a medieval executioner.

"What do you want?" she squealed. "Leave me alone."

It often got him how stupid some people were. What did he want?

It was pretty fucking obvious to him.

He told her, "Just making a film, honey. Just what you do all day long. Only there's one difference: You tease. This is for real. This film's going to show your soul."

"You're . . ." Her voice was soft, shook with sickening terror. "This is a snuff film, isn't it? Oh, God . . ."

He pulled more rope out of his bag. He paused for a moment, studying her.

Nicole began to scream.

Tommy took an S & M gag—a lather strap with a red ball attached to it—and shoved it into her mouth. He tied it tight behind her head.

"They sell so much garbage. You know, leather panties. Face masks, jockstraps out of latex. You ask me it's too complicated. I go for the simple stuff myself. You got to get it just right. It's sort of a ritual. You do it wrong, they don't pay. This customer of mine—I'm making twenty-five thousand for this, by the way—he likes the knots to be just right. They're very important, the knots. One time, this guy wanted redheads only. Man, that's not easy. So I cruised two, three days along Highway 101. Finally found this student from some community college. Get her into this shack and made the film. I thought it was pretty good. But the customer was pissed. Know why? She wasn't a natural redhead. Her pussy hair was black. I only got five thousand. And what'm I gonna do? Sue?"

He finished the elaborate knotting, then rummaged through his bag. He found a whip, a leather handle with a dozen leather strips hanging from it. He took a long pull of vodka from the bottle. He checked the time. The customer was paying for a two-hour tape. Tommy'd make it last for two hours. He believed in the adage that the customer is always right.

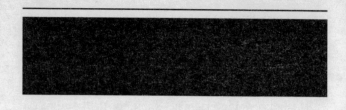

CHAPTER TWENTY-ONE

Sam Healy and Rune lay in bed, watching the lights on the ceiling, reflecting off the Hudson River.

Healy was feeling pretty good. He wanted to say, Not bad for an old guy. Or something like that. But he was remembering about times like this—and that was one thing he remembered clearly: You didn't talk about yourself.

Now, for this moment, maybe *only* for this moment, there were two of them and that was all that mattered. He could talk about her or about both of them. . . . But then he remembered something else: Sometimes it's best not to say anything at all.

Rune was curled against him, twirling his chest hair into piggy tails.

"Ouch," he said.

"Do you think people live happily ever after?"

"No."

She didn't react to that and he continued. "I think it's

like a cycle. You know, happy sometimes, unhappy others."

She said, "I think they can." A tug went by. Healy pulled the sheet over him.

"They can't see in. . . ." She pulled the sheet down and kept twisting hair. "Why do you disarm bombs?"

"I'm good at it."

She grinned and rubbed her head against his chest. "You're good at other things too but I hope not professionally."

There. *She* was talking about *him*. That was okay.

"It sets you apart. Not many people want to disarm bombs."

"IEDs," Rune corrected. "Why'd you become a cop in the first place?"

"Gotta make a living doing something."

Rune disappeared for a moment and came back with two beers. The icy condensation dripped on him.

"Hey."

She kissed him.

He said, "You want a present?"

"I like Herkimer crystals and blue topaz. Gold is always good. Silver if it's thick."

"How about information?"

Rune sat up. "You found a suspect in a red windbreaker?"

"Nope."

"You found fingerprints on one of the Angel letters?"

"Nope. But I did find out something about the explosives in the second bombing."

"And you're going to tell me?"

"Yep."

"Why?" she asked, smiling.

He didn't know. But at least this was something *he* was saying about *her*. And it seemed to make her happy.

"Because."

"What about them?" she asked.

"They were stolen from a military base. A place called Fort Ord in Monterey. Whoever did it got away with—"

"California?" Rune asked, sitting up, pulling the sheet off Healy and around herself.

"Right."

She was frowning. "Monterey is where Shelly and Tommy used to live."

"Who?"

"Tommy Savorne. Her old boyfriend. He still lives there."

Healy tugged back more of the covers. "So?"

"Well, it's just kind of a coincidence, doesn't it seem?"

"The explosives were stolen over a year ago."

"I guess." Rune lay back down. A moment later, she said, "He's in town, you know."

"Tommy?"

She nodded. "He's been in town since before the first bombing."

A tug hooted.

One of the Trump helicopters cruised low, making its run from Atlantic City.

Rune and Healy looked at each other.

███████

Healy stood at the pay phone across from the dock while Rune tugged at his arm.

"He might have been in Nam. He's about that age. He'd know how to—"

"Shhh." Healy motioned at Rune, then began speaking into the phone, "Officer Two-five-five on a landline. Patch me into ops coordinator at the Sixth."

"Roger, Two-five-five. He's in the field. Give me your number we'll have him call back on landline."

"Negative, Central. This is urgent. I need that coordinator now."

A long pause, then static, then a voice saying, "Hey, Sam. It's Brad. Whasshappenin'?"

"I may have a suspect in the porn bombings. Check CATCH, National Crime Database and Army CID. Tell me what you got on a Thomas or Tommy Savorne. I'll wait."

"Spelled?"

Healy looked at Rune. "Spelled?"

She shrugged.

"Guess."

Two minutes later the ops coordinator came back on the line.

"Got yourself a bad boy, homes. Thomas A. Savorne, private first class, LKA Fort Ord in California. Present whereabouts unknown. Dishonorably discharged a year and a half ago as part of plea bargain with JA's office for an agreement to drop court-martial proceedings. The charge was theft of government property. A codefendant was court-martialed and served eleven months on one count of theft and one count of weapons possession. Sam, the codefendant still lives out there and is believed to be dealing in arms. FBI hasn't been able to nail him yet."

"Damn . . . What'd Savorne do in service?"

"Engineer."

"So he knows demolition."

"Something about it, I'd guess."

Healy spun to Rune. "Where is he? You have any idea?"

"No . . ." And then she remembered. "Oh, Jesus, Sam—he was going over to Shelly's friend's place tonight. Maybe he's going to hurt her too." She gave him Nicole's name and address.

"Okay, Brad, listen up," Healy said. "Got a possible Ten-thirty in progress, one-four-five West Fifty-seventh. Apartment?"

He looked at Rune, who said, "I don't remember. Her last name's D'Orleans."

Healy repeated the name. "Subject probably armed, maybe with plastic, and it looks like a possible hostage situation."

"I'll get ESU rolling."

"One other thing . . . The guy's probably emotionally disturbed."

"Oh, some kind of fucking wonderful, Sam. An EDP with plastic and a hostage. I'll do *you* a favor someday. Ten-four."

"Two-five-five out."

Rune was getting her arguments ready—to talk him into letting her come with him. But there was no problem with that. Healy said, "Come on, let's hustle. I'll get a squad car at the Sixth."

━━━━

West Fifty-seventh Street was lit up like a carnival. Flashing lights, blue-and-white cars and Emergency Service Unit trucks parked in the street. The big Bomb Squad truck, with its TCV chamber on a trailer, was parked near the canopied entrance.

But there wasn't much of a sense of urgency.

Two of the ESU guys, holding those black machine guns—like they used in Vietnam—leaned against the doorway, smoking. Their hats were on backwards. They looked awfully young—like stickball players from the Bronx.

So, Rune understood, they'd gotten here in time. They'd moved fast and caught Tommy. It was all over. She looked for Nicole. What a surprise she'd have had. The knock, the door bursting open, cops pointing guns at Tommy.

He'd been the one all along, the killer. How had she read him so wrong? How had he looked so innocent? The one in the red windbreaker. Ah, the cowboy hat too. And the ruddy face—not from a tan at all but from the tear gas.

Jealousy. He'd killed her out of jealousy.

Healy stopped her as they got close to the building. "Hold up here. This isn't for you."

"But—"

He just waved his hand and she stopped. He vanished into the building. The night was punctuated with radio messages broadcast over the police cars' loudspeakers. Lights whipped around in elliptical orbits.

Rune turned on the camera and opened the aperture to take natural-light shots of the scene of them bringing Tommy out.

Motion. Men appeared.

She aimed the camera toward the door.

But he wasn't in handcuffs. God, they'd shot him! Tommy was dead, on a gurney, covered with a bloody sheet.

She felt her legs weaken as she kept the camera on the door, trying hard for a steady shot—the matter-of-fact attendants wheeling Tommy's body down from the apartment.

A grim, moving end to the film.

And Shelly Lowe's murderer died just the same way he had killed—violently. It is a fitting epitaph from the Bible—fitting for someone who concocted religious fanatics to cover up his crimes: He who lives by the sword dies by the sword. . . .

The image through the viewfinder went black as a figure from the crowd walked up to her.

Rune looked up.

Sam Healy said softly, "I'm sorry."

"Sorry?"

"We didn't make it in time."

Rune didn't understand. "You mean to get a confession?"

"To get him."

"But?—" Rune nodded with her head toward the back of the ambulance.

"Tommy was gone when they got here, Rune. That's Nicole's body."

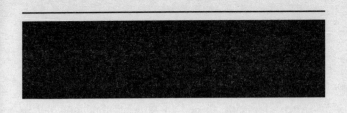

CHAPTER TWENTY-TWO

Another cop stood next to Healy. He wore a light suit that was mostly polyester, and he stood with the tired, unrushed posture of a government worker. Thin, humorless. His eyelids were heavy from fatigue and boredom.

Heavy from years of interviewing reluctant witnesses.

From years of kneeling over bodies in their graves of gutters and car seats and SRO hotels.

From seeing what he'd witnessed upstairs.

Rune whispered, "She's dead?"

The other cop was answering, but to Healy. "DCDS."

"What?" Rune asked.

Healy said, "Deceased confirmed dead at scene."

Deceased.

The cop kept speaking to Healy as though Rune weren't there. She thought maybe Healy had introduced her to this somber man. She wasn't sure. She thought

she'd heard a name but all she remembered was Homicide. "Looks like torture, strangulation, then mutilation.
There was some dismemberment." He shook his head and
finally showed some emotion. "What that goddamn business does to people. Porn . . . Like any other addiction.
Keep having to go for more and more to get a high."

Then Homicide turned to Rune. "Could you tell us
what you know, miss?"

A rambling explanation. She did her best and the man's
narrow fingers wrote quickly in a small, dime-store notebook. But she stopped quite a bit and had to throw in a
lot of "uh's" and "No, waits." She thought she knew the
story of Nicole D'Orleans better than this. But a distrac-
tion kept intruding.

It was an image of Nicole.

There was some dismemberment. . . .

She told him about her film, how she'd known Shelly,
about the film company. Then about how Tommy had
been in love with Shelly and she'd dumped him and
moved to New York and how he'd been a demolition
expert and had stolen explosives from the army—Healy
had broken in here with details. And how he must have
been so furious at Shelly for leaving him, and so crazy,
that he had contrived the idea of the Sword of Jesus and
the bombings to cover up his murder. He'd probably figured Shelly and Nicole were lovers and picked her to
ritually murder—again from jealousy.

Rune finished the story and gave him a description of
Tommy.

The detective's cheap pen danced in blotching ink over
the paper. He took it all down, in sweeping handwriting,
a man who didn't understand a thing about her documentary, about Nicole, about Shelly, about the movies they
made. He wrote without a flicker of emotion on his thin,
gray, inflexible face. He wrote down her answers, then
looked around.

Homicide waved to a scrawny Hispanic-looking wreck of a man wearing a blue headband to keep his black curls at bay.

Healy asked, "ACU?"

"He was working the crowd. Didn't know we had a positive suspect. I'll send him back with a description."

Homicide nodded to Rune. He walked to the ACU man and they began talking, their heads bent toward the ground. Neither looked in the other's eyes as they spoke.

"He's a cop?" Rune asked, staring at him.

"He's anticrime unit. Undercover. Today's ACU color is blue—see his headband? They wear that so we know he's one of us. After a murder they go into the crowd and eavesdrop, ask questions. Now that we know the suspect's ID, though, he'll just show his shield and interview them."

"Yo, bus is coming through!" a voice shouted. The EMS ambulance eased forward. Healy stepped aside. Rune shouldered the Sony and taped the boxy orange-and-blue truck as it wound through the crowd, carrying Nicole's body to the morgue.

Healy walked with her to the corner. She leaned against an express mailbox and squeezed her eyes shut.

"We were talking together, Tommy and me. I was two feet away from him. As close as you and me . . . A man like that, a killer. And he seemed so normal."

Healy was silent, looking back at the revolving lights. Though he wasn't as calm as Homicide had been, not at all. He'd seen her, Nicole, and it shook him. It occurred to Rune that one of the advantages of bomb detail was that you dealt with machines and chemicals more than people.

In a soft voice Rune said, "I was supposed to be there tonight. He wanted me to come too."

"You?"

"He said he was making a film. A legitimate film. Christ, Sam, why did he do it? I just don't understand."

"Guy blows up a dozen people just to cover up killing his girlfriend, then slaughters somebody like that . . . I don't have any answers for what makes him tick."

"When did he leave, do they think?"

"There was no postmortem lividity. No rigor mortis. Probably twenty minutes, a half hour before we got here."

"So he's still in town."

"Doubt it. People know him, people can place them together. My bet is he got a car and'll drive to some small airport, then grab a connecting flight to California. Hartford, Albany, White Plains."

"You've got to call them. Get a description—"

"We can't lock up every airport in the Northeast, Rune. They've got a citywide out on him now but he'll probably make it out of the area. They'll get him when he gets home—where is it? Monterey? The MPs'll be after him too. And theft of government property and interstate flight'll bring in the FBI."

"Oh, Sam." She pressed her head against his chest.

He held her, which made her feel good, but what made her feel even better was that they were standing in front of a half dozen of the guys he worked with and he was still hugging her, not glancing around or making it look like she was just an upset witness. He held her tight and she felt some of the horror shift away to him and she let it go. He knew what to do; he could dispose of it. That was his job.

They walked.

South, into the Theater District, then through the geometric shapes of cold neon in Times Square. Down Broadway. Past a wolf pack of four black kids wearing throwaways, with round heads and shaver-cut streaks in their hair, looking innocent and sour. Past businessmen and businesswomen in running shoes. Past hawkers, past a couple—German or Scandinavian tourists—dressed in

nylon running suits, carrying Nikons. Their heads, covered with stringy blond hair, looked around them, their
expressions asking, *This* is New York?

Past the billboards on which the fifty-foot models, re-
clining sexily, sold liquor and jeans and VCRs, past a porn
theater that gave off the smell of Lysol (maybe Shelly or
Nicole was performing on screen at that moment). There
was no way of knowing what the movies were; the marquee promised only that there were three superhot hits
showing.

"You know," Rune said, speaking her first words since
they'd started to walk. Her voice snagged. "You know that
Thirty-fourth Street used to be the big entertainment
strip? All the theaters and burlesque shows. I'm talking
turn of the century. A long time ago."

"I didn't know that."

"Times Square's pretty recent."

They walked past a big monument, a statue of a
woman in wings and robes. She gazed down at pigeons
and a dozen homeless people.

Who was she?

A Greek or Roman goddess?

Rune thought of Eurydice, then of Shelly. A captive in
the Underworld. There was no Orpheus and his lyre
nearby, though. The only music was from a scratchy rap
song on a tinny boom box.

When they came to the Flatiron Building, they
stopped.

Rune said, "I should go home."

"You want some company?"

She hesitated. "I don't need—"

"I didn't ask *need*. I asked *want*."

Rune said, "Your house?"

"It's small, ugly. But homey."

"Tonight, I think I could go for homey."

"I've got to help with some of the paperwork—you

want to meet me there? I'll give you the keys." He wrote down the address. She took the slip of paper and the keys.

"I oughta go pick up some things at my place."

"I shouldn't be any longer than an hour or so. You all right?"

Rune tried to think of something funny and flippant to say, something a tough lady newscaster would sling out. But she just shook her head and gave him an anemic smile. "No, I'm not."

He bent down quickly and kissed her. "You want a cab?"

"I walk, I feel better." He turned away. She said, "Sam . . ."

He paused. But there was nothing at all she could think of to say.

In the houseboat Rune stacked up the tapes she'd shot—the rough footage for *Epitaph for a Blue Movie Star*—and set them on her shelf, but put the script for the narration in her bag. That was something she could ask Sam about. Tell him to pretend he was in the audience and read it to him.

But not tonight.

In the morning.

That would have to wait till the morning.

She glanced into her purse and saw the script—the one she'd stolen from Arthur Tucker's office. She picked it up, flipped through it. Hell, she'd forgotten all about it. And now that he wasn't a suspect she ought to get it back to him. Mail it anonymously. She tossed it on the table and walked into the bedroom, to her dresser. She packed a skirt, T-shirt, blouse, socks, underwear (no Disney characters, girl; go for the lacy, uncomfortable pair). She added her toothbrush and makeup and began turning out lights.

Rune paused at the living room window, looking out at the lights of the city.

Nicole . . .

Of the two—Nicole and Shelly—wasn't Nicole's the more tragic death? she wondered. Rune felt sorrier for her. Shelly, because she was smarter, more talented, an artist, was also the risk-taker. She could choose to walk right to the edge. Hell, she'd *chosen* to date Tommy. Nicole wouldn't appreciate the risks so much. She was sweet, and—despite her line of work—innocent. She'd do her nails, she'd fuck, she'd dream about opening the shoe store, dream about the advertising executive she could marry. She—

The smell.

Rune sensed it suddenly, though she understood in that instant that she had been aware of it for a long time, ever since she'd returned to the houseboat. It had a familiarity about it, but a scary one. Like the sweet-sick chemical scent that bothers you an instant before you remember it's the smell of a dentist's office.

Cleanser? No. Cologne? Maybe. Perfume.

Rune's thoughts began jumping, and she didn't like where they arrived.

Incense! Sandalwood.

The smell of Tommy Savorne's apartment.

She thought: Run, or get the tear gas?

Rune turned fast toward the front door.

But Tommy got there first, and leaned up against it. He was smiling when he locked the latch.

CHAPTER TWENTY-THREE

She fought him.

Knees, elbows, palms . . . everything Rune remembered about self-defense from a tape she'd watched over and over again because the black-belt tae kwon do instructor was so cute.

But she didn't get anywhere.

Tommy was very drunk—she realized why Warren Hathaway had thought he was older and why he'd been so winded as she'd chased him from the Pink Pussycat theater. And she was able to dodge away from his groping hands.

She grabbed a pole lamp and hit him so hard it made the flesh on his arm shake. But even though it made him uncoordinated, the liquor also anesthetized him, and Tommy just grunted, knocked the pole aside, then swiped his forearm across her face. She went to the floor hard. She tried for the tear gas but he slung her bag across the room.

"Bitch." He grabbed her by the ponytail and pulled her over to a straight-back chair, then shoved her down into it and wound brown doorbell wire around her wrists and ankles.

"No!" she screamed. The wire dug into her flesh and hurt terribly.

He sat back on his heels, rocking slowly, and studied her. His hair was greasy. The tiny crevices and cracks in his fingers were stained dark red, like Chinese crackle pottery, his shirt was stained with sweat and his jeans were dark with black shapes that Rune knew were Nicole's blood.

He leered at her. "Was she good?"

"What do you want?"

"Was it worth it?"

"What are you talking about?"

"Making love to Shelly. You were her girlfriend, weren't you? You and Nicole both were." His eyes were unfocused. "She slept with Nicole—I've seen the movies. I could see in her face how much she liked it! Did she like it with you too? Did *you* enjoy it?" Tommy squinted, then asked calmly, "Will you think about it while you die?"

"I didn't take Shelly away from you. I hardly knew her. I just—"

He opened his bag and took out a long knife. There were dark stains on the wooden handle. Something else was in his hand: a videocassette. He looked at Rune's TV set and VCR, started them both and, after three tries, slipped the tape in. A crackle, then a hum, and the screen became a fuzzy black-and-white.

He watched the set, almost incidentally, as he began mumbling, reciting a mantra. "Way I see it, pornography is art. What is art exactly? It's creation. The making of something where there was nothing before. And what does pornography show? Fucking. The act of creation." He tried to find the fast forward on her VCR but couldn't.

He turned back to her. "When I figured that out it was like a revelation. A religious experience. You *write* about fucking and it's not real. But with movies . . . you can't fake it. You are watching, like, the whole act of creation in front of you. Fucking amazing."

"Oh, God, no." Rune, staring at the screen, began to cry.

Watching:

Nicole, hanging from the rack.

Nicole, twisting, futilely, away from the swinging whip.

". . . but with film, it's so different. The artist can't lie. No way. I mean it's all right there. You've got the beginning of life right in front of you. . . ."

Nicole, begging with her eyes, maybe screaming through the gag.

Nicole, crying tears that sloughed off her makeup in brown and black stripes across her face.

Nicole, closing her eyes, as Tommy walked forward with a knife.

". . . also religious. In the beginning God *created* . . . See, created. That's a fucking wild coincidence, wouldn't you say? God and the artist. And pornography brings it all together. . . ."

Nicole, dying.

Rune surrendered to her sobbing.

Savorne watched the tape with sad, hungry eyes. "I really loved Shelly," he said in his slurred voice. "When she left me I died. I couldn't believe that she'd actually gone. I didn't know what to do. I'd wake up and there would be the whole day ahead of me without her, hours and hours without her. I didn't know what to do. I was paralyzed. At first I hated her. Then I knew she was sick. She'd gone crazy. And I knew it wasn't all her fault. No, it was other people too: people like Nicole. People like you. People who wanted to seduce her."

"I didn't seduce her!"

Rune's words didn't register. Tommy set up his camcorder, then he paused. "I'm tired. I'm so tired. It's hard. People don't understand how hard it is. It's like working in a slaughterhouse, you know? I'll bet those guys get tired of it sooner or later. But they can't quit. They've got a job to do. That's how I feel."

He switched the lights on. The sudden brilliance made Rune scream.

"When they die," he said softly, "part of me dies too. But nobody understands."

He looked at her and touched her face. Rune smelled the metallic scent of blood. Tommy said, "When you die, part of me will die. It's what an artist has to go through. . . . There was one night . . ." He seemed to forget his train of thought. He sat down, his hand on the small camera, staring at the floor. Rune squirmed. The wire was thin but it didn't give.

He finally recalled his thought. "There was one night, we were living in Pacific Grove then. Not far from the beach. It was a weird night. We'd been doing okay with the movies, making some good money. I was directing then. We were watching a rough cut, Shelly and me, and what usually happened was she got turned on watching herself and we'd have a wild time. Only this time, something was wrong. I put my arms around her and she didn't respond. She didn't say anything. She just looked at me in this eerie way. She looked like she'd seen her own death. It wasn't long after that she left me.

"I spent hours and hours thinking about it. Seeing her that way, the expression on her face . . ." He gazed at Rune, a sincere face, intense. A man talking about important things. "And I finally understood. About sex and death—that they're really the same."

He was lost in a memory for a moment, then he focused on Rune, almost surprised to see her. He dug the vodka bottle out of his bag and took another hit. He smiled. "Let's make a movie."

Tommy turned on the camera and focused it at Rune.

The sweat from the heat of the lights ran down from his eye sockets and he made no attempt to wipe it away.

Rune was sobbing.

He caressed the knife. "I want to make love to you."

He stepped forward and rested the blade on Rune's forearm.

He pressed it in and cut a short stroke.

She screamed again.

Another cut, shorter. He looked at it carefully. He'd made a cross.

"They like this," he explained. "The customers. They like little details like this."

He lifted the knife to her throat.

"I want to make love to you. I want to make love to—"

The first shot was low and wide. It took out a lamp.

Tommy was spinning, looking around, confused panic in his eyes.

The second was closer. It snapped past his head, like a bee, and vanished through the window, somewhere into the dark plain of the Hudson.

The third and fourth caught him in the shoulder and head, and he just dropped, collapsing, slumping from the waist, like a huge bag of grain dumped off a truck.

Sam Healy, breathing hard, his service Smith & Wesson still pointed at the man's head, walked up slowly. His gun hand was shaking. His face was pale.

"Oh, Sam," Rune said, sobbing. "Sam."

"You all right?"

Tommy had fallen against Rune, his head resting on her foot. She was trying to pull away. She said, panicky, through her tears, "Get him away! Get him off me. Please, get him off!"

Healy kicked him over, made sure he was dead, then

began undoing the bell wire. "God, I'm a lousy shot." He was trying to joke but she could hear the quaver in his voice.

When Rune was free, she fell against his chest.

He kept repeating, "It's okay, it's okay, it's okay."

"He was going to kill me. He was going to tape it. What he did to Nicole, he was going to do that to me."

Healy was speaking into a Motorola walkie-talkie. "Two-five-five to Central."

"Go ahead, Two-five-five."

"I have a DCDS on houseboat in the Hudson River at Christopher. Send Homicide, an EMS bus, and a tour doctor from the ME's office."

"Roger, Two-five-five. Just the DCDS? You have injuries too?"

Healy turned to Rune, and asked, "You all right? You need a medic?"

But she was staring at Tommy's body and didn't hear a word he said.

■

It was very domestic.

That was the eerie part.

Rune had wakened at seven-thirty. She'd been having a nightmare but it wasn't about Tommy or Shelly. Just some kind of forgetting-to-study nightmare. She had those a lot. But she relaxed at once, seeing Sam asleep next to her. She'd watched him breathing slowly, the slight motion of his chest, then climbed out of bed and walked into the house.

Pure burbs, pure domestic.

She made coffee and toast and looked at all the beer bottles and cheese slices and junk food in the refrigerator. Why did he refrigerate Fritos?

No, this whole thing didn't seem right. *She* ate junk food, sure, but he was a man. And a policeman. It seemed that he ought to eat something more substantial than beer and corn chips. In the freezer were TV dinners, three stacks, each different. He must work his way from right to left, she figured, so he wouldn't have the same thing twice in a row.

She walked around an ugly yellow kitchen, with huge daisies pasted on the refrigerator and pink Rubbermaid things all over the place—wastebaskets, drying racks, paper-towel holders, dish drains. Pictures of Adam were everywhere.

Rune studied it all, as she made coffee and burned bread into toast.

Was this what it was like to be a wife?

Probably what it was like to be a Cheryl.

Rune wandered through the one-story house as she sipped coffee from a white mug that had cartoons of cows on it.

One bedroom was a study. There were odd gaps in the room where furniture should have been. Cheryl had done okay, it seemed; from the looks of what was left she'd taken the good stuff.

In the white shag-rugged living room she looked at the bookcases. Popular paperbacks, textbooks from school, interior design. *Explosive Ordnance Disposal—Chemical Weapons.* . . . *The Claymore Mine: Operations and Tactics.*

The last one was pretty battered. It was also water-stained and she wondered if he'd been reading it in the bathtub.

Improvised Detonation Techniques was right next to *Mastering the Art of French Cooking.*

Sam Healy might be an easy person to fall in love with, and have fun with, but Rune could see it'd be tough to be married to him.

She walked back into the kitchen and sat at the table, which was covered with diseased Formica, and stared out into the backyard.

Nicole . . .

Nicole, suckered in by the glitz and bucks and hot lights. The coke. God, that teased hair, the glossy makeup, the dangerous fingernails, the aerobic thighs . . . A sweet simple girl, who had no business doing what she did.

Shelly and Nicole.

The Lusty Cousins . . .

Well, they were both gone now.

It seemed awful to Rune, to stumble into your death like that. It'd be better to face death head-on, to meet it, even insult it or challenge it some, rather than have it grab you by surprise. . . .

For a moment, Rune regretted the whole business—her film, Shelly, Nicole.

These porn films—it was a shitty little business and she hated it. Not a good attitude, dear, you want to make documentaries but, goddamn it, that's how she felt.

Images from last night returned. Tommy's face, Nicole's—worse, the red-stained sheet. The network of blood on Tommy's hands. The heat of the lights, the steady, terrifying eye of the camera lens aiming at her as Tommy walked forward, the sound of the bullet hitting his head. She felt her hand shaking and a terrible spiraling churn begin deep inside her.

No, no, no . . .

Sam Healy's sleepy voice called from the other room and broke the spell. "Rune, it's early. Come back to bed."

"Time to get up. I made breakfast." She was about to add, Like a good wife, but figured why give Cheryl a plug? "We do the final cut of that House O' Leather job today. The one I told you about? I've got to be at work in an hour."

"Rune," Healy called again, "come here. There's something I want to show you."

"I burned toast just for you."

"Rune."

She hesitated, then stepped into the bathroom and brushed her hair, then sprayed on perfume. Rune knew a lot about men in the morning.

CHAPTER TWENTY-FOUR

█████ *She didn't intend her life to be violent. She certainly didn't intend to die violently. But Shelly Lowe was an addict— addicted to the power that the films she made brought her, addicted to that raw urge that perhaps all artists feel to expose herself, in every sense, to her audiences.*

And just like for all addicts, Shelly ran the risk that that power would overwhelm her.

She understood that risk, and she didn't back away from it. She met it and she lost. Caught between art and lust, between beauty and sex, Shelly Lowe died.

Carved into her simple grave in a small cemetery in Long Island, New York, is the single line: "She lived only for her art," which seems a fitting epitaph for this blue movie star.

FADE OUT To:

CREDITS . . .

"What do you think?" Rune asked Sam Healy.

"You wrote that?"

Rune nodded. "It took me a hundred tries. Is it too, you know, flowery?"

Healy said, "I think it's beautiful." He put his arm around her. "Is it ready to go?"

"Not hardly." Rune laughed. "I've got to find a professional announcer to do the voice-over, then spend about three weeks editing it all together and cutting about ten hours of tape down to twenty-eight minutes. Shooting was the fun part. Now the work begins. . . . Hey, Sam, I was thinking. Anybody ever done a documentary about the Bomb Squad?"

He kissed her neck. "Why don't you call in sick today. We can talk about it."

She kissed him quickly, then rolled out of bed. "I'm already in the doghouse with Larry and Bob. I didn't bring in fresh croissants the other morning."

"This is for House O' Leather? Is that name for real?"

"I just make the commercials. I'm not responsible for the client's poor taste."

She finished her coffee. She sensed him looking at her.

No, it was more of a stare.

No, it was worse than that; it was one of those sappy gazes that men give women occasionally—when they get overcome with this *feeling,* which they think is love though it usually means they're horny or guilty or feeling insecure. You can die of suffocation under one of those gazes.

Rune said, "Gotta go." And started toward the door with a coquettish smile that sometimes had the effect of throwing cold water on men who were sloppy drunk on love.

"Hey," he said in a low way that made him sound like a cop.

I'm not going to stop. Keep it cool. Keep the distance. There's no hurry.

"Rune."

She stopped.

What I'll do is wink at him, on my way out the door, all flirty and bitchy.

"Come here for a minute."

Wink, girl. Come on.

But instead she walked back to him slowly. Deciding that she wasn't really *that* late. . . .

———

Rune sensed it the moment she walked into the office, and what she noticed was not a good feeling.

Rune hung her coat up on the peeling, varnished rack and glanced around.

What was it?

Well, first: The mail was still on the floor. Larry usually carried it to Cathy's desk—well, Rune's desk now—and looked through it.

And there was the coffee machine, which Larry always got going right away, but which was now unplugged and wasn't giving off its usual sour, scorched smell.

And there was Bob.

Who was already in the office—at 9:45! Rune could see him though the bubbly-glass partition.

Something big was up.

Two heads moved, distorted by the fly's-eye effect of the glass. Larry was in too but *that* wasn't unusual. Larry always got in early; he was afraid client checks would dissolve if he didn't pick them up early.

"It's 'er." The voice was soft, but came clearly over the partition.

Her. That tone was not good.

"Right. Less 'ave a talk."

The door opened and Larry motioned to her. "Rune. You come in for a minute?"

She walked into the office. They both looked tired and

rumpled. She began an inventory of recent screwups. It was a long list but included mostly minor infractions.

"Rune, sit down."

She sat.

Bob looked at Larry, who spoke: "What's happened is we got us a call from the client."

"Both of us," Bob threw in. "At nine this morning."

"Mr. Wallet?"

Son of a bitch, the postpro house missed the shipment. She said, "I told the postpro to ship it right away. I threatened him. He absolutely guaranteed me—"

"The tape got delivered to the client, Rune. The problem was they didn't like it."

They want me to take a cut in pay. That's what it is. House O' Leather's talked down the fee and they're going to cut my salary.

She sighed. "What was it he didn't like? It was the dominoes, right? Come on. I did the setup three times. I—"

Larry was playing nervously with a coin in his hand. "No, I think the dominoes were okay. " 'E said the logo was still a bit, you know, dodgy. But 'e could live with that."

Rune said, "The transitions? I did the dissolves real carefully. . . ."

Bob said to Larry, "Show 'er what he wasn't too 'appy about."

Larry hit the play button of the Sony three-quarter-inch tape player. A colorful copyright slate appeared. The countdown from ten began, each second marked off with an electronic beep. At three, the screen went blank. Then:

Fade in: the smiling daughter, explaining how House O' Leather wallets were handcrafted from the finest cowhide, treated and dyed according to old family traditions.

Cut to: Factory workers making wallets and billfolds and purses.

Cut to: The daughter caressing a wallet (Model HL/ 141).

Dissolve to: The dramatic domino shot.

Cut to: Two women performing oral sex on a water bed as the closing credits for *Lusty Cousins* come on the screen.

Rune said, "Oh."

Fade out.

Larry said, " 'E fired us, Rune. They aren't paying the fee, they aren't paying expenses."

Rune said, "I guess something kind of got mixed in."

"Kind of," Larry said.

Bob added, "So we're out the profits and also out of pocket about seventy-five thousand."

"Oh."

Larry said, "I know it was an accident. I'm not suggesting it wasn't but . . . Rune, you're a sweet kid. . . ."

"You're firing me, aren't you?"

They didn't even bother to nod.

"You better pick up whatever you got 'ere and 'ead out now."

"We wish you the best of luck," Bob said.

He didn't mean it, Rune could tell, but it was nice of him to at least make the effort.

Didn't mean she was no good.

Rune walked along the Hudson, staring at the olive-drab shadows stretching outward into the rippled texture of the water. Seagulls stood on one leg and hunched against the cool morning breeze.

After all, didn't Einstein get kicked out of school for failing math? Didn't Churchill fail government?

They went on to show everybody.

The difference was, though, that they had a second chance.

So that was it: no distributor. And no money for editing, voice-overs, titles, sound track . . .

Rune had thirty hours of unedited tape whose value would go to zero in about six months—the time when the world would stop caring about Shelly Lowe's death.

She went home to her houseboat and stacked up all the tape cassettes on her shelf, tossed the script on top of them and walked into the kitchen.

She spent the afternoon sipping herbal tea as she sat on the deck, browsing through some of her books. One that she settled on, for some reason, was her old copy of *Dante's Inferno.*

Wondering why that volume—not the one about purgatory or the one about paradise—was the best-seller.

Wondering about the levels of hell people descend to.

Mostly she meant Tommy as she thought this. But there were others, too.

Danny Traub, who, even if he donated money to a good cause, was a son of a bitch who liked to hurt women.

Michael Schmidt, who thought he was God and destroyed a fine actress's chance for no good reason.

Arthur Tucker, who stole Shelly's play after she'd died.

Rune wondered why descent seems the natural tendency, why it's so much harder to go upward, the way Shelly was trying to do. Like there's some huge gravity of darkness.

She liked that, *gravity of darkness,* and she wrote it down in her notebook, thinking she wished she had a script to use the phrase in.

If she hadn't died would Shelly ever have climbed out of the Underworld like Eurydice?

Rune dozed and woke at sunset, the orange disk squeezing into the earth over the Jersey flatlands, rippling in the angle of the dense atmosphere. She stretched and took a shower, and ate a cheese sandwich for dinner.

Afterward, she walked to a pay phone and called Sam Healy.

"I got fired." She told him the story.

"Oh, no. I'm sorry."

"My one regret is that we didn't ship it to the networks," she joked. "Can you imagine? *Lusty Cousins* on an ad during prime time? Boy, would that've been wholly audacious."

"You need any money?"

"Aw, this is no big deal. I get fired all the time. I think I get fired more often than people hire me. Probably doesn't work that way but it seems so."

"Well, you want to go out and get drunk?"

"Naw, I've got plans," she said. "Let's make it tomorrow."

"Fair enough. My treat."

They hung up and Rune took a couple dollars in quarters out of her pocket, called directory assistance.

She needed most of the coins. It took her quite a while to find a dance school that promised to make her an expert Texas two-stepper in just one night.

———

The place didn't exactly live up to that promise. It took a while to convince them she wasn't interested in signing up for a series of Latin dances or the "Chic to Chic" Fred and Ginger special.

But after the lessons got under way she picked up the moves pretty fast and she figured she could hold her own. The next night she surprised Healy by showing up at his place in a gingham skirt and blue blouse.

"I look like Raggedy Ann. I'll never be able to show myself south of Bleecker Street—I hope you're happy."

They went to his Texas club again and danced for a couple hours, Rune impressing the hell out of him with what she'd learned. Then an amateur caller got on stage and started an impromptu square dance.

"Enough is enough," Rune said. They sat down and started working on a plate of baby back ribs.

At eleven a couple of cops Healy knew came in and in a half hour the place was so crowded that they all left and went to another bar, a dive of a place on Greenwich Avenue. She expected them to talk about guns and dead criminals and bloodstains but they were just normal people who argued about the mayor and Washington and movies.

She had a great time and forgot they were cops until one time there was a truck backfire out on the street and three of them (Sam wasn't one) half-reached for their hips, then a second later, when they understood it was just a truck, dropped their hands, never missing a beat of the conversation and not laughing about what they'd done.

But that made Rune think of Tommy and that reminded her of Nicole and the evening went sour. She was happy to get home and into bed.

The next day she applied for unemployment at the office on Sixth Avenue, where she knew most of the clerks by name. The lines weren't long—she took that as a barometer reading of a good economy. She was out by noon.

Over the next week she saw Healy three times. She sensed he wanted to see her more but one of her mother's warnings was about men on the rebound. And getting too involved with an *older* man on the rebound didn't seem real wise at all.

Still, she missed him and on Thursday when she called she got a pleasing jolt when he said, "Tomorrow's my day off, how about we go—"

"Blow things up?"

"I was going to say, have a picnic someplace."

"Oh, yeah! I'd love to get out of the city. The streets

smell like wet dogs and it's supposed to hit ninety-seven.
The only thing is I've got this interview at a restaurant."

He said, "You're making a movie about a restaurant?"

"Sam, I'm applying for a job as a waitress."

"Postpone it for a day. We'll get out of the city."

"You're twisting my arm."

"I'll call you tomorrow with details."

"I haven't said yes."

"Tomorrow."

He hung up.

"Yes," she said.

CHAPTER TWENTY-FIVE

████████ Kent was a small town in Putnam County, sixty-seven miles north of New York City, near the Connecticut state line. The population was 3,700.

The town hadn't changed much since the day it was incorporated in 1798. It was too far from New York or Albany or Hartford for commuters, though a few people drove to and from Poughkeepsie for work at Vassar. The residents mostly made their money from farming and tourism and the staples of small-town economics: insurance, real estate and building trades.

Travel books about the area generally didn't mention Kent. The *Mobil Guide* gave the restaurant in the Travel-lodge near the Interstate a couple of stars. The Farming Museum got mentioned. So did a spring flower festival.

It was a quiet place.

Outside of the small downtown, about a mile from the last of the seven Protestant churches in Kent, was an old rock quarry. The huge pit did double duty: a Saturday night hangout for teenage boys who had either dates or six-packs of Bud, and an informal shooting range during the day. This afternoon, three men stood at a disintegrating wooden board that served as a table for bench-resting rifles and for holding ammo and targets and extra magazines.

All three were in the NRA-accepted standing firing position—right foot back, parallel to the target, left forward and pointed downrange. They were tall men with short-cut hair sprayed into place. Two of the men had graying hair and were thin. The other, a younger man with black hair, had a beer belly, though his legs were thin and his shoulders broad. They all wore light-colored shoes, light slacks (two pink and one gray) and short-sleeved dress shirts with ties kept in place with a tack or bar. In the shirt pocket of the fatter man was a plastic pen-and-pencil caddy.

They all wore teardrop-shaped shooting sunglasses tinted yellow and made out of impact-resistant glass. In their ears were flesh-colored earplugs.

One thin man and the fat man held Kalashnikov assault rifles, whose clips they had just finished emptying at paper targets 150 feet away. They rested the guns on the ground, muzzles up, and began picking up the empty brass cartridges, which they would reload themselves on the weekend.

The third man held a square, ungainly Israeli Uzi, which he fired in two-second bursts. The muzzle ended in a ten-inch sound suppressor, and the gun made a sound like a hushed chain saw.

All three guns were fully automatic and therefore in violation of federal and state law. The suppressor was a separate offense. None of the men, however, had ever even seen an agent from the FBI or BATF in this part of the county and they weren't any more secretive with these guns than they were with their favorite .30-06 deer rifle or Remington side-by-side.

The man with the Uzi aimed carefully and emptied the clip.

He took his earplug out and said, "Cease fire," although the others had already laid the guns on the bench, muzzles downrange. There were just the three of them present but they'd been raised in the protocol of firearms and adhered to formalities like this—the same as when they'd arrived, an hour before, and this man had glanced at the others and said, "Ready on the left, ready on the right, ready on the firing line . . . commence fire."

These were rituals they respected and enjoyed.

He set down the Uzi and went downrange to pick up targets. When he walked back to the shooting stations they picked up their guns, pulled out the clips, opened the bolts, put the safeties on and started toward the parking lot. The guns disappeared into the trunk of a Cadillac El Dorado.

The ride took only ten minutes. The car pulled into the black gravel driveway of a white colonial, which had been built with money from the man's insurance business. The three men walked around a fieldstone path to the entrance of a den. Inside the large room, decorated with dark green carpeting and wormwood walls, they rolled a gray tarpaulin out on the floor and laid the guns on the thick canvas. Battered metal cleaning kits appeared and the sweet smell of solvent filled the room.

In thirty seconds the guns were stripped down into their component parts and the three men were swabbing the bores with patches threaded through eyelets in the tips of aluminum rods. They lovingly cleaned their weapons.

One of the thin men, John, looked at his watch and walked to the desk—this was his house—and sat down. In seven seconds the phone rang and he answered. He hung up and returned to the blanket. He began to rub oil on the sling of his Kalashnikov.

"Gabriel?" asked Harris, the dark-haired man, the fatter one.

John nodded.

"Has he figured out what happened?"

"Yes, he has," John said.

The third man, William, said, "Who climbed on our bandwagon?"

"It seems there was a man who wanted that girl killed, the one in those filthy movies. He planted the second bomb. He was killed by the police."

"The press thinks he was behind all the bombings?" William asked.

"It seems so. To cover up what he did."

"Media," said Harris. "Blessing and a curse."

John finished assembling the Kalashnikov, closed the bolt, put the safety on and stacked the gun on a rosewood rack next to a Thompson submachine gun, a Remington pump shotgun, an Enfield .303, an M1 carbine and a .30-06 bolt-action. "What do you two think?"

Harris said, "All Gabriel's work is wasted if they think someone else did the bombings. . . . You know, though, it is a good smoke screen. There's no pressure on him now. It's a good thing we picked up the count with the passage about the third angel, after the second bomb."

William used a tiny periscope to study the bore of his gun, looking for any bits of gunpowder he'd missed. "We can't just stop. Brother Harris is right."

"No. We can't just stop," John said slowly. He poured water into a Mr. Coffee and began to brew a pot of decaf. Like the others here he felt caffeine was a sinful stimulant. "But I'm not sure I agree about Gabe. The police aren't going to ignore the other bombings. The experts will finish their reports, and they'll find out that someone else was behind them."

Harris said, "Gabriel will stay to see things through. He won't hesitate to sacrifice himself."

John said, "But he shouldn't. He's too valuable."

"Then let's give up on New York," William said. "Send him to Los Angeles. Hollywood. I've said all along we should have begun there. Nobody knows Gabriel in California. All his connections are in Manhattan."

"With all respect," John said, "I think we've got to finish what we started." He spoke softly, as if it pained him to disagree.

John's aura of gentleness was misleading. Harris and William hunted for deer and geese with that excited, hungry love of the hunt. John did not. John had been a marine in Nam and had never once spoken about his tours of duty. Harris and William knew that the ones who didn't talk about killing were the ones who had the most personal relations with it.

John said, "We can't leave New York yet." He shrugged. "That's how I feel."

William hawked and spit into a linen handkerchief. "All right. How does Gabriel feel?"

Harris snapped home the bolt of his machine gun. "He'll do whatever we want him to."

"But he should act fast."

John poured coffee into mugs and handed them to William and Harris. "Oh, he will."

William nodded, then said, "What's the target going to be?"

John's eyes flickered to an illuminated crucifix above his desk, then he looked at the other men.

"I sometimes feel great temerity at times like this," Harris said. "Deciding who should live, who should die."

"He told me about someone, Gabriel did. I think it's an interesting idea."

"Let's go with his thoughts then," Harris said, nodding. "Agreed."

"Let's pray for his successful mission."

Their eyes closed tightly as they dropped to their knees and the three men that made up the council of elders of the New Putnam Pentecostal Church of Christ Revealed, known—though only to themselves—as the Sword of Jesus, prayed. And they prayed so fervently, their grim lips moved with silent words and tears came into their eyes.

Ten minutes later they rose from the floor, feeling refreshed and cleansed, and John placed a call to Gabriel, waiting for their message in the terrible city of Sodom.

███████

Sam Healy didn't sound quite right.

Rune wasn't sure what it was. Maybe he was standing next to a five-pound wad of C-4 or a land mine.

"So. What's it going to be? Sunshine and sand? Mountains? I need fresh air and wildlife, skunks and badgers, even worms and snakes. Where're we going?"

The rush-hour traffic sped past the phone booth. It was eight a.m.

"Uh, Rune . . ."

Oh, boy. Do I know *that* tone.

"Something's sort of come up."

Sort of, yeah.

"What? You on an assignment?"

Silence.

Healy said, "I want to be honest with you. . . ."

Oh, shit. She hated that word: *Honest.* It was like *Sit down, dear.* Right up there with *There's something we have to talk about.*

"Cheryl called," Healy said.

Hey, not the end of the world.

Not so far.

"Is Adam okay? Is anything wrong?"

"No. Everything's fine."

Another pause.

"She wanted to see me. To talk about . . . our situation."

He's told her about me? A warm burst of pleasure in her stomach. Rune asked, "Our . . ."

"I mean, Cheryl and me," Healy said.

"Oh." That *our*.

"I know we made plans but I thought I ought to . . . I wanted to be up-front with you."

"Hey, not a problem," Rune said cheerfully. I'm not going to ask. No way in the world am I going to ask. . . . Where they go, what they do, that's their business. *I will not ask.* Rune asked, "Is she going to spend the night?" Oh, shit, no, no, no . . . "I'm sorry, it's none of my business."

"No, she isn't. We're not even going to have lunch or anything." He laughed. "We're just going to talk. On neutral ground."

Discuss their situation? The bitch dumped him. That's not a situation; that's warfare.

As politely as possible: "Well, I hope you both get everything resolved."

Big grin on my face. I'm so proud of myself.

"I'll call you tomorrow," he said.

"No phone, remember?"

"You call me?"

"Will do."

"You don't sound pissed . . ."

Don't I? I'll try harder. . . .

". . . but you probably are. The thing is, I like you a lot, Rune. I didn't want to lie to you."

"Honest, yeah, I appreciate honesty, Sam. That's very important."

They hung up.

"Fuck honesty," she said out loud.

He should've lied through his teeth. Told me he was

dismantling bombs. That he had to have his gallbladder out. That he had tickets to take Adam to the Mets.

She leaned against the phone stall for a moment, looking at the graffiti sprayed on the clear glass sides of the booth. A motorcycle went past. A voice called, "Wanna ride?" But the Honda didn't slow down.

Sweat ran, tickling in streams down her face. She wiped it away and walked west toward the river. She stepped in a blob of tar that grabbed her shoe. It came away with thick black strings attached.

Rune sighed and sat down on the curb, wiping off what she could.

Picnic, she was thinking. Beach. Mountains.

He could have told me he had a headache. Or he got a stomach flu.

Talk about their situation . . .

Dump her, Healy, Rune thought. She's no good for you.

She knew, though, where it would end up.

He'd go back to the wife.

It was so hyperobvious. Back to Cheryl, with her daisy contact paper. Cheryl, with her white silk blouses and big boobs. The Darling-I'm-making-eggplant-casserole-for-the-Andersons Cheryl. Who was probably a perfectly fine person and who only walked out after he refused her tearful and perfectly reasonable request to get out of bomb detail.

She'd be decent, sweet, a good person. A perfect mother.

How I hate her. . . .

Rune had canceled the restaurant interview, thinking she'd be on her way to the beach. She didn't have any money to work on her film. She was stuck in deserted New York over a blistering hot August weekend. And her only boyfriend was going to shack up with his wife that night.

Aw, Sam . . .

It was then that she glanced up to a storefront window and saw an old sign, faded and warped, that advertised tax return preparation by a CPA.

Rune looked at the sign, smiled, and said, "Thank you, Lord."

She stood up and left black footprints of tar all the way back to the phone.

■■■■

Rune opened the door of her houseboat and let Warren Hathaway, carrying several beach bags, inside. In sports clothes—shorts, a dark green Izod shirt and tennies—he was much less of a nerd than he had been in the suit.

"Hey, Warren, you're looking pretty crucial."

"Crucial?"

"Jazzed? You know, cool."

"Well, thanks." Hathaway laughed.

"You like?" Rune did a pirouette. She wore a miniskirt and red tank top over her bikini.

"You're looking pretty crucial yourself. What are those on your skirt? Electric eels?"

She looked down at the squiggly lines radiating from larger squiggly lines. "It's from South America. I think they're landing pads for spaceships."

"Ah. Spaceships, sure."

Rune slung her leopard-skin bag over her shoulder and locked the front door.

"I was really glad to hear from you. I was going to call. I mean, I *did*—at that place you used to work. But they said you didn't have a phone at home. I'm glad you called. I didn't know if I'd ever hear from you again."

No way was she going to say that she'd been stood up or—at least until he had a few drinks in him—that she needed some backing for her film and had he thought any more about the investment idea? So she just said, "I thought it might be fun to get some fresh air. I didn't mean to wheedle a trip to Fire Island. You have a place out there?"

They walked down the wharf to his car.

"I wish. I'm in a summer share. A lot of the people from the firm go in together. When you said you wanted to get out of the city I thought about the Island.

"I've never been there. Why do they call it that, I wonder. Fire Island."

Hathaway shrugged. "I'm not sure. I'll look it up and give you a call."

Rune looked at the frown on his face as he memorized his task. Seemed like he still needed a little work at loosening up, according to mother's instructions.

They loaded their bags into the trunk and got into the car.

"Put your seat belt on," he said.

"Yessir."

He started the car and drove out onto the highway, heading south.

Rune didn't even have to bring up the topic. Before they'd gone a half mile Hathaway said, "I've run a lot of numbers on documentary films. They're kind of encouraging. It's not a gold mine. But it looks like there's money to be made. We'll go over the details if you want."

"Well, sure."

He signaled and checked his blind spot as he cautiously changed lanes.

In two hours they climbed off the ferry and trekked over the sandy sidewalks to his vacation house, halfway between Kismet and Ocean Beach on Fire Island. The place was a cheap assembly of sharp-angled gray wood and glass and yellow pine with polyurethane so thick the grain was distorted by the lens of the coats. When Warren finally got the door open—he had key trouble—Rune was disappointed. The windows were filthy. The grit of sand

and salt was everywhere. The stench of Lysol and the sour scent of mold fought for supremacy.

A crummy house, a romantic beach—and an accountant . . .

Thanks tons, Sam.

But, hey, life could be worse. At least he was a rich accountant, almost ready to invest in her documentary film.

And besides, they had a fierce yellow sun and a case of Budweiser and potato chips and Cheez Whiz and Twinkies and the restless Atlantic Ocean.

Who needed anything but that?

■■■■■

Arthur Tucker, no longer dressed in his workaday suit but in an old work shirt and slacks and rubber-soled shoes, sat forward in the back of a taxicab and told the driver to go slower.

They were cruising along the West Side Highway.

"What're we looking for?" the man asked in a thick accent.

"A houseboat."

"Ha. You kidding."

"Slower."

"Here," he said. "Stop here."

"You sure?" the driver asked. "Here?"

Tucker didn't answer. The Chevy pulled to a stop. He climbed out of the cab, picked up the heavy canvas bag beside him and paid the driver. He made a point of not asking for a receipt; the less evidence, he knew, the better.

CHAPTER TWENTY-SIX

■■■■■ Harris said, " 'These are they which came out of great tribulation, and have washed their robes, and made them white in the blood of the Lamb.' "

John ran his finger along his tattered King James. " 'God shall wipe away all tears from their eyes, and there shall be no more death, neither sorrow, nor crying, neither shall there be any more pain. . . .' "

The two men, along with William, said a perfunctory "Amen."

John sipped his lemonade and marked the passage. There were no priests in their church. Since God's terrible and just will touched every soul (every believing, nonsinning, white soul, that is) equally, there was no need for ordination. Laymen gave sermons and conducted services. John was a favorite speaker.

He looked at his watch and glanced at the other two, who nodded. He then made a long-distance phone call.

On the fourth ring, it was answered.

"Gabriel? How are things? . . . Good. So pleased to hear it. Brothers Harris and William and I are here together. Our thoughts are with you. . . . We're ready to do what you asked."

John listened, nodding. His graying eyebrows lifted and his face flushed with excitement. "What's the number?"

He jotted down a phone number in New York.

He hung up the phone and turned to Harris. "He's had a brilliant thought. Since no one believes we exist he said he's decided to create a living testament to the will of God." He looked at the phone number and began to dial.

―――

The room seemed smaller with his wife in it.

Healy's impression was that she'd grown. But maybe it was just that rooms are always smaller with your ex in them.

"How you doing?" Healy asked.

"Not bad. You?" Cheryl responded. "You've gained weight."

"I don't work out like I used to."

"You're not spending three nights a week at the gym?"

He didn't answer and she didn't comment further.

"Adam tells me you have a girlfriend."

"Not a girlfriend really."

"She's young, he says."

"You were the one—" Oops. Watch that.

"I'm not saying anything. I didn't expect you to be celibate."

"We're just friends."

"Friends." Cheryl was wearing a pink dress. She looked like she could be in a Betty Crocker commercial. Cheerful and efficient, smacking a sifter to dislodge bits of flour.

Healy thought she should look more, well, suicidal about the breakup.

They sat close together on the couch. Healy decided he'd have to get more furniture. He asked, "You want anything? A drink?"

"Nope."

He said, "I haven't gotten the divorce papers yet."

"I haven't had my lawyer serve them."

"I thought you were in a hurry," he said.

"I'm not sure I'm in a hurry."

"Oh."

The sunlight fell in a familiar pattern on the white rug. He remembered the day they bought it. They'd bought shag because it seemed ritzier even though it was cheaper than pile. He remembered the salesman. A young man with razor-cut black hair and eyebrows that formed a single band across his face. He and Cheryl had gone out to the food court in Paramus Mall afterward and made love when they got home. On the old carpet.

Today they talked for an hour.

Healy wasn't sure how the words were going. It seemed familiar terrain, though the tone was different this time. He didn't feel defensive. He wasn't desperate or confused. Maybe it was because he'd been seeing Rune, maybe because he felt that somehow the equilibrium of the house had shifted and it was now *his* home more than it was *theirs*. Every so often they'd fall back into the roles of adversaries. Boy, that was familiar: *Hey, that was you, not me. . . . If you'd said anything, I could have . . . That wasn't my fault. . . . Sure, say it all you want, you know it's not true. . . .*

The old arguments . . . I'd rather deal with a pipe bomb any day. . . .

But neither of them had the urge to go for the throat. And once that harmless sparring was done they were just having a good time. Healy got some beers and they began to reminisce. Cheryl was talking about the time an old friend called up to say they couldn't make it for dinner because his wife just left him but could he come tomorrow, only without the casserole because he didn't know how to make one.

And Healy mentioned the time they came home and found the dog standing in the middle of the dining room table, peeing on the candlestick.

And they both laughed about the night they were staying at Cheryl's parents' house, and remember, on the billiard table in the rec room?

"Like I could forget? . . ."

Then there was silence and it seemed that they had come to the point where a decision was supposed to be made. Healy didn't know what the choices were, though, and he was stalling. He left it to Cheryl but she wasn't much help, either. She sat with her hands together, looking out the window she'd cleaned a thousand times at the yard he'd mowed a hundred.

Healy finally said, "Honey, you know, I was thinking—"

The phone rang.

He wondered if it would be Rune and how to handle it.

It wasn't.

"Sam?" the ops coordinator from the squad asked. "We got a live one."

"Tell me."

"A call from those Sword of Jesus assholes. The device is in a bag on a houseboat in the Hudson—"

"Houseboat? Where?" His heart thudded.

"Around Christopher. Maybe Eleventh."

"That's my friend's," he whispered.

"What? That girl who was in here?"

"Yeah."

"Well, don't panic. We've got a clean frozen zone and the boat's empty. She's not there."

"Where is she?"

"I don't know but we searched the boat."

"What's the device?"

"Different this time. The portable got a look at it before he called us. Looks like it's a bit of C-3 or C-4 embedded with ball bearings. Not much charge. Only a few ounces."

"So, antipersonnel." Ball bearings or coins were added to explosive to cause the most damage to human flesh.

"Right."

"Can the robot get it?"

"Nope. It's on the deck. Too narrow."

Healy pictured Rune's boat. Knew it would have to be a hand entry.

"Hell, get a bomb blanket over it and let it detonate."

"Only one problem. Your girlfriend didn't realize it, I assume, but she's docked right next to a barge that's filled with five thousand cubic yards of propane. That bomb goes and takes out the barge—that'll ignite three square blocks of the West Side."

"Hell, tow it out there."

"I made a call and it'll take two hours to get a tug there and get the barge rigged to move. It's bolted to off-loading pumps on shore. You can't just move the damn thing."

"And how much time do we have till the device goes?"

"Forty-five minutes."

"I'll be right there."

"One thing, Sam. It's weird."

"What's that?"

"The Sword of Jesus . . . they didn't just call in a threat. They said, 'Get the Bomb Squad over to this houseboat in the Hudson at Christopher.' It's like that was the most important thing, getting somebody from the detail there."

"That's why it's antipersonnel, you think?"

"Yep. I think it's directed at us."

"Noted," Healy said. He hung up. Turned to Cheryl, who'd heard the conversation.

He wondered if she was going to give him one of

her exasperated looks. The Here-he-goes-again look. The shield against his stubbornness and selfishness. But, no, Cheryl was standing up, letting her white patent-leather purse fall to the floor, then walking straight to him. She eased her arms around him. "Be careful." He was surprised at how tightly he found he was holding her.

———

Breathing hard, in the bomb suit.

Walking up the gangplank onto Rune's houseboat. Trying not to think about the last time he was here. About them lying in bed together. About the stuffed toy, Persephone, falling to the floor.

He saw the bag, peeked inside.

Okay. Problems.

It was one of the most sophisticated bombs he'd ever seen. There was an infrared proximity panel so that if a hand got close it would detonate. And it had a cluster shunt—twenty or thirty fine wires running from a shielded power source to the detonator. With a typical two-wire shunt, if you cut them simultaneously, you might be able to disarm. But it was impossible to cut this many shunt wires. The timer was digital, so there was no way to physically gum up the mechanism.

And to top it off, there was a mercury rocker switch in the middle of the shuts.

Great, a rocker switch in a bomb on a houseboat . . .

Healy gave these details to the ops coordinator, who along with Rubin and several other members of the squad huddled behind sandbags at the end of the pier. They'd made the decision to bring only a few officers here; if the propane barge went up, whoever was within two blocks would be killed, and they couldn't risk losing the majority of the squad.

"I could cut the rocker switch," he said, breathing

heavily. It wasn't shunted. "But I can't get into the bag. The proximity plate'll set it off."

"How sensitive's the rocker?" Rubin asked through the radio.

"Pretty," he replied. "Looks like anything over three or four degrees'll close the switch."

"Could you freeze the mercury?"

"I can't get anything into the bag. The prox switch."

"Oh, right."

"I'll just have to move it out slowly."

Healy surveyed the scenario. He'd move the bomb to the gap in the houseboat railing where the gangplank was. That would be all right; the bag would stay relatively flat. But then he'd have to pick it up and carry it, by hand, down the gangplank and then to the TCV, which had been driven out onto the pier, ten feet from the house-boat.

That'll be the longest ten feet of my life.

He glanced at the timer. Seventeen minutes left.

"I need some oil."

"What kind?" Rubin asked.

"Any kind."

"Hold up. . . ."

Fifteen minutes . . .

He was startled when Rubin appeared beside him with a can of 3-In-One oil.

Healy shook his head in thanks—Rubin wasn't wired into the radio any longer—and poured the oil on the painted deck of the houseboat, to minimize the friction when he moved the bag. He tossed the can aside and then reached out and gripped a corner of the canvas. Thought of Adam, thought of Cheryl, thought of Rune. He started to pull it toward him.

Rune watched Warren Hathaway walk down the path to the beach, where she was sunning on a large towel.

"I've just been on the phone with some investors. Here's what I've arranged. Not great but, considering you don't have a track record making films, I think you'll be happy."

The way it would work was this: Warren Hathaway would loan her the money to finish the editing and post-production work. It would be a straight loan at just eight percent interest. He'd said, "Prime is twelve but since you're a friend . . ."

She'd hugged him.

"I'd go lower but the IRS imputes income if the interest isn't market value."

What*ever* . . .

Then, he explained, they'd do something called a joint venture, a phrase Rune had never heard before and that started her giggling. When she'd caught her breath he'd told her that he'd underwrite the cost of finding a distributor, then they'd split the profits. She'd get eighty percent, he'd get twenty. Was that okay with her?

"More than okay. Hey, this sounds like real business. Adult, grown-up business."

"I'll go let them know."

Then he'd gone into the house and left her on the wide beach, dozing, thinking about Sam Healy, then about her film, then dozing again, then trying *not* to think about Sam Healy. She heard the water crash and the gulls hover overhead, squawking. Rune fell asleep to that sound.

An hour later she woke up, with the first sting.

Rune looked at her arm.

Oh, brother. . . .

I have dark hair and dark skin and I've got a half inch of sunscreen on me. There's no way I should have a third-degree burn.

But she felt the blisters forming on her back—a crawling, chill, damp sensation.

She slowly sat up, dizzy, and threw a blanket over her shoulders. She walked toward the house.

Maybe she could ask Warren to rub some Solarcaine on her, but she decided that one thing would lead to another. . . . Not that he wasn't cute, not that she wouldn't love to make Sam Healy a little jealous. But with Warren's interest in her film she figured that no sex made the most sense. Keep it professional.

Her back pricked with an infuriating itching and she danced over the hot concrete of the patio into the house.

Warren was inside, looking into his gym bag.

"I hope you've got Solarcaine in there," she said. "Or Bactine. I'm lobster woman."

"I think I've got something to fix you right up."

She looked around. "Didn't you have two bags?"

"Yeah," he said matter-of-factly. "I left one at your houseboat."

"Oh, too bad."

"No, I did it on purpose." He rummaged, squinting into the bag.

"You did, why?"

"To keep the Bomb Squad busy."

And he took a red windbreaker from the bag, unwrapped it carefully and set a fist-sized wad of plastic explosive and detonator on the tacky driftwood table.

CHAPTER TWENTY-SEVEN

███████ She got as far as the glass door.

Hathaway looked soft but he was tougher than coat-hanger wire. He latched onto her wrists and wouldn't let go, then dragged her back into one of the wood-paneled bedrooms. Just like on the pier. He was the one who'd followed, he was the one who'd attacked her!

He slapped her hard and she spiraled down to the ground. She couldn't get her hands up for protection. Her head hit first. She lay for a moment, stunned, the pain radiating from her eyes back into her skull. She felt a punch of nausea.

"Warren—"

"Gabriel," Hathaway said, as cheerfully as if he'd just picked her up at a church social. He stepped out of the bedroom to collect the bag and the explosive. As he walked back, sipping his iced tea, he said to her, "You can call me Gabriel."

Rune whispered, "The Sword of Jesus . . . There really *is* a Sword of Jesus. . . ."

"And we're very upset that people think we were just the creation of some psychotic murderer. We have you to thank for that. You and that film of yours."

"What do you want? What are you going to do to me?"

Hathaway began taking tools and wire and small boxes out of his canvas bag. "You have to understand I don't feel we can eliminate sin and evil. There've always been whores, there's always been sin. But there have also been those who fight against it, even if they have to sacrifice their own life." He looked at her carefully and when he spoke, the reasonable tone in his voice was somehow as terrifying as Tommy Savorne's craziness had been. "We're like advertising in a way. We get the message across. What people do with that message is up to them."

Rune said, "You weren't a witness at all. The first bomb—you planted it."

"As I was leaving the theater, a man stopped me. He called me 'brother.' He had a kind face. I thought I could help him, I could get him to repent and accept Jesus. Even if we both died in the blast he'd be entering the Kingdom of God. That would have been such a marvelous thing. Unfortunately, what he was looking for wasn't salvation at all but twenty dollars for a blow job. As I turned to leave the bomb went off. It removed most of his head but what was left of his body saved my life. That's ironic, I suppose. God works in strange and wonderful ways."

And the injuries on her face—part of that was the tear gas.

Rune realized too that he'd lied about the man in the red windbreaker being older—to shift suspicion away from himself. And he'd worn the hat to cover up his bald head.

Hathaway continued. "I saw you outside the theater. Saw you with the camera. I thought you were one of those sinners. I was going to kill you. But then I thought maybe we could use you." He nodded around the room. "And I guess I was right."

"What are you going to do with me?"

"Make you a living testament to the will of God."

"Why me? I don't make those movies."

"You were doing this film about a pornographic actress. You're idealizing her—"

"No I'm not. I'm showing what the business did to her."

"She got exactly what she deserved. You should make your movies about missionaries, about the glory of God—"

"I'll show you my film! There's nothing glamorous about it."

Hathaway looked at her and smiled. "Rune, we all have to make sacrifices. You ought to be proud of what's going to happen to you. I think the press coverage should last a year. You're going to be famous."

He sat down on the small bed, spreading out the components of the bomb, examining each one carefully.

She eased forward, her feet sliding under the bed slightly.

Hathaway said, "Don't think about jumping at me." The box cutter she remembered from the first attack on the pier was in his hand. "I can hurt you in very painful ways. It's why I wear a *red* windbreaker—I sometimes have to hurt people. They sometimes bleed."

Rune sat back on the bed.

Hathaway spoke in a soothing tone as he pressed a white cylinder into the middle of the wad of explosive. "This is about three ounces of C-3." He looked up. "I wouldn't go into this detail normally but since you're going to be my partner in this project I thought you'd like to know a little about what to expect. It's not fair to let you think you can just pull the wires out and wait for help." He held up a black plastic box, which he pressed the explosive into. "And what we have here is very clever. A rocker box. It has a liquid mercury switch. If you pick it up and try to pull the detonator out the switch sets off the explosive. The battery's inside, so you can't cut the power." He ran wires to another small black box with a clock on it. "The timer. It's set and armed electronically. There's a shunt. If you disconnect the wire or cut it the detonator senses a drop in voltage and sets off the bomb." He smiled. "God gave men such miraculous brains, didn't he?"

"Please, I'll do whatever you want. Do you want me to make a movie about God? I can do that."

Hathaway looked at her for a moment. "You know, Rune, there are clergy that will accept repentance at any time, whether the sinner's acting of his own will or whether he's, say, being tortured." He shook his head. "But I'm funny. I need a little more sincerity than this situation warrants. So in answer to your question: No, I don't want a little whore like you to make a movie about God."

Rune said, "Yeah? And what do you think *you* are—a good Christian? Bullshit. You're a killer. That's all you are."

Hathaway's eyes lifted to her as he picked up the wire. "Swear all you like. God knows who His faithful are."

He stood back. "There we go." He placed the assembly of boxes and wires on the night table and slid it into the middle of the room. "Now let me tell you what's going to happen." He was proud. He looked critically at the ceiling and walls. "The explosion will take out most of the inner walls—they're only Sheetrock—and the floor and ceiling too. The outer wall is structural and shouldn't collapse. On the other hand you wouldn't want to be caught between that wall and the bomb."

Hathaway bounced on the floor near the bomb.

"Wood." He shook his head. "Hadn't counted on that. Splinters are going to be a problem. Fire too. But you'll just have to hope for the best. Now, there's easily enough explosive here to kill you. In fact, I'd say you've got a twenty percent chance of getting killed outright. So I would suggest you take the mattresses and springs and lay them over you. . . ." He looked around. "In that corner there. You'll be blown into the living room. It's hard to know exactly what'll happen but I can guarantee that you'll be permanently deafened and blinded. When C-3 goes off it spreads poisonous fumes. So even if you aren't blinded by the explosion you will be by the smoke. I think you'll probably lose an arm or leg or hand. Lung burns from the fumes. Can't tell for sure. Like I was saying, the splinters are going to be a problem. That's how most sailors were killed in nineteenth-century naval warfare, by the way. Splinters, not cannonballs. Did you know that?"

"Why are you doing this to me? What's the point?"

"So you'll tell everyone about us. People will believe us and they'll be afraid. You'll live off charity, you'll live off God's grace. You might die, of course. In fact, you can always choose that. Just pick it up." He gestured to the box. "But I hope you won't. I hope you realize what kind of good you can do, what kind of message you can leave for our poor sinful world."

"I know who you are. I can tell—"

"You know Warren Hathaway, which isn't, of course, my name. And how are you going to pick me out of a lineup without eyes?" He laughed, then nodded at her and said, "You have thirty minutes. May God forgive you."

Rune stared back at him.

Hathaway smiled and shook his head and left the room. She heard a half-dozen nails slamming into the frame of the door. Then there was silence. A moment

later, the black box clicked and a red light came on. The
hand of the clock started moving.

She ran to the window and drew her hand back to
smash through the glass with her palm.

Suddenly the window went black and she gave a soft
whimper as Hathaway began nailing the thick plywood
sheet over the glass.

"No, no," she was crying, afraid the huge booming of
the hammering would set off the bomb.

███████

Ten minutes.

The canvas bag was at the gap by the gangplank.

Sam Healy took a deep breath. Looked at the containment vehicle.

The longest ten feet . . .

"How you doing, buddy?" the ops coordinator asked
through the radio headset.

"Never been better," Healy replied.

"You got all the time in the world."

Breathing. In, out. In, out.

He bent over the canvas bag and carefully closed the
top. He couldn't keep it level holding it by the strap so
he'd have to grip the base with both hands and pick it up.

He backed down the gangplank, then went down on
one knee.

Breathe, breathe, breathe.

Steadiest hands in the business, someone had once said
about Healy. Well, he needed that skill now. Fucking
rocker switches.

He bent forward.

"Oh, Jesus Christ," came the staticky voice in the radio.

Healy froze, looked back.

The ops coordinator, Rubin and the other men from
the squad were gesturing into the river, waving madly.
Healy looked where their attention was focused. Shit! A

speedboat, doing thirty knots, was racing along, close to the shore, churning up a huge wake. The boater and his passenger—a blonde in sunglasses—saw the Bomb Squad crew's gesturing and waved back, smiling.

In ten seconds the huge wake would hit the boat, jostle it and set off the rocker switch.

"Sam, get the fuck outa there. Just run."

But Healy was frozen, staring at the registration number of the speedboat. The last two numbers were a one and a five.

Fifteen.

Oh, Christ.

"Run!"

But he knew it would be pointless. You can't run in a bomb suit. And besides, the whole dock would vanish in the fiery hurricane of burning propane.

The wake was twenty feet away.

He bent, picked up the bag with both hands, and started down the gangplank.

Ten feet from the houseboat.

Halfway down the gangplank.

Five feet.

"Go, Sam!"

Two steps and he'd be on the pier.

But he didn't make it.

Just as he was about to step onto the wood of the pier the wake hit the houseboat. And it hit so violently that when the boat rocked, the gangplank unhooked and fell two feet to the pier. Healy was caught off balance and pitched forward, still clutching the bomb.

"Sam!"

He twisted to the side, to get his body between the bag and the propane barge, thinking: I'm dead but maybe the suit'll stop the shrapnel.

With a thud he landed on the pier. Eyes closed, waiting to die, wondering how much pain he'd feel.

It was a moment before he realized that nothing had happened. And a moment after that before he realized he could vaguely hear music.

He sat up, glanced at the sandbags, behind which the squad stood immobilized with shock.

Healy unzipped the bag and looked inside. The rocker switch had closed the circuit. What it had set off, though, wasn't the detonator but apparently a small radio. He pulled the helmet off the bomb suit.

"Sam, what're you doing?"

He ignored them.

Yeah, it was definitely music. Some kind of easy listening. He stared at it, unable to move, feeling completely weak. More static. Then he could hear the disc jockey. "This is WJES, your home for the sweetest sounds of Christian music. . . ."

He looked at the explosive. Pulled off the glove and dug some out with his fingernail. Smelled it. He'd have recognized that smell anywhere—though not from his bomb disposal training. From Adam. The explosive was Play-Doh.

███████

Rune didn't waste any time trying to break through the walls. She dropped to her knees and retrieved what she'd seen under the bed when he'd first dragged her into the room.

A telephone.

When Hathaway had seen her ease forward on the bed, it wasn't because she was about to leap. It was because she'd seen an old, black rotary dial phone on the floor. With her feet she pushed it back into the shadows under the bed.

She now pulled it out and lifted the receiver. Silence. No!

It wasn't working. Then her eyes followed the cord.

Hathaway, or somebody, had ripped the wire from the wall.

She dropped down to the floor and, with her teeth, chewed off the insulation, revealing four small wires inside: white, yellow, blue, green.

For five minutes she stripped the four tiny wires down to their thin copper cores. Against the wall was a telephone input box with four holes in it. Rune began shoving the wires into the holes in different order. She was huddled, cramped on the floor, the receiver shoved under her chin.

Finally, with the last possible combination, she got a dial tone.

The timer on the bomb showed twelve minutes.

She pressed 911.

And what the hell good is that going to do? Did they even *have* a fire department on Fire Island? And how could she even tell them where she was?

Shit!

She depressed the button and dialed Healy's home number.

No answer. She started to slam it down, then caught herself and cautiously pressed the button again—feeling as if she had only a few dial tones left and didn't want to waste them. This time she called the operator and told her in a breathy voice that it was an emergency and asked for the 6th Precinct in Manhattan. She was astonished. In five seconds, she was connected.

"It's an emergency. I need to speak to Sam Healy, Bomb Squad."

Static, someone near the switchboard telling a Polish joke, more static.

"Patch it through," Rune heard. More static. The punch line of the joke.

Static.

Oh, please . . .

Then, Healy's voice.

The operator was saying, "Central to Two-five-five. I've got a landline patch for you. Emergency, she says. You available?"

"I'm in the field. Who is it, what does she want?"

"Sam!" she shouted.

But he didn't hear.

CHAPTER TWENTY-EIGHT

■■■■■■ "Tell him Rune," she shouted to the dispatcher. "Hurry!"

A moment later the condition of the line improved, though it was still filled with static.

"Sam." She was crying. "He's got me in a room with a bomb. The Sword of Jesus bomber."

"Where are you?"

"A house on Fire Island. Fair Harbor, I think. He's put a bomb here."

Seven minutes.

"Where's the guy who set it?"

"He left. It's that Warren Hathaway . . . the witness in the first bombing. He's going back to Bay Shore on the ferry."

"Okay, I'll get a copter on its way. Describe the house." She did. Healy broke the line for a terrifyingly long twenty seconds.

"Okay, what've we got?"

"A big handful of—what is it?—C-3. There's a timer. It's set to go off in about six minutes."

"Christ, Rune, get the hell out—"

"He's nailed me in."

A pause for a moment. Was he sighing? When he spoke, his voice was soothing as a Valium. "Okay, we're going to get through this just fine. Listen up. Okay?"

"What do I do?"

"Tell me about it." Rune told him what Hathaway had said about the bomb. It seemed he whistled when she explained it, but that may have been just static.

Five minutes.

"How big is the room?"

"Maybe twenty by fifteen."

A pause.

"All right, here's the deal. You get far enough away and cover yourself up with mattresses or cushions, you'll probably live."

"But he said it'll make me deaf and blind."

There was silence.

"Yeah," he said. "It may."

Four minutes, twenty seconds.

"The thing is, you try to disarm it yourself, and it goes, it'll kill you."

"Sam, I'm going to do it. How? Tell me how."

He was hesitating. Finally he said, "Don't pull the detonator out of the explosive. There's a pressure switch in it. You'll have to bypass the shunt and cut the battery cord. You need enough electricity to keep the galvanometer fooled into thinking the cord isn't cut."

"I don't know what that means!"

"Listen carefully. Look at the bomb. There'll be a little box near the battery."

"It's gray. I see it."

"With two metal posts on it."

"Right."

Healy said, "You have to run a piece of wire that's very narrow gauge—"

"What's *gauge*?" She was crying.

"Sorry . . . I mean, it's got to be real thin. Run a piece from one lead of that box to the main terminal connecting the battery to the cable. See what I'm saying?"

"Right."

"Then you cut the wires to the timer."

Three minutes, thirty.

"Okay," she said.

"Find a piece of wire, strip the insulation off, and wrap one strand—not all of them, just one strand—around the terminal of the gray box and then the other around the terminal on the timer. Then cut the other wires from the timer."

"Okay, I'll do it." She stared at the plastic components. Picturing it.

Healy said, "Remember, you can't override the rocker switch. So don't move the bomb itself."

Through her tears she said, "They're called IEDs, Sam. Not bombs."

"The helicopter's on its way. There'll be county police meeting the ferry in Bay Shore. And we'll send one out to Fair Harbor."

"Oh, Sam. Should I just hide under the mattress?"

He paused. The static rose up like a storm between them. Then he said, " 'Believe in what isn't as if it were until it becomes.' "

Two minutes.

"I'll see you soon, Sam." Rune yanked the wires from the phone. Then, with her teeth, stripped the insulation off one of them—the white wire—and wound one strand around the two terminals, the way Healy had told her.

Ninety seconds.

Now cut through the battery cables. She bent to the bomb, smelled the oily scent of the explosive, just inches from her face, and took one of the black wires in her teeth. She began chewing. Tears fell on the plastic.

It was thicker than she thought.

Fifty seconds.

A tooth chipped and she felt an electric jolt of pain and surprise. Her breath hissed inward.

Forty.

Thirty . . .

The wire snapped.

No time for the other one. Had he said to do both of them? She thought he had. Shit. She backed away from the bomb, pulled the mattress and springs off the bed and lay down on the floor in the corner the way Hathaway had told her. Blind and deaf . . .

Thirty twenty-nine twenty-eight twenty-seven . . .

She prayed—to a God she hoped was a lot different from the one the Sword of Jesus claimed as theirs.

Fourteen thirteen twelve eleven . . .

Rune tucked her head against her chest.

Warren Hathaway was proud of his precision. When not building bombs he was in fact a bookkeeper—though not a CPA—and he enjoyed the sensuality of the act of filling in the numbers on the pale green paper with a fountain pen or a fine-tipped marker—one that did not leave indentations on the sheet. He enjoyed the exactness and detail.

He also enjoyed watching big explosions.

So when the windows of the beach house did not disintegrate in a volley of shards and the sandy earth did not jerk beneath him from the huge jolt of the bomb he felt his stomach twist in horror. He didn't swear—the thought never would have entered his mind. What he did was pick up the hammer and walk the hundred yards back into the house.

The trials of Job . . .

He knew he'd set the system properly. There was no doubt that he knew his equipment. The cap was buried in just the right thickness of plastic. The C-3 was in good condition. The battery was charged.

The little whore had ruined his handiwork.

He walked inside and then slammed the hammer down on the wooden boards barring the door. He struck them near the nails to lift their heads and then caught them in the claw. With a loud, haunted-house creak the nails began coming out.

With the first nail: He heard the girl's voice in a panic, asking who was there.

The second nail: She was screaming for help. How silly and desperate they were sometimes. Women. Whoring women.

The third nail: Silence.

He paused. Listening. He heard nothing.

Hathaway pulled the rest out. The door opened.

Rune stood inside the room, in front of the table, looking at him defiantly. Her hair was stuck to her face with sweat, her eyes were squinting. She drew the back of her hand across her mouth and swallowed. In her other hand was a leg wrenched from a table or chair.

He laughed at it, then frowned, looking past her at the bomb. He studied it with professional curiosity. She'd bypassed the shunt.

He was frowning. "You did that? How did you know—?"

She held up the club.

Hathaway said, "You whore. You think that's going to stop me?"

He stepped forward toward her. He got only six inches before he tripped over the taut strands of telephone wire Rune had strung across the bottom of the doorway.

Hathaway fell heavily. He caught himself but his wrist

bone snapped with a loud crack as it struck the floor. He shouted in pain and struggled to his feet. As he did Rune brought the club down on his shoulders as she ran past him through the doorway. It hit hard and he fell forward on his bad hand with a cry.

Hathaway was trying again to stand, supported by one knee and one foot planted on the floor, reaching into his pocket with his good hand for the box cutter. Staring at her as if she were the Devil come to earth. He started to his feet.

■■■■■■

Rune waited for just a moment, then flung the leg of the table past Hathaway.

After that, the images were just a blur:

Rune's diving fall as she threw herself to the floor against the baseboard in the living room.

Hathaway's awkward, panicked attempt to grab the leg before it hit its intended target.

Then—when he failed to stop it—the cascading flash and ball of flame as the leg struck the bomb and the rocker switch set off the C-3.

Then the whole earth joined in the blur. Sand, splinters, chunks of Sheetrock, smoke, metal—all tossed in a cyclone of motion.

Hathaway had been right about the walls. The outer one held; it was the interior walls that shattered and whistled around Rune like debris in a hurricane. The floor dropped six inches. There was no fire, though the smoke was as irritating as he'd promised. She lay curled up in a ball until her throat tightened and the coughing became too violent, then she rose to her feet—without looking into the bedroom—and staggered outside.

Deafened, eyes streaming, she dropped to her knees and crawled slowly to the beach, coughing and spitting out the bitter chemical smoke.

Fire Island was empty on weekdays; there was no one even to be enticed by the bang. The beach here was completely deserted.

Rune dropped to the sand and rolled onto her back, hoping that the surf would rise closer and closer and touch her feet. She kept urging it on, and didn't know why she felt an obsession for the touch of the water. Maybe it was primal therapeutics; maybe she needed to feel the motion of something that seemed to be alive.

At the first brush of the cold water Rune opened her eyes and scanned the horizon.

A helicopter!

She saw it coming in low, then another.

Then a dozen more! All cruising directly toward her, coming in for an urgent rescue. Then she was laughing, a deep laugh she couldn't hear but which ran through her whole body, as the helicopters turned miraculously into fat seagulls that didn't pay her the least attention as they cruised down for their ungainly landings on the firm sand.

CHAPTER TWENTY-NINE

██████ Rune spent the next couple weeks by herself. That was the way she wanted it. She saw Sam Healy a few times but she thought it was best to keep things a little casual.

And professional. There'd been some follow-up. Rune had told the police that she'd heard Hathaway on the phone not long before he'd locked her in the bedroom. He might have been talking to the others in the Sword of Jesus. The New York State Police traced the call and started an investigation of their own. Three days after Gabriel was blown to pieces three senior members of the Sword of Jesus were arrested.

There was also the matter of Arthur Tucker. When Rune arrived back at her houseboat from Fire Island she saw that it had been broken into. Nothing was missing, she thought at first, until she noticed that the script she had lifted from Arthur Tucker's office was gone.

She'd called him, threatened to call the police and tell

them that he'd stolen a dead woman's plays. The crotch-ety old man had told her, "Call away. It's got your finger-prints on it and I've already got a police report filed about a break-in a week ago—just after you came to interview me. And I'm not very happy that you told half the world I was a suspect in the case. That's slander."

Their compromise was that neither would press charges and that if he made any money from the plays, he'd donate a quarter of it to the New York AIDS Coali-tion.

Then something odd happened.

Larry—the Larry who was half of L&R—had appeared at the door of her houseboat.

"No bloody phone. What good are you?"

"Larry, I've had my abuse for the week."

"It's a bleedin' 'ouseboat."

"Want a drink?"

"Can't stay. I came by to tell you, 'e's an arse, Mr. House O' Leather, what can I tell you?"

"I still lost you the account, Larry. You can't give me my job back."

He snorted an Australian laugh. "Well, luv, that wasn't *ever* gonna 'appen. But truth is, there's this guy called me, 'e's got some ins at PBS and seems there's this series on new documentary filmmakers they're looking to do. . . ."

"Larry!"

"All right, I recommended you. And they got a budget. Not much. Ten thousand per film. But you can't bring it in under that you got no business being a film maker."

He wrote down the name. She got her arms most of the way around him and hugged him hard. "I love you."

"You fuck it up, I don't know you. Oh, and don't tell Bob. What 'e does is 'e 'as this little doll and it's got your name on it and every night 'e sticks pins—"

"That's a load of codswallop, Larry."

"Rune, that's Brit, not Aussie. Work on your foreign languages some, right?"

Five minutes after he'd left Rune was on the phone. The distributor had been pretty aloof and said, real non-committally, to submit a proposal and they'd make their decision on funding.

"Proposal? I've got rough footage in the can."

"You do?" He sounded more impressed than a film person ought to. "Everybody else has these one-page treatments."

Two days later, when she called, he told her he'd sold *Epitaph for a Blue Movie Star* to PBS. It was slotted for September, on a program about young film makers. A check for all her postproduction work would be sent shortly.

Sam Healy emerged again and began spending more and more nights on the houseboat. He complained about the rocking motion for a while, though that was mostly for effect; Rune figured something inside of him felt it was better for the woman to move into his homestead, rather than the other way around.

He saw Cheryl some, too. He told Rune about it— *Honesty, goddamn honesty*—but it seemed that their get-togethers were to discuss the sort of nitty-gritty details appropriate for people on the verge of divorce. Nonetheless, dear Cheryl still hadn't filed papers and once or twice when Rune stayed over at his place he took calls late at night and talked for thirty, forty minutes. She couldn't hear what he said but she sensed that it wasn't Police Central he was talking to.

Adam decided he liked Rune a lot and asked her advice on which rock groups were current and where to get good chic secondhand clothing. ("It's all right, Sam. You don't want him to be a geek, do you?") The two of them went to a Mets game once after Healy'd bought tickets but couldn't make it because of a travel alarm ticking away in a suitcase in a Port Authority locker. Rune and Adam had a great time; when somebody had tried to pick her up by telling her what a cute brother she had Adam had said, "Don't talk about my mom that way."

They laughed about the guy's reaction for a good portion of the trip home.

Tonight was Sunday and Sam Healy had stayed the night. He was watching the ball game as Rune looked through the *Times* working up the courage to actually cook breakfast and wondering how risky it would be to make waffles. She noticed an article, read it, sat up suddenly.

Healy looked at her.

She pointed to the story. "That guy they found in the trunk of the car at La Guardia a couple of days ago?"

"Somebody with the Family?"

"Yeah."

"What about it?" Healy asked.

"The medical examiner said the autopsy showed he'd been dead for a week."

Healy turned back to the game. "The Yankees're behind by seven and you're worried about dead hit men."

"The assistant medical examiner who did the autopsy—his name is Andy Llewellyn."

But Healy was directing all his attention to help the boys from the Bronx rally back in the eighth.

"I've got a couple errands to run," Rune said. "You'll be here when I get back?"

He kissed her. "They can do it," Healy said.

She looked at him.

"The Yankees," he said.

"I'll keep my fingers crossed," Rune said sincerely.

████

Rune went for a long walk and ended up—surprised to find herself there—in Times Square. She walked into the old Nathan's Famous and ordered a Coke and a cardboard carton of crusty French fries, which she covered with sauerkraut and ketchup and mustard and ate as best she could with the little red skewer they give you instead of a fork.

She hadn't quite finished when she got up suddenly and went outside to a pay phone. She made two long-distance phone calls and in five minutes was in a cab on the way back to her houseboat, wondering if Sam would loan her the money for a plane ticket.

■

Beneath the 727, the sheet of Lake Michigan—so much bluer than New York Harbor—met the North Shore somewhere near Wilmette. The fragile lattice dome of the Baha'i temple rose just above the dark green sponge of late-summer trees.

Rune, looking through the viewfinder of the little JVC video camera, lost sight of the temple as the plane eased out of its bank. She released the shutter. The wheels lowered with a quivering rush of protest against the slipstream, bells sounded and lights came on and in five minutes they were on the ground at O'Hare. With the roar of the reverse thrusters, the final-approach thoughts of mortality vanished.

"Welcome to Chicago," the steward said.

I don't know about that, Rune thought, and unbuckled her seat belt.

■

"This city is flat. . . . It's not like New York, where all the energy is crowded onto a rocky island. It's a sprawl, it stretches out, it's weak, it's . . ." Rune's voice faded; the miniature tape recorder sagged.

"Dissipated?" The cabdriver offered.

"Dissipated?" *Click*. She shut off the recorder.

Rune glanced at his head, balding on top but hair pulled back from the sides and tied into a long ponytail. In the rearview mirror she noticed he had a demonic goatee.

"Diffused?" he tried.

Click.

". . . It's weak and diffused. . . . Great expanses of land stretch between the pockets of . . ."

"How about *extend*?" the driver said. "You used *stretch* earlier."

"I did?" The train of her poetic thought vanished. Rune dropped the tape recorder in her bag.

"What are you, a writer?" he asked.

"I'm a film maker," she said. Which she wasn't exactly, she figured, if being something had to do with making regular money while you did it. On the other hand, *filmmaker* had a lot more class than *occasional waitress at a bagel restaurant on Sixth Avenue,* a job she'd just accepted.

Anyway, who was going to check?

The driver—actually part-time student, part-time driver—loved movies and concluded by the time the cab cruised past Lawrence Avenue that Rune should do a film on Chicago.

He shut off the meter and for the next half hour took her on a tour of the city.

"Chicago means 'Wild Onion,'" he said. "That'd be a good way to open the film."

He told her about Captain Streeter, the Haymarket Riots, Colonel McCormick, William Wrigley, Carl Sandburg, Sullivan and Adler, the Sox and the Cubs, the Eastland boat disaster, the Water Tower, Steve Goodman, Big Bill Thompson, Mayor Daley, the ugly Picasso monkey woman, snow and wind and humidity, Saul Bellow and Polish, German and Swedish food.

"Kielbasa," he said with admiration in his voice.

He talked a lot about the Great Fire and showed her

where it began, west, near the river, and where it ended, up north.

"Hey, that'd be great." He looked back at her. "A film about city disasters. San Francisco, Dresden, Nagasaki . . ."

They arrived at her hotel. Rune thanked him and decided that, while she appreciated his thoughts, it was a film she'd never make. She'd had enough cataclysm.

They exchanged names and phone numbers. He wouldn't take a tip but she promised to get some footage of him to use for atmosphere if she ever needed to.

Rune checked into the small hotel just off Lincoln Park. The room overlooked the lake and she sat looking at it for a while.

The bathroom was fantastic—enough towels so she could dry every limb with a different one. Enough mirrors so that she found she had a birthmark in the small of her back that she'd never known she had. Rune used the tiny scented cake of soap to wash her face, then the little bottles of shampoo and conditioner. That was a real treat; at home she used an old bar of Ivory for everything, including dishes. She stole the complimentary shower cap. After the shower Rune put on her one dress—a blue silk number her mother had sent her four years ago (but since she'd only worn it three times she figured it still qualified as new).

She looked at herself in the full-length mirror.

Me, in a dress, staying in a hotel that overlooks a beautiful lake with rocking, blue-green waves, in a city that burned down and has come back from the ashes . . .

Rune then turned on the desk lamp and took out her makeup kit. She began to do something she hadn't done for almost a year—put on nail polish. A dark red. She wasn't quite sure why she'd picked this shade, but it seemed sophisticated, cultured—the color you'd want to wear if you were going to the theater.

▬

"That's where John Dillinger bought the big one," a square-jawed, sandy-haired young man told her. She was eating a hamburger in a half-deserted folk music club. He'd leaned along the bar and pointed to the old Biograph movie house across the street.

"He was betrayed by a woman in a red dress," the man said, adding some flirt to his voice.

But Rune scared the guy off when she asked with gleaming eyes if you could still see the bloodstains.

The Haymarket Theater was in a small two-story Victorian building, on Lincoln Avenue, just north of Fullerton, up the street from the Biograph. She picked up her ticket at the box office and wandered into the small auditorium. She found her seat and thumbed through the program. At one minute after eight the lights went down and the curtain rose.

Rune wasn't sure what to think about the play. As much as she loved movies, she generally didn't like plays very much. Just when you started to believe the painted sets and the funny way everyone talked and walked, the two hours were up, and you had to go back to reality. It could be very jarring.

But this wasn't bad at all. At least, unlike a lot of modern plays, it had a story you could follow. It was about a young woman—played by a pretty brunette actress named Rebecca Hanson—who kept postponing her romantic life because of her family. The major incident in the play was her decision to leave home at the age of thirty-two.

There was some very clever stuff in it, like the scene where one actor's talking to another actor who suddenly becomes someone else in a flashback. It was funny in parts, then sad, then funny again. Rune cried when the actress left her small-town boyfriend and headed off for Europe.

The audience loved it and about half of them gave the star a standing ovation. The play was long; by the time the curtain calls were over, it was 10:45. The audience, all except for Rune, left soon after the lights came up.

She waited until the actors and actresses had disappeared, then strolled backstage.

No one stopped her.

Rebecca Hanson's dressing room was at the end of the corridor.

Rune paused in front of it, collected herself, then knocked.

"Yes?"

Rune opened the door.

Shelly Lowe finished wiping the cold cream off her face and gave Rune a smile. It was pretty bleak, Rune decided.

"I thought I saw you in the audience," she said. "Well, I guess we better have a little talk."

CHAPTER THIRTY

███████ The two women walked down Lincoln Avenue past the closed shops and mostly empty bars to the broad intersection at Halsted and Fullerton, then they turned east.

In front of them the street and apartment lights disappeared into an expanse of blackness. Rune wondered if that void was the lake or the park or the sky.

She glanced at Shelly, who was wearing blue jeans, a silk blouse and Reeboks.

"You don't quite look the same. Close, though."

"A little plastic surgery. Eyes and nose. Always wanted it bobbed."

"Arthur Tucker knew all along, didn't he?" Rune asked.

"It was his idea, in a way. About six months ago he found out about my movie career—of course, I didn't exactly keep it a secret. We had this terrible fight."

"I met him. He doesn't like pornography very much."

"No, but it wasn't the morality of it. He thought making the movies—what's the word?—diminished me. That's what he said. That it was holding me back from being great. It dulled me creatively. Like drinking or drugs. I thought about it. He was right. I told him, though, I couldn't afford just to quit cold. I wasn't used to being poor. I said I'd have to be crazy to quit what I'm doing. Crazy, or dead.

"He said, 'So, die.' Well, I thought about disappearing the way Gauguin did. But every city that was big enough to have good theater would also have a porn market; there was a risk I'd be recognized. Unless .. . ." She smiled. "Unless I was actually dead. A week later, that religious group set off the first bomb in the theater. The news report said some bodies had been unidentified because the blast was so bad. I got into fantasizing about what if someone had mistaken that body for me. I could go to San Francisco, L.A., even London. . . .

"I began to obsess over the idea. It became a consuming thought. Then I decided it might actually work."

"You got the bomb from Tommy's army buddy? In Monterey? The one who was court-martialed with him?"

Shelly cocked a single eyebrow. It was hard to see her as a brunette. Blonde had definitely been her color. "How did you know that?" she asked.

"Connections."

"He sells black-market munitions. He'd been a demolition expert. I paid him to make me a bomb. He explained to me how it worked."

"Then you waited. For someone like me. A witness."

She didn't speak for a moment. The park was ahead of them, off to their left; couples were walking through the trim grass and oaks and maple trees. "Then I waited," she said softly. "I needed someone to see me in the room where the explosion was."

"You tried to get me to tape it. I remember you asking

that. Then it went off. Only you were gone and the body that Andy Llewellyn'd gotten for you was next to the phone."

Shelly smiled, and Rune thought it was a smile of admiration. "You know about him? You found that out too?"

"I saw his name on your calendar. Then I saw a story in the paper the other day about a murder. It mentioned that he was a medical examiner. I figured he'd be a good source for a body."

After a moment, Shelly said, "The body . . . I remembered this guy—Andy—who'd picked me up at a bar one time. He was really funny, a nice guy—for someone who does autopsies all day. He was also making a nice low salary, so he was happy to take thirty thousand cash to get me a body and arrange to do the autopsy and fake the dentals—to identify the corpse as me. They aren't all that hard to come up with, did you know? Dozens of unidentified people die in the city every year."

She shook her head. "That night I was on some kind of automatic pilot. The body was in the room at Lame Duck where Andy and I had put it that evening, before I came over to your place for the taping session. The bomb was in the telephone. You were outside. I called to you, then went into the back of the studio and pressed a couple of buttons on this radio transmitter. The bomb went off.

"In my bag I had what was left of my savings, in cash, an original-edition Molière play, a ring of my mother's, some jewelry. That was it. All my credit cards, driver's license, Citibank cash card letters, were in my purse in the room at Lame Duck."

"Aren't you afraid somebody here will recognize you?"

"Yes, of course. But Chicago's different from New York. There are only a couple adult theaters here, a few adult bookstores. No Shelly Lowe posters, like you see in Times Square. No Shelly Lowe tapes in the windows of the bookstores. And I had the surgery."

"And dyed your hair."

"No, this is my natural color." Shelly turned to her. "Besides, you're talking to me now, a few feet away—what do you think? Do I seem like the same person you interviewed on your houseboat?"

No, she didn't. She didn't at all. The eyes—the blue was there but they weren't laser beams any longer. The way she carried herself, her voice, her smile. She seemed older and younger at the same time.

Rune said, "I remember when I was taping you, you started out being so tough and, I don't know, controlled."

"Shelly Lowe was a ballbuster."

"But you slipped. Toward the end you became someone else."

"I know. That's why . . ." She looked away. They started walking again, and Rune grinned.

"That's why you broke into my houseboat and stole the tape. It gave away too much."

"I'm sorry."

"You know, we thought Tommy was the killer."

"I heard about it. About Nicole . . . That was so sad." Her voice faded. "Danny and Ralph Gutman and all the others—they were just sleazy. But Tommy was frightening. That's why I left him. It was those films of his. He started doing real S & M films. I left him after that. I guess when he found he couldn't get off on just pain alone he started doing snuff films. I don't know."

They walked for a few minutes in silence. Shelly laughed sadly, then said, "How you tracked me down, I'll never understand. Here in Chicago, I mean."

"It was your play. *Delivered Flowers.* I saw it on Arthur Tucker's desk. He'd crossed out your name and written his in. I thought . . . Well, I thought he'd killed you—to steal your play. He really had me fooled."

"He's an acting coach, remember. And one of the best actors you'll ever meet."

"He gets an Oscar for that performance," Rune said. "I remembered the name of the theater. The Haymarket. It was written on the cover of the play. I called the theater and asked what was playing. They said *Delivered Flowers*."

Shelly said, "That was his idea, the play. He said that we'd pretend he wrote it. A play by Arthur Tucker would be a lot more likely to be produced than one by Becky Hanson. He sends me the royalties."

"None to the AIDS Coalition?"

"No. Should he?"

Rune laughed and said, "Probably he should. But things've changed since we made our deal." Thinking: Damn, that man *was* a good actor.

"Arthur got the company here to produce it and arranged for me to get the lead. . . . I thought about it afterward. It was very strange. Here, I'd had the chance to direct my own death. My God, what an opportunity for an actress. Think of it all—a chance to create a character. In the ultimate sense. Create a whole new person."

They walked along Clark Street for a few minutes until they came to a Victorian brownstone. Shelly took her keys out of her purse.

Rune said, "I don't know a whole lot about plays, but I liked it. I didn't, you know, understand everything, but usually, if I don't understand stuff all the way, that means it's pretty good."

"The reviewers like it. They're talking of taking a road company to New York. It'll hurt like hell but I won't be able to go with them. Not now. Not for a few years. That's my plan, and I'll have to stick to it. Let Shelly rest in peace for a while."

"You happy here?" Rune asked.

She nodded her head upward. "I'm nearly broke, living in a third-floor walk-up. I pawned my last diamond bracelet last month because I needed the cash." Shelly shrugged, then grinned. "But the acting, what I'm doing? Yeah, I'm happy."

Rune looked at the twisty wrought-iron gate. "We've got kind of a problem."

"What's that?"

"There's a film about you."

"The one you were working on when I was killed?" Shelly looked at her curiously. "But after the bombing . . . Well, there was nothing more for you to make a film about. You stopped working on it, didn't you?"

Rune leaned against the grille and turned to face Shelly. "It's slotted on PBS."

Shelly's eyes went wide. "Oh, Rune, you can't . . . PBS is national. Someone here could see it."

"You don't look like you."

"I look enough like me so people could make the connection."

Rune said, "You used me. You weren't honest with me."

"I know I don't deserve to ask—"

"You didn't want to help me make my film at all. You just used me."

"Please, Rune, all my plans . . . They're just starting to work out. For the first time in my life I'm happy. No one knows what I did—the films. I can't tell you how wonderful it is, not to be looked at like a thing. It's so wonderful not to be ashamed. . . ."

Rune said, "But this is *my* one big chance. I've lived with this film for months. It's gotten me fired and nearly gotten me killed a couple times. It's all I've got, Shelly. I can't let it go."

Tears formed in the actress's eyes. "Remember in your houseboat, we were looking through the mythology book. The story about Orpheus and Eurydice? Shelly Lowe is dead, Rune. Don't bring her back. Please, don't." Shelly's eyes were round and liquid with tears. Her hand closed

on Rune's arm. "Look at me, Rune! Please. Like Orpheus.
Look at me and send me back to the Underworld."

■■■■

The Hudson was choppy; a storm was coming. Rune was
afraid she'd lose electricity.

That's all I need tonight. My television premiere and all
of New York has a blackout.

A flash of lightning over Jersey froze the image of Sam
Healy, opening two cans of beer at once.

The rain began, whipped against the side of the houseboat by fast, surprised sweeps of wind.

"I hope the moorings hold," Rune said.

Healy looked out the window, then back at the dinner
resting on Rune's blue Formica coffee table. The cold an-
chovy pizza seemed to bother him more than an un-
planned voyage into New York Harbor.

"They pay you much for your film?"

"Naw. This is public television—you do it for love,"
Rune said, turning on the TV. "And because, if I'm lucky,
a lecherous producer with a ton of money he's dying to
give away is gonna be watching."

"You use your real name?"

"You don't believe Rune's my name?"

"No." He sipped the Miller. "Is it?"

"The credit line is Irene Dodd Simons."

"Classy. So *that's* your real name."

"Maybe, maybe not." Rune smiled mysteriously and sat
back in the old couch she'd bought from a Goodwill shop.
It was still uneven from the time she'd cut through a lot of
the stuffing looking for hidden money but if you settled
yourself enough it got to the point where it was pretty
comfortable.

Healy tried the couch, then sat on the floor, picking
anchovies off half the pizza and dropping them onto the
other half.